HER HUSBAND'S SECRET

A gripping crime thriller full of twists

JANICE FROST

JOFFE BOOKS

Published 2016 by Joffe Books, London.

www.joffebooks.com

© Janice Frost

ISBN-13: 978-1-911021-91-9

kicked his duvet aside and swung his legs over the side of the bed. He was already fully clothed. He retrieved a bag from under his bed, a small backpack that he'd packed earlier for his night-time excursion. It contained a torch, a pair of gloves and his mobile phone.

He crept along the landing to the stairs. The second to last stair creaked in two places and he trod carefully and sighed with relief when he reached the bottom without making the slightest sound. He put on his coat and wellies. Any sound now would bring his mum to the top of the stairs in a heartbeat.

Belle, the family's honey-coloured Labrador, cocked an ear at Zak when he entered the kitchen. Fortunately, Belle only barked at unfamiliar sounds, and although Zak creeping into the kitchen after midnight was not a common occurrence, Belle took it in her stride. Even so, the sound of her toenails tip-tapping on the ceramic floor tiles as she padded across to greet him seemed to ricochet around the room.

He reached for her lead and signalled to her to be quiet. Fortunately, Belle wasn't the sort of dog who made a fuss and after enduring some obligatory tail-wagging and hand-licking, Zak was able to lead her out of the kitchen, through the utility room and then outside into the garden without much commotion.

At the garden gate, Zak hesitated. The wrought-iron structure seemed to represent a psychological as well as a physical barrier and once through, there would be no going back.

"It's freezing," Zak said, his teeth chattering. He looked down at Belle, who yawned. The moon was full and bright enough to read by. Zak turned off his torch, gently lifted the latch on the gate and pushed it open halfway — any further and it would squeak. Belle was first through, the lead tangling around her legs as she charged ahead of Zak.

They walked a little way and Zak told Belle to "sit." He looked around. Frost glistened on the tops of the hedgerows and the moonlight cast eerie shadows across the lane from the overhanging trees. Suddenly Belle growled. Zak jumped, then shushed her. "It's only Rowan, silly."

A girl appeared through a gap in the hedgerow and grinned at Zak.

"Where have you been? I've been here for ages. I can't feel my feet anymore," Zak said.

"Liar. I saw you and Belle coming out of your garden a minute ago."

"Well, it seemed like ages."

"My dad was still up with my baby brother when I left. I sneaked out the side door."

"Yeah, well, Holly's covering for you, isn't she?" said Zak.

"She didn't want to. She wanted to come. I've had to give her a whole week's pocket money to keep her quiet."

"Let's just go, or we won't have time," Zak said, exasperated. Rowan was in his class at school. She lived in the house nearest to his and their mothers were friends. They were friends too. Lately Zak's feelings about Rowan had started to change, to become more complicated somehow. She felt it too, he was sure, but tonight none of that mattered. Tonight they were just simple friends again, out on an adventure.

At the end of the lane they passed through a kissing gate and entered a field that adjoined a dark wood. They followed the perimeter of the field for a bit and then veered off to the right. Another gate, another field and they arrived at their destination, the site of a ruined eleventh century abbey on the edge of the Stainholme lime wood. A life-sized monk carved out of wood stood at the entrance, welcoming them. Someone had hung a little bag of dog poo from the fingers of the monk's hand. Belle strained on her lead and sniffed at it before Zak tugged her sharply away. "What now?" he said.

"Now we wait." Rowan pushed Zak into the field and they tramped over the rime-hardened ground towards a craggy stone structure. It was all that remained of the monastery that had dominated the landscape almost a millennium ago. There was a jagged stone tower, three or four crumbling arched walls and some mounds of earth, sites of buildings lost long ago. It was a lonely spot. Zak had been here many times, but never at night. "We can hide in the trees over there and still have a perfect view of the ruin," he said, pointing at the wood fringing the field.

"Can you hide from a ghost?" Rowan asked.

"I don't know, but I'll feel safer if we're not right out in the open. Anyway, you know it's not the kind of ghost that harms people. It just sort of floats between the arches."

They were talking about the White Monk, so-called because of the white robes worn by his order. He was reputed to haunt the abbey ruins. Zak's class had gone on a ghost tour in Stromford a few weeks ago and when he'd heard that they lived near the ruins of Stainholme Abbey the tour guide had told them about the White Monk. Of course they had heard the legend many times before. An eleventh century abbot had been accused of practising Satanism and as punishment he had been bricked up alive in the walls of the abbey. At night, especially when the moon was full, his ghostly spirit could be seen drifting among the abbey ruins.

The tour guide, whom their teacher claimed had once been a famous actor, told the story so vividly and with such theatricality that Zak immediately decided to see the White Monk for himself. He planned to catch him on film and send it to one of those ghost-hunting programmes on the telly. He enlisted Rowan as his accomplice.

"He was a devil-worshipper. You don't know if his ghost will harm you or not — just cos it hasn't so far

4

doesn't mean it won't go for us if it finds out we're spying on it," Rowan reasoned. So they headed for the trees, pulling Belle along in their wake.

"We probably shouldn't talk. It might hear us and be put off," Zak said. "Let's just stand here and watch." He glanced nervously into the wood behind them. It looked dark and full of hidden dangers. He'd sooner be seen by the ghost than go in there, even with his torch.

They had not anticipated the sheer tedium of waiting in the cold and dark with nothing to do but stare at a single fragment of wall. Excitement soon gave way to boredom. After what seemed an interminable amount of time — in reality only about twenty minutes — Zak broke the silence with an explosive fart. Rowan shushed him immediately, and then creased in silent laughter, which set Zak off too and for several minutes they held their hands to their mouths to stifle the noise.

"There's no chance of it coming out now," whispered Rowan at last. "You've contaminated the area."

"It's only methane gas — it'll think we're cows." More stifled laughter.

Another ten minutes went by.

"We can't stay much longer," said Zak at last. "We'll get hypothermia. Maybe we should call it a night." His hands were tingling with cold and he hadn't been able to feel his toes since ten minutes after he'd left the cottage.

They stared at the ruin. It certainly looked spooky. Frosty moonlight shone through the single intact stone archway of what had once been the abbey's nave. The lower part of the wall was black. In the wood at their backs, tree branches stirred, night creatures rustled in the stiffened undergrowth and from somewhere far off came the sound of a fox yipping. Suddenly, an owl hooted overhead. Zak and Rowan started and Belle growled.

Then they heard a different sort of noise, one that was more familiar. The purring sound of a car engine was followed soon afterwards by the yellow glow of dipped headlights.

"What is it? A tractor?" Rowan asked.

"No, it's a car. It's stopping. It must have come down the track from the road."

Belle growled again, her body alert. Zak and Rowan exchanged puzzled glances. Zak gripped Belle's collar and shushed her. They watched from the treeline. They heard the unmistakable sound of a car boot being slammed shut and then a figure loomed into view. He stood quite still and looked around him. Then he disappeared and emerged from behind the car a couple of moments later, making grunting sounds and straining under the weight of something heavy and cumbersome. Belle's hackles rose and she stiffened. Zak sank to his knees beside her and whispered to her to be quiet.

"He's pulling something along," Rowan muttered. "D'you think he could be a poacher?"

"Shh," Zak answered. They watched as the man hauled his burden across the ground.

Zak and Rowan looked at each other, saucer-eyed. Zak whispered, "That's a dead body he's dragging, I'm sure of it." His voice quivered. "He's brought it here to bury it in the woods."

"We have to get away from here. If he sees us he'll kill us too, to keep us quiet." A frightened pause. "What if Belle starts barking?"

"She won't," Zak whispered fiercely. "I won't let her." Belle seemed to understand the need for silence. She sat still, alert but obedient.

The man's face was concealed under the fur-lined hood of a parka. His grunts became louder as he drew nearer.

"Come on. Let's go," Zak said, panicking. He grabbed Rowan's arm. Already jumpy, she recoiled, and took a step backwards . . . onto Belle's tail. Belle yelped. No one could have blamed her for that. The man stopped in his tracks.

"Who's there?" he called, looking around. And now he began striding straight towards them, his long, powerful legs covering the short distance at an alarming pace.

"Run!" Zak cried. He pushed Rowan ahead of him further into the trees. Belle began to bark. Pulling the dog along behind him Zak charged after Rowan, his heart racing, breath coming in big, laboured gasps. Zak had asthma. Pounding through the woods in the middle of a frosty night, already breathless with panic provided a perfect storm of circumstances to induce an attack. He felt the familiar tightness grip his chest.

"Rowan!" he cried, gasping.

Rowan turned around and ran back to join him.

"Use your inhaler!" she said.

Zak fumbled in his coat pocket. Finding what he was looking for, he sucked greedily.

Rowan's face looked surprisingly calm. "Hide," she said to him fiercely.

Zak's mouth opened to form a silent "no," but something about the determined set of Rowan's face cautioned him to obey.

"Belle and I can lead him away, then you can cut round the other way to Badger's Field. We'll meet up with you there. He won't know he's not following us both." Rowan pushed Zak sideways off the path. She tugged Belle's lead from his hand, encouraging her to bark loudly to draw the man away from Zak.

Zak darted into some bushes and crouched down, hoping he was not visible. The man charged straight past his hiding place, focused on pursuing the sound of the barking dog ahead. Zak shrank further back into the bushes. He could still make out the man's bulky shape crashing through the trees, led on by the dog's frenzied barking. Then, by some miracle, the man came crashing to his knees and Zak heard him swear. The man got up slowly, perhaps shaken by his fall. Every second, Belle's barking was becoming more distant. The man cursed again and bent double, hands on knees. Then he began to retrace his steps. At the spot where Zak had stopped to fish out his inhaler, the man halted abruptly and bent down. He picked something up and examined it in the light of his torch. His face was turned away from the beam but Zak felt that there was something familiar about his size and shape. With mounting horror, Zak saw that the man was holding part of his inhaler. Instead of discarding it, the man slipped it into his pocket, before going back to where he had abandoned the body.

It took some time for Zak to stop shaking. He waited a while in case the man changed his mind and returned, then rose unsteadily to his feet, and ventured out from the safety of the bushes. As soon as his legs felt less wobbly he began to run. He didn't stop until he reached Badger's Field.

"Rowan! Belle!" Zak called. He caught sight of them crouched by the hedgerow between Badger's Field and the road. Only ten minutes or so had passed since they had parted, but it had been the longest ten minutes of Zak's life.

"Zak!" Rowan and Belle were upon him now and for several joyous moments the friends clung to each other in relief. Gradually, their fear and relief changed to excitement.

"Did you see the size of him?"

"We'd have been dead for sure if he'd caught us."

"You were a hero leading him away like that."

"Who do you think he killed?"

"We have to get home straightaway and tell Mum to call the police," Rowan said, at last.

Zak looked at her in panic. "Don't be stupid! My mum'll ground me for the rest of my life if she finds out we've been out at this time of night."

"But, Zak, he murdered someone. What if he finds out who we are and comes after us?"

"That's not going to happen."

"How do you know?"

"Because, dummy, he doesn't know who we are."

"He could work it out."

"How?"

"I dunno, but he's probably smart, isn't he?"

"He won't find out, Rowan."

"The police should know about the body. It could be ages before they find out. Hardly anyone comes up here in winter."

Zak deliberated. "We could call them," he said at last. "Anonymously."

"Alright. I'll do it if you tell me what to say. I can disguise my voice."

"Okay, but not when my mum's around. Agreed?"

Rowan nodded. Zak added, "And we'll wait a bit, okay? Someone else might find the body first, then we won't need to say anything."

Rowan looked a little unsure about this but Zak stared her down. All at once, he yawned and Rowan followed suit. "Come on. Let's get home or it'll be Mum who calls the police if she wakes up and finds we're not there."

Chapter 2

Ava Merry was feeling restless. She had been back at work for a few days now. She had spent the Christmas break at home with her younger brother, Ollie. Ollie had recently moved in with Ava and was attending Stromford grammar school where he was studying A levels. Any doubts Ava had harboured about her new domestic arrangement had been rapidly dispelled when she discovered that her little brother was a gifted cook. Ollie had slaved away happily in the kitchen on Christmas day, encouraging Ava to put her feet up and watch TV. She had been happy to comply. Normally, she would have insisted on helping, but the case she'd been working on before the holiday had been intense — and harrowing. She was still bruised and sore from her tussle in the back seat of a car with a killer who had left her partner, DI Jim Neal, cradling his gravely wounded sister in his arms. The emotional fallout from the case had been exhausting.

On Boxing Day, Dr Joel Agard had turned up at Ava's cottage with a festive bouquet, a gourmet food hamper and a bottle of champagne. His generosity made Ava feel at once delighted and embarrassed at having nothing but a pack of Homer Simpson socks to offer him in return. They had only been on a couple of dates since they'd met at Stromford county hospital, when Ava and Neal had turned up to interview suspects in their last case. Ava and the doctor both worked long, unsocial hours that seemed never to coincide. As a junior doctor, Joel was supposed to be working shifts at A&E throughout the holiday, but somehow he'd managed to wangle a couple of days off. He'd ended up staying Boxing Day night — much to Ollie's amusement. On the following day they had driven out to the coast and taken a long, bracing walk along a deserted beach. Icy sea-spray from the incoming tide stung their faces and the wind off the sea had chilled them half to death but they'd thawed out in a cosy café before driving back to Stromford. It should all have been very romantic, but the attack on Maggie Neal still loomed large in Ava's mind and her concern about Jim Neal and his sister dominated her thoughts. She hoped Joel hadn't noticed her distractedness.

On her first day back at work, Ava had sat down at her desk and stared at Jim Neal's empty office. She felt his absence keenly, not least because she was worried about his state of mind. She knew that Neal blamed himself for his sister's injury. She wished that before he went off on leave she could have assured him one more time that none of it was his fault. Her words would have bounced off him as they had done the first couple of times, but at least they would have been the last words he'd heard from her.

Neal had attempted to talk to the killer, to appeal to her humanity. Ava's instinct had been to charge forward, all guns blazing, and overwhelm Maggie's attacker. Of course, with the benefit of hindsight, Ava appreciated that her tactic could have led at best to the same outcome, at worst to a tragedy.

Ava settled at her desk to work through her long list of unopened emails, most of which seemed to be from her friend and colleague Polly 'PJ' Jenkins. Nothing from Neal, who was still on leave. She had heard that he was going up to Scotland for the holiday and that DCI George Lowe had cautioned him not to return 'until his head was in a better place.' No one could accuse George of mincing his words. Ava had not learned this from Neal, but from her other colleagues when she returned to work.

She had hoped he might at least have texted her to let her know how Maggie was faring. Maggie had been discharged from hospital a couple of days before Christmas and she, Neal and Neal's son Archie, had departed for Edinburgh the same day. Ava had visited Maggie in hospital the day after her attack when she was in the ICU. Drugged up with pain medication, Neal's sister had begged Ava to convince her brother that he wasn't to blame. But Ava hadn't managed to see Neal again.

What if he didn't come back to work? He could transfer to Edinburgh, couldn't he? Ava pondered that for a couple of moments, then put it out of her mind. It wasn't her normal practice to shy away from confronting her feelings head on but what was the point, she reasoned, in wasting time analysing a situation that might never arise? *He's coming back,* she said aloud.

"Who's coming back?"

Ava turned around. "What? Hey, PJ! Happy New Year!"

"Happy New Year!" PJ was almost unrecognisable in a quilted jacket that Ava had not seen before. It was long, padded and not exactly stylish.

"I know. It's dreadful, isn't it? Christmas present from Steve. When he told me he was getting me something really hot for Christmas, I thought he meant from Ann Summers."

"It's very practical. Looks really cosy."

"Yeah, well. His taste in jewellery is better," PJ said, showing Ava a pretty silver ring. "You were thinking about Inspector Neal just now, weren't you, when you said that?"

There was no point in denying it. "Yeah."

"Have you heard anything?"

"Only that he's taken leave for a few weeks."

"Has he been in touch with you?"

"No. Why should he?" Ava said, too quickly.

"Well, you are partners," PJ reminded her.

"Yeah."

"So, A little bird told me you saw the lovely Dr Agard on Boxing Day."

Ava smiled. She had no idea how PJ had heard that particular piece of information. "You should ace your detective constable exam, Peej. Nothing gets by you."

"Not when young Ollie is so willing to divulge your whereabouts to anybody who asks. I rang the day after Boxing Day. He told me Joel spent the night and that you'd gone in search of a romantic beach to walk on in the freezing cold."

"He didn't say you'd called."

"I told him not to. It was only to ask if you wanted to come over for the evening. Steve was on duty and I thought you might be at a loose end if the men in your life were unavailable."

Ava pretended not to notice PJ's use of the plural. She also made a mental note to speak to Ollie about the need to be more discreet.

The telephone on Ava's desk rang and after a brief conversation she turned to PJ. "That was DCI Lowe. He wants me upstairs. Catch you later."

George Lowe's office was on the second floor. Ava took the steps two at a time, eager to find out what Lowe had to say. It had to be a new case, and she was relieved at the prospect of being busy. Lowe looked up as she entered his room. Ava had the distinct impression that she was being scrutinised and — unusually for her — she felt uncomfortable. Lowe had a reputation for being results-driven, which was understandable considering the pressures to stay within budget while ensuring that Stromfordshire received appropriate policing. Not an easy job given the very different needs of the urban and rural areas of the county. Ava knew that Lowe was not a great fan of hers. He had been unhappy with her unprofessional behaviour on the first case she and Neal had worked on, and only Neal's intervention had saved her from disciplinary action.

There was no preamble. No good morning, no small talk. "Sit down, Sergeant," Lowe said, his hand waving loosely at a chair. "I spoke with Hammond Bell earlier. He's the Wildlife and Rural Crimes officer for the Wolds area. He had a bit of a garbled report earlier this morning about a body being dumped out at the old abbey ruin near Stainholme. He thought it might be a hoax at first, because the anonymous caller apparently sounded like a kid . . ."

Lowe's phone rang. Ava leaned forward in her seat, listening to his side of the conversation. Lowe's expression gave nothing away.

". . . Finish securing the scene and I'll get a team out there," he looked at his watch, "within the hour."

He put the phone down and nodded at Ava. "Not a hoax then, as you've probably gathered. Bell was just letting me know that he thinks we've got a suspicious death. The body is that of a man in his late twenties or early thirties. No ID. No obvious sign of violence."

Ava felt a prick of excitement. She waited for Lowe's order to drive out to Stainholme as part of the investigating team. Her chief also seemed to be waiting. There was a knock on the door, Ava turned round and her heart sank. DI Reg Saunders walked into the room and greeted Lowe, ignoring Ava completely. Saunders was twice Ava's age. He was an experienced detective, but he was retiring in a matter of months and it was no secret that he was counting the days, any real enthusiasm for the job having been wrung out of him years ago. Allegedly he had been a good enough cop back in the day, but somewhere along the line he'd become jaded. He also had a reputation for being a bit old school. Not Ava's idea of a dream substitute for Jim Neal, but it was what it was.

"DS Merry, I believe you've met DI Saunders?"

Ava summoned a smile and a nod. Saunders reciprocated.

"I'd like you to work with DI Saunders on this investigation for now, Merry."

Ava nodded again, suppressing her disappointment. She wanted to ask if Lowe had heard from Neal, whether he'd be taking over from Saunders upon his return or at least working the case with them. Instead she replied, "I look forward to working with you, DI Saunders." Saunders cocked his head in acknowledgement. If he was looking forward to working with Ava, he kept it to himself.

* * *

It was a forty-minute drive out to Stainholme. The conversation between Ava and Reg Saunders was one-sided and mostly consisted of Saunders pontificating about how different things had been when he started out in the force in the seventies. From time to time he dropped a remark that made Ava cringe. She tried not to judge him. It was thirty-five years since he had started out as a young constable. Ava had a sense that he was testing the water, seeing how far he could go before he overstepped and got a rise out of her. It wasn't the first time she had come across people like this. Publicly, they kept within what was considered acceptable, but their attitudes remained unchanged. Every so often they would betray themselves with an unconsidered word or gesture. Ava suspected that Saunders was far too clever to say anything that could get him into real trouble.

Saunders's other favourite topic appeared to be his forthcoming retirement and how he would be spending his time. Mostly, 'trying to forget all the shit cases' he'd spent his working life investigating. Listening to him made Ava feel disheartened. She hoped that at the end of her own career in the force she would look back on her achievements and remember them with pride.

"Rural and animal welfare bloke's my nephew," Saunders said. "Normally the bodies that turn up on his patch have got four legs."

Ava nodded and gave a polite smile. The more rural areas of the county tended to be policed by local officers based in the market towns. They dealt with everything from hare coursing and poaching to theft of livestock, agricultural machinery, diesel and pesticides as well as conflict between local populations and the seasonal migrant workers who worked the harvests. More and more, rural crime was becoming the preserve of gangs of organised criminals, and violence was becoming more common. Murder was the remit of the serious crimes unit based in Stromford itself.

"Bloody bleak out here, isn't it?" Saunders commented. They were on the outskirts of the Wolds now, the landscape ahead of them beginning to swell gradually, as they left vast acres of flat wintry fields behind them.

"On a day like this, I suppose," Ava said, her eyes on the grey sky pressing around them. "I bet it's really pretty in the summer, though. I've been meaning to drive out here and do a bit of biking or running. Maybe even some walking."

"I heard you were a bit of an exercise fanatic."

"Yeah, I like to keep fit."

"Can't be bothered myself. I walk the dog a couple of times a day and that keeps me fit enough. Can't be arsed with all these faddy diets, either. Although I like that seafood one. Ever heard of it?"

"See food and eat it." Ava forced a smile.

"That's the one. Whatever doesn't kill you makes you stronger, that's my motto."

Judging by the size of Saunders's gut he saw a lot of food, not to mention booze. And he was a smoker. The unmistakable smell of stale cigarette smoke lingered in his car and on his clothes. She supposed she should be thankful hadn't lit up already.

"At least you're not a bleedin' vegetarian. You're not, are you?" Saunders turned a worried face in Ava's direction.

"No. I try to avoid red meat but I eat white meat and fish," Ava reassured him.

"Yeah, well, live and let live. Be a boring world if we were all the same now, wouldn't it, Sergeant."

Ava agreed, wondering if Reg Saunders ever ran out of platitudes.

Saunders took a left turn off the main road and drove into what looked like a dirt trail leading nowhere. The car bumped and rattled over the frost-hardened ground following a track alongside a tall hedgerow that concealed their view of the field on the other side. Saunders braked near a gap in the hedge.

"Are we here?" Ava asked, straining to see any sign of the ruined abbey.

"Yeah. Can't see it from here. Not that there's a lot to see. Ham's probably parked on the road at the other side of the field. I thought it might be just as easy for us to cut across the field as drive all the way round."

"Ham? Is he the rural and wildlife officer? The one you said was your nephew?"

"That's him. Hammond Bell. He was the ex's sister's boy. Bit of a weirdo, if you ask me. Building his own sustainable home out in the sticks, him and his wife. They're living in a caravan in the woods until the house is finished."

"Sounds interesting."

"Yeah, well, each to his own, I suppose. I'm quite happy with my bachelor pad on the Oakwoods estate. Know it?"

"Yeah," Ava replied. She had heard PJ say that she and her boyfriend Steve were thinking about buying a starter home there. It was a large, unimaginative estate with a hotchpotch of new homes squashed in over the site of an old Victorian hospital. Some of the original buildings had been converted into flats and studios which sold as luxury accommodation at inflated prices. Ava would rather have moved into one of Ham's eco homes than live there.

They left the car and trudged over the field, entering a wood. Ava was surprised by the sudden stillness, the lack of light. Some lines from a poem she'd read at school popped into her head, something about the woods being, 'lovely, dark and deep.' She wasn't so sure about the lovely. She'd always found woods a bit creepy. Jim Neal would probably know who the poet was. He seemed to like that sort of thing.

The abbey ruin loomed up in front of them suddenly, as they broke through the wood and emerged into the field on the other side. Ava wasn't sure what she'd been expecting. Fountains Abbey it was not. Only one wall and a crumbling stone tower remained of whatever structure had existed previously. She looked around. A series of information posts and earthworks marked the locations of lost buildings attached to the original monastery. A refectory, an infirmary, a dormitory. Once, long ago, this must have been a thriving community. Now it was a desolate spot, but also beautiful in a stark and lonesome sort of way. A police car was parked on the other side of a fence enclosing the site.

"There's Ham," Saunders said, waving to an officer getting out of the vehicle. Ham strode over to join them. He nodded at Saunders and grinned. "I've been waiting in the car, it's brass monkeys today. It's not as if the scene's likely to be contaminated. You only get the occasional walker or history buff out here at this time of year." He turned to Ava.

"This is DS Ava Merry," Saunders said.

Ham extended his hand. "PC Hammond Bell." His smile was friendly, reaching his hazel eyes and making them twinkle. Ava had noticed him appraising her as he walked towards them from his car, and she'd given him the once-over too, deciding she liked what she saw. *He's married and you're seeing someone*, she reminded herself. Still, it was okay to look.

"Where's your body, then, Hamster?" Saunders asked, stamping his feet.

"It's on the other side of the monument," Bell said, colouring at what was obviously a family nickname. Ava noted his respectful description of the ruin as a 'monument,' guessing that Bell had more than a passing interest in the ruined abbey's history.

They stepped through one of the stone arches. Bell pointed at a mound of earth about twenty feet away. The body lay beside it

"Male. Aged around thirty, I'd guess. No ID on him."

"What's your feeling?" Saunders asked Bell.

Bell pursed his lips. "Looks well-dressed, so it's unlikely he's a vagrant. He's not local, that much I can tell you. I know most of the folk in the villages around here and I've never seen him about. He's a long way from anywhere if he wasn't staying with someone local, though."

Instinctively, Ava scanned the ground around the body. Ham saw her looking. "The ground's hard owing to the frost but there's enough evidence of disturbance to the grassier areas to suggest he was dragged from the opening in the hedge near where I'm parked," he said.

"Why dump him out in the open?"

"Maybe he was planning on dragging him a bit further." Ham nodded in the direction of the woods."

"So why change his mind? Unless he was disturbed by someone."

"Or something," Ham added. Ava caught Ham's wink to Saunders. "This is a spooky place. They say it's haunted."

"Yeah, right. Headless horseman? Casper . . . ?"

"Satanist Premonstratensian monk, actually. Bricked up in the abbey walls. What you're standing on is the site of a second abbey, built two hundred years after the original one was destroyed by the Vikings in 870. More than three hundred monks were slain, so this place is no stranger to murder."

"I don't believe in ghosts," Ava said.

"Nor did I until I saw one," Ham replied.

Ava waited for him to elaborate.

"I was scouting around this area one night last July, following a series of reports about badger-baiting in the area and I saw a figure dressed in flowing white robes flitting between those arches over there." Bell waved an arm in the general direction of the ruin.

"One of the murdered monks?" Ava raised a sceptical eyebrow.

"I raced over and there was no sign of a living soul. And no way could anyone have made it across to the wood that quickly. I'm not easily spooked, Sergeant, but I legged it back to the car like my arse was on fire."

Ava laughed.

"Have you searched the wood?" Saunders asked Bell.

"Only as far as the treeline."

Saunders extracted a pair of gloves from his pocket and knelt down beside the body. He moved the head from side to side, while Ava stood by nervously, concerned about contaminating the scene before forensics arrived.

She hoped that the backup team would arrive soon. She shivered. It was going to be a long, cold morning and her feet were already turning to ice.

"I don't suppose there's anywhere a person could grab a coffee around here?" she asked Ham without hope.

Saunders overheard and piped up. "There's a bleedin' Costa round back of that bush over there, Merry. I'll have a cinnamon latte and a bloody croissant."

"No harm in asking," Ava said unabashed.

Bell whipped out his phone. "Rosie?" he said. "Think you could fix up a flask of coffee and some bacon butties for three? I'm up at Stainholme Abbey with Reg Saunders and his DS. Looks like we're going to be a while . . . Yes, a body . . . Sorry, love, I can't give you any details. Thanks, babe, you're a star." Bell grinned at Ava. "My wife's day off today. I'll stop by and collect our provisions in half an hour or so."

"You've got a good 'un there, Hamster boy," Saunders said.

"Yeah. She's a keeper," Bell agreed, beaming.

"I hear you're building an eco-friendly house," said Ava. "Is it one of those cool little underground hobbit homes?"

"Don't get 'im started on the bleedin' environment, Merry, unless you've got a spare lifetime or two."

Bell shook his head. "It's above ground. Rosie and I designed it ourselves with a bit of help from a local architect. We're using locally-sourced materials and it's going to be very eco-friendly. Come and see it, if you like. You'd get on well with Rosie, I reckon."

Before Ava could say that she'd be interested, a couple of police vans arrived at the scene and from then on it was down to routine police work — securing the scene, accompanying the CSIs as they scoured the immediate area, looking for anything that might help piece together how their John Doe might have ended up here. Ava donned a coverall and combed the wood. From time to time she looked across at Saunders, who seemed more interested in chatting with one of the female SOCOs and smoking roll-ups. Ava felt a bit alone. She didn't even recognise any of the SOCOs. Dan Cardew, a shy young CSI who was sweet on Ava wasn't part of the team today. Working with Neal wasn't a laugh a minute, not for nothing had he earned a reputation for being dour, but Neal was dedicated to the job in a way that Saunders clearly was not. Moreover, she trusted Neal and they had an attachment of sorts, though Ava preferred not to define exactly what it was.

Unlike Saunders, Hammond Bell appeared to be one of those people who live for their jobs, although Ava thought he would be even more at home as some kind of environmental scientist. When she suggested as much, Bell shook his head. "I've never been very academic. Wanted to be a copper for as long as I can remember. I did a pre-uniform course at college until I was old enough to join the force. I grew up on a farm. My dad was a labourer so I knew a thing or two about animals, and this seemed a good way to combine my two passions. Besides," he looked over at Reg Saunders, "Being a copper's in my blood."

"You're only related to DI Saunders by marriage, aren't you?" Ava pointed out.

Ham grinned. His phone rang. "That's great. Thanks, babe, I'll be about ten minutes." He gave Ava the thumbs up. "Coffee and butties are nearly ready. I'll swing home and collect them." Ava gave him a look of gratitude that came right from the tips of her frozen toes.

A search of the wood was important if it proved to be the case that the body had been abandoned because the killer had been disturbed. Even at this time of year, you could expect to find some evidence of people passing through, Ava knew. She sighed, thinking of the stiffened body. Whoever the man was, he had lain in this lonely spot overnight. Ava wondered if anyone had missed him. Was there a loved one somewhere wondering and worrying, already fearing the worst? Checking missing persons would be a first port of call. She thought of what Ham had said about him not being a local. She tried to summon up an image of his face and found that she could not.

Something crunched under Ava's foot. She bent down and raked her hands through the dead leaves. And picked up the cover of a salbutamol inhaler snapped in two. Not necessarily a piece of relevant evidence, but she took it and deposited it in an evidence bag anyway. It looked as though it hadn't been outside for long. She handed the bag to one of the SOCOs. "Looks like the cover to an asthma inhaler, I think. Might be worth checking it?"

Ava looked around for Saunders, and not seeing him, she made her way back to the body, determined to take a good look at his face. The problem was, she saw only an average-looking man with no distinguishing features. There was nothing at all to make him stand out in a crowd. He was the kind of person you passed every day on the street and didn't notice. Ava was disappointed in herself. As a detective, she had trained herself to be observant, to notice what others would not. The man lying on the ground before her had not been killed because he was ordinary, she thought. He had provoked strong emotions in his killer, who had not looked at him and seen a bland, bearded everyman. With a sigh, she turned away, disappointed at her failure to connect with the victim.

"Bet his mother loved him."

Ava started. She had not realised Reg Saunders was standing behind her. Where had he been a few moments ago when she'd been searching for him?

"Funny how some victims give you that choking feeling and others just . . . don't." Saunders was only echoing more or less what Ava had been thinking. Still, she disliked his tone, his blatant lack of respect.

She turned on him, momentarily forgetting their respective ranks. "That's a person lying there. You could show a little respect."

"Come on, Blondie, you're only getting excited because you feel the same way. Only you don't care to admit it." In a mocking tone, he added. "He had *feelings*, and somebody *loved* him, yada, yada, yada."

"My name's Ava."

"So what? I like to give people nicknames. You should be flattered, not everyone gets a cute one. Lighten up, Sergeant." He blew cigarette smoke in her face and walked away.

Ava stared after him in disbelief. Trouble was, he hadn't said anything all that offensive. It was his tone and the narrowing of his eyes, daring her to challenge him. She wouldn't give him the satisfaction of accusing her of being priggish . . . *Let it go*, a warning voice inside her head cautioned, and she listened. For once.

At that moment, Hammond Bell returned with the coffee and butties and Ava had to restrain herself from running up and hugging him. They ate in Ham's car. Ava listened with interest as Ham related some of the history of the site. Stainholme had been only one of seven monasteries scattered across the Strom valley, all within a few miles of each other. "Because of the River Strom," Ham explained. "The monks — all the different orders — some of them Benedictine, others Cistercian and Premonstratensian — relied on the trade links it provided with Stromford and the ports to Europe. Their livelihood came from trading — wool, mostly."

"What happened to them?" Ava asked.

"Er . . . Henry VIII? Remember your history?"

"Oh, yeah, right." History hadn't been her favourite subject at school. Jim Neal would be fascinated by all this. No doubt he already knew all about it. She felt herself warming to Hammond Bell. He was clearly a person with genuine passions for the environment and local history.

Saunders finished his coffee and left them to it. Ava watched him walk across to the body and pace around it slowly. He looked more like a predator circling its prey than a police officer examining a crime scene. Ham saw her looking. "Don't let him get to you," he said quietly. "He was married to my mum's sister but they've been divorced for years. My mum doesn't speak to him because of the way he treated my aunt Karen. He's my uncle but I don't really know him well."

"It's not your fault that you're related to him." They both smiled.

After a flying visit from pathologist Ashley Hunt, who declared that he could tell them nothing until he got the body back to the lab, the unknown man was bagged and tagged and removed from the scene. Ava breathed a sigh of relief as she trudged back over the frozen field to Saunders's car, glad to escape the forsaken ruin. She guessed conversation between her and Saunders would be sparse on their drive back to Stromford and was proved right when he put on a CD as soon as she belted up. Two can play at that game, Ava thought, pulling her iPod from her pocket and sticking her ear buds in under her hat. Even though she could still hear Saunders's music above her own, she felt she had scored a point.

Chapter 3

James, aka Jock, Dodds, was watching him. Neal was pretending to be asleep. He didn't want another conversation about how he was feeling. How he was feeling was still angry. At his sister Maggie's attacker, certainly, but his anger was also turned inwards, on himself, which, as Jock kept reminding him, was not a healthy way to deal with powerful emotions.

Jock was feeling pretty emotional himself, Neal suspected. He had always liked Maggie and the news of her attack had given him a shock. Perhaps almost losing her would make him act on his feelings at last.

He caught Jock's eye and scowled at him.

Jock shook his head. "You spend half the night pacing up and down, the other half tossing and turning. You've hardly spoken for days and you look like hell. Oh, aye, and you're starting to smell.

"I know this trip was my idea, Jimmy . . ."

"Aye, that it was."

"Fresh air, exercise . . ."

"The restorative power of nature. Just what the doctor ordered."

"Aye, something like that." They'd driven up from Edinburgh the previous afternoon, a long journey, and the conversation had been hard going. Neal had stared out of the window most of the time, eyes on the view, mind elsewhere. And not just anywhere, but at a particular time and place, watching the blade of a knife slicing into his sister's throat over and over.

Jock grunted. "I'm going into Fort William to get some supplies. Are you coming?" Jim shook his head. "Take it easy today then, Jimmy. Tomorrow we'll have a wee walk."

The 'wee walk' Jock had in mind was a ten hour hike to the summit of Ben Nevis, reached, not from the tourist route, but via the summit of its neighbouring Munro, the majestic, Carn Mor Dearg.

"See you later!" Jock called as he left Neal to his gloomy thoughts.

As soon as Jock was out the door, Jim Neal felt a pang of guilt. He was aware that his friend was concerned for him, but Jock's constant attempts at elevating his mood were becoming annoying. He should never have agreed to the walking trip. It hadn't been part of the plan when he, Archie and Maggie decided to see in the New Year in Scotland like they always did.

Neal looked at the clock and wondered what his son was up to. He'd stayed behind in Edinburgh with Maggie. Both of them were excited about a trip to the zoo to see the pandas. Neal stood up, stretched and crossed to the window. Maybe tomorrow would be better, he thought, gazing out at the darkly brooding mountain range. One step at a time makes good walking, Jock had said to him on the drive up from Edinburgh. As if a long walk was all that was needed to lift Neal's spirits. But maybe Jock was right. Perhaps his low mood would lift as he made the arduous ascent to the summit of the Ben tomorrow.

* * *

After three hours of steady walking, Jim Neal and Jock Dodds reached the dramatic, narrow arête connecting Carn Mor Dearg to its more famous peak, Ben Nevis. Before them, the north face of the Ben was threaded with wispy clouds. Both men stooped to attach crampons to their boots, a necessary precaution at this time of year on the snow-sprinkled ridge.

"This is where you're glad you avoided the tourist route," Jock said. "Look at those views, man.

Makes you feel proud to be Scottish."

Neal didn't respond. With a referendum on Scottish independence looming large, every other person he'd met was on political high alert.

"Better crack on. Make the most of the light," Jock said. For a while the only sound was their laboured breathing and the crunch of their footsteps in the snow. It required concentration and focus to avoid a fall. Lachie weaved ahead of them finding his way surefootedly around the granite stones and boulders. Every now and again he stopped to check they were still behind him. On the few occasions he strayed from the ridge and slipped in the scree, Jock cautioned him with a, "Lachie! Mind how ye go, you stupid canine."

As he concentrated on scrambling over the piles of rocks and boulders, Neal found respite from the negative thoughts that had been plaguing him since Angie Dent's chilling assault on his sister.

A herd of red deer in the Coire Leis valley below caught his eye. He tracked them for a few moments, then picked out a camp of three brightly-coloured tents and a small group of hikers eating breakfast around a campfire. Neal took a deep breath of mountain air into his lungs and held it until he felt light-headed. A feeling vaguely reminiscent of joy stirred in his heart.

A cairn at the end of the knife-edge ridge marked the beginning of the Ben's north face. The sheer size and bulk of the mountain took Neal's breath away and he stood beside Jock, gazing up in awe at the imposing mass of solid volcanic rock. Even Lachie stood still, his roving spirit momentarily tamed.

"It's a humblin' sight, right enough," said Jock quietly. "Ye canna but respect it." Turning to Neal, he added, "Ready for the long hard trudge to the summit?"

Jock wasn't joking. The last part of the walk was not difficult, but it was a relentless slog and once again, Neal found that the sheer physical exertion and focus required to reach the top of the boulder-strewn slope drove all other thoughts from his head.

* * *

"Not often you get a view like this up here, especially at this time of year," Jock remarked. He was unpacking provisions from his backpack — a small flask of tea, a water bottle, sandwiches, and fruit and some chicken and biscuits for Lachie. Neal joined him on his boulder and unpacked a similar feast. They ate in silence, absorbing the views.

Neal was aware of Jock giving him sly glances from time to time. Any conversation on the route up the Ben from Torlundy had been instigated by Jock. Neal made no apologies for his taciturnity. He knew that Jock neither expected nor needed any. The two of them had known each other so long that they were entirely comfortable in each other's company. They were brothers in all but blood.

It was Lachie who coaxed Neal to utter his first unprompted remark. He watched the dog lick chicken from Jock's fingers and couldn't help commenting. "Ach, you shouldn't let him do that. It's unhygienic, man."

Jock gave a bellowing laugh. "I'm a bloody doctor, Jimmy. I know a wee bit about hygiene."

"You could have fooled me."

"Lachie's the cleanest dog in Scotland, aren't you, pal? Anybody ever tell you that you can be a right grumpy bastard, Jimmy?"

"Aye, you, often enough." Neal smiled and it felt good. Maybe it was true that simply exercising the facial muscles involved in smiling released the endorphins. He stood up, stretched, and stamped some feeling back into his numbed feet.

The Romantic poets had been right, Neal thought on their descent, there was a restorative power in nature that could balance our darkest thoughts.

By the time they were walking through Glen Nevis on the lower slopes of the Ben, the light was beginning to fade, but Neal's mood was brighter than it had been for weeks.

* * *

"You ready to talk yet?" Jock asked him later, over a fish supper in a cosy pub in Fort William. Neal glowered at him. But he realised he was no longer angry.

"You're a cardiologist, not a bloody psychiatrist, Jock."

"Come on, Jim. You know you're like a brother to me."

"Aye, I know. And you to me."

"Right, well, now that's out of the way, tell me you're not still blaming yourself for what happened to Maggie."

A sigh. "I just keep going over it in my head and wondering what would have happened if I'd handled things differently. Or if the ambulance hadn't got to her so quickly."

"Let it be, Jimmy. Maggie's alive. Do you know how many lives I've seen slip through my fingers on the operating table? If I blamed myself for every patient that ended up dead, I'd give up the job. Then where would the patients I could have helped be?"

Neal nodded. On one level he knew that his friend was right, but there was a part of him that refused to accept it. "I thought about resigning. I'd never really considered that my job could put the people I care about in danger."

This was quite an admission and Neal could tell from Jock's silence that he appreciated the confidence.

"Are you still thinking along those lines?"

Neal shook his head. "Like you said, it's all a question of balance. Fancy another pint?" Neal could feel Jock watching him as he crossed to the bar. Jock was well aware of his tendency to brood. It was all very well to say forget about the past, but time and time again in his work, Neal had seen how the past could affect or infect the present. He wasn't a great believer in all this letting go — or any of that psychobabble that kept the counsellors in business. All of us are made up of elements of our past, they make us what we are and we forget them at our peril, he thought. But the truth was he was growing weary of running the attack on Maggie over and over in his head until it hurt.

Maggie's attacker was heading for a long jail sentence — or a high security hospital. Seeing justice done would go a long way to restoring the balance. And Maggie had thanked him for saving her life, not blamed him for almost getting her killed. Maybe it was time to move on.

Neal thought suddenly of his colleague, Ava, who seemed to have no problem with moving on. In their first case she'd nearly killed a man and seemed to have had no regrets. Her sessions with the police counsellor had left her seemingly untroubled. He could do with a bit of her self-belief. With a pang of regret, he recalled Ava's attempt to reach out to him after the attack on Maggie. He'd been too self-absorbed to acknowledge her concern. It occurred to him that Ava might have troubled feelings of her own about the incident. Sooner or later, he'd have to talk to her. The barman put two pints of beer in front of him. Neal paid, lifted the glasses in the air and nodded at Jock. He walked back to their table.

Then he grinned, plonking Jock's beer in front of him. "So when are you going to ask Maggie out?"

Chapter 4

The discovery of the body at Stainholme was reported on the local evening news. A police artist's sketch accompanied a description of the man. It was said that the police were treating his death as suspicious and the usual appeals were made for information. Ava watched, hoping someone would come forward quickly. She looked at the drawing of the man's sallow, bearded face on the screen and wondered if anyone seeing the same image was reacting with shock, recognising a loved one in the artist's carefully drawn outlines.

"That the bloke you saw this morning?" her brother Ollie asked.

"Yeah. It's a pretty good likeness." She was glad that she remembered his face after all.

"How do you go about finding out who he is?"

"Well, if we're lucky, someone might recognise him and get in touch."

"And if they don't?"

"It takes a bit longer."

"DNA, dental records, fingerprints, that sort of stuff?"

"Maybe. But that only works if the victim's details are in the system. We also do routine things like checks of missing persons to see if we can find a match. Of course, it can take a while for someone to be reported as missing and not just absent. Our victim might not have been missed yet. But to be honest, there have been instances where it's taken years to identify a murder victim. But, hey, let's be positive and hope someone comes forward in this case."

* * *

Ava had barely walked into her office when Reg Saunders summoned her to his part of the building. "We know who our John Doe is," he said by way of greeting.

Ava was surprised. "Has someone identified him from the sketch or the description we put out?"

"No. There was a robbery out at Ridgeway Farm the night before last. Thieves made off with a truckload of pesticides and some farm machinery." Ava listened, wondering what this had to do with their body. "Local police searching the area found a discarded wallet in the woods bordering onto the farm. Cash and cards had been taken but there was a mini statement still inside with the account number on. And a driver's licence. Got his details from the DVLA. His name is Ewan Cameron, from Edinburgh."

"Was he one of the thieves?" Ava asked.

"Don't know yet. His bank account's in Edinburgh and his home address is there too, so you wouldn't think so. But who knows? I'm about to contact the Edinburgh police to see if they can help."

"DI Neal's in Edinburgh," Ava said.

Saunders gave her a blank look. "So?"

"He could make some enquiries on our behalf."

Saunders shrugged. He looked hungover. "Contact him if you like."

His lack of enthusiasm seemed odd to Ava. It was a lucky break to discover their victim's identity this quickly. She would have expected his mood to be a bit more upbeat. She recalled his attitude the day before, how he had stood smoking and chatting while she and the SOCOs combed the wood, acting like the whole case bored him.

Glad to have a reason to get in touch, Ava sent Jim Neal a text asking him to contact her. His reply was instant, but it was a phone call not a text and it took Ava off guard. Hearing his voice made her edgy. They hadn't spoken for a couple of weeks, not since that time in the hospital when he had all but ignored her.

"Hello, sir," she said, tentatively, unsure how she'd find him. To her surprise, there was genuine warmth in Neal's tone when he greeted her. After wishing Neal a happy New Year, Ava moved quickly to business, not wishing any awkwardness to arise between them. "We had a John Doe. Out at Stainholme — you know, the old abbey ruin where they used to hold concerts back in the eighties?"

"Yes, I know it. Fascinating history. Archie's class did a project based around it in Year Five. Suspicious circumstances?"

"Looking that way." Ava explained about the wallet. She paused. "I know you're on leave, sir, it's just that the victim's wife lives in Edinburgh and I wondered . . ."

"You wondered if I could break the news to her?"

"I know the local police could do it, sir, but we really need to have a positive ID on the body as soon as possible and . . ."

"I'll do it," Neal said. "As long as the local force are in agreement. Email me the details."

Ava sent them immediately, including the wife's name and her current address. She attached a copy of the artist's sketch of Ewan Cameron. Would their conversation end as soon as Neal received her message, she wondered, or could she risk a question? She cleared her throat and took the plunge. "Er . . . how are you, sir? I mean after the . . . after Maggie's . . . um . . ."

Not unexpectedly, the silence from the other end extended into seconds. Just as Ava was about to stammer her apologies, Neal said in a gruff voice. "I'm fine, thanks, Ava. And Maggie's fine too. She's seen a consultant up here and she told her she's unlikely to suffer any lasting damage. Physically, at any rate."

"I'm glad to hear that, sir. Will you be returning to work soon?" She bit her tongue.

"Yes. Who are you working the case with?"

"Reg Saunders."

"Ah." Neal's tone was telling. "How's that working out?"

"I think we got off to a bit of a bad start. I don't think he likes me much." Tactfully, she left out what she thought of Saunders. She waited for advice from Neal on how best to handle working with Saunders, but none was forthcoming.

"I'll call you when I've spoken with this . . . Laura Cameron," Neal said.

"Thanks, sir. Enjoy the rest of your leave." Another gaffe. Neal was not on leave to enjoy himself. He had gone away to recover from the trauma of seeing his only sister almost bleed to death in his arms. At least she hadn't said 'holiday.'

It had been good to hear Neal's voice again. She'd missed his soft Scots accent, the way he sometimes slipped in words she'd never heard before, or said 'aye' instead of 'yes,' when he wasn't thinking. There were other things she missed about him too. Jim Neal was not the sort of person who wore his emotions on his sleeve. He had a kind of brooding aura about him, a way of thinking deeply about the most straightforward things. Straightforward to Ava, at any rate. She tried to avoid over-analysing, life was too short. Despite the differences between them, Ava sensed that she had feelings for Jim Neal, but they were complicated and Ava didn't like complications in her life. Life was too short for those too.

Her phone rang again and Ava was pleased to hear Dan Cardew's voice. "Hi, Dan. Have you got something for me?"

"Hi, Ava. A ranger in the lime woods area near Stainholme has reported finding an abandoned car. Ham Bell's been out to take a look and he's confirmed it belonged to our victim. I'm going out there now to give it the once-over and take some photographs. We'll carry out a full examination of the vehicle when we get it back here, of course. Just thought you'd like a heads-up in case you want to come meet us out there."

"Thanks for that, Dan. I'll probably see you at the site. Does DI Saunders know about this?"

Dan told Ava that he'd leave it to her to liaise with Saunders. She got the impression that Dan's opinion of Reg was about the same as her own.

Finding abandoned vehicles, particularly farm vehicles stripped of their parts, wasn't unusual out in the countryside. It was a mistake to underestimate the extent and nature of crimes committed in rural areas and the level of violence they could involve. Thefts of tools, ATVs and quad bikes, oil and diesel and pesticides, high-value agricultural equipment, machinery and livestock were common. Tractors had been stolen in Stromfordshire only to turn up in Eastern Europe or sold on to developing nations. Far from being a rural idyll, the countryside was fast becoming a hotbed of organised crime. Even hare coursing involved high levels of organisation and surprisingly large amounts of money were connected to gambling or good breeding dogs. Murder was less common but it happened every so often. A shotgun used in self-defence during a burglary, domestic violence resulting in the death of one of the partners. Then there were the cases of manslaughter resulting from road traffic accidents, or farm labourers killed by faulty machinery. It wasn't outside the realms of possibility that Ewan Cameron had stumbled upon some night-time criminal activity and lost his life because he happened to be in the wrong place at the wrong time. Ava put in a quick call to Saunders and was relieved to hear that he was tied up in court for the rest of the day.

* * *

The Stromfordshire lime woods lay in a stretch of the Stromfordshire Wolds designated as an area of outstanding natural beauty. They had once been a vast ancient forest and still covered almost three per cent of the land in the county. Nowadays though, they were no longer a single forest but a collection of woodlands interspersed with fields and roads, rural villages and hamlets. The wood at Stainholme Abbey where Ewan Cameron's body had been dumped made up only a tiny area of the lime woods. The location Dan had given Ava for the abandoned car lay a little farther to the east and was in a larger, denser stretch of woodland.

Ava found the ranger station at the entrance to the wood. She could see Dan Cardew's van parked in a small staff car park and she pulled up alongside it. One of the rangers was inside the station working at a PC. She looked up as Ava knocked and entered.

"Police?" she asked. Her name was Faye Wellings and she explained that the head ranger, Bran Gallagher, was out showing 'that nice forensics boy' where the car was.

"Was it Mr Gallagher who discovered it?" Ava asked.

"No. Actually, I did. I was down at the lake taking some water samples when a glint of metal in the sunlight caught my eye. It was concealed in the trees. I expect your people would have found it when they got around to searching this part of the woods.

"You discovered it this morning?" Ava asked.

"Yes. Sorry, I don't know how long it'd been there. It could've been dumped overnight. You'd be surprised what gets dumped around here."

Probably not, Ava thought. They'd already found a dead body. "Maybe forensics will be able to tell how long it had been there."

Faye Wellings's face lit up. "Yeah, it's just amazing what they can do nowadays, isn't it?" The CSI effect again. These shows had duped the public into believing that there was no crime that forensic science couldn't crack. To those actually doing the day job, forensics complemented good, solid investigative police work. It didn't substitute for it.

"Has there been any unusual activity in the area lately?" Ava said.

Faye considered the question. "Not really, just the usual stuff."

"The usual stuff being?"

"Dumping of all sorts in the lake, minor vandalism, poaching, destroying bird boxes and other wildlife habitats. The farmers hereabouts get their share of thefts. There was one the same night as the murder, as a matter of fact. Did you know that?"

Ava nodded. "Do you live locally?" she asked Faye Wellings.

"Yes."

"Are people talking about the murder?"

Faye rolled her eyes. "What do you think? We don't get that many murders hereabouts." She screwed up her face. "So, yeah, there's been a bit of talk." Ava waited patiently. People seldom needed encouragement to gossip or speculate.

"Everybody's a bit shaken up, to tell the truth. A lot of us around here live some way off the beaten track. Even the houses in the village are quite far apart from one another. My friend, Olivia Darby, lives alone with her young son and I know she's nervous. She was trying to keep the news from Zak, but of course kids always get to hear about these things."

"Do you think you could point me in the direction of the car?" Ava asked.

"I'll take you down there myself." Faye shut down her computer and stood up. She looked dubiously at Ava's immaculate brown suede ankle boots.

"You might want to borrow some wellies. The ground's hard but there are still a lot of soggy parts, especially down by the lake." She disappeared into a cupboard and emerged holding up two pairs of wellies for Ava to try. Neither fitted, but Ava would have worn size tens to spare her beloved new boots, which had cost an absurd amount of money.

Faye Wellings locked up behind them. "We're not officially open to the public in the winter months, but people who want to talk to us at this time of year generally manage to find us. We run guided walks and talks and classes in the spring and summer months and during school holidays, depending on the weather."

As they made their way across a wide clearing, Faye told Ava about the history of the lime woods and their continued importance.

"The interesting thing about these woods is that they've been continuously managed by people since the eleventh century. Longer, really. Coppicing has been going on probably since Neolithic times. Deer management's a part of our job, too," she explained.

"Deer management? Does that include culling?" Ava asked.

"Nobody likes the word, but managing the deer population is a necessary evil. Deer can have a devastating effect on other wildlife in the woods. We shoot them, it's the most humane way. Poachers are less kind."

Ava grimaced, images of Bambi flitting through her head. She wouldn't be able to shoot a deer, she knew, and she was squarely on the side of the foxes when it came to hunting. Probably just as well she hadn't plumped for a career in wildlife 'management.'

They saw Dan Cardew and one of the other forensics people emerging from a heavily-wooded area at the other side of the clearing. Another man was with them, and Ava had an impression of immense size and hirsuteness. He waved at Faye as they approached.

"That's Bran Gallagher. He's the big chief around here. No one knows these woods better than him."

Bran Gallagher was a huge bear of a man, dressed like a lumberjack in a tartan shirt and jeans and a big suede jacket. He could have been the twinkly-eyed woodcutter from a children's book except that, rather disconcertingly, he was holding a chainsaw. Ava felt slightly intimidated.

Faye introduced Ava and the small party entered the wood. The car was half-hidden from view in a fringe of trees skirting the meadow. To reach the spot it must have been driven across the clearing from the woodland track and rammed into the thicket.

"Look at the damage to the saplings!" Faye exclaimed.

"Why go to such an effort to conceal the car after dumping the body in a public place?" Ava mused aloud.

"How did Mr Cameron die?" Faye asked. "I know he was murdered, but what happened to him?

"We're not sure how he died yet."

"Where do you even start?" Faye asked. "I mean his car in the woods, his body over at Stainholme. I take my hat off to you lot." Ava noticed that Faye was addressing Dan, who seemed totally oblivious of it.

"I expect the officers are keen to get on with their jobs," Bran Gallagher said tactfully. "If you need us we'll be down at the pond taking water samples." He pointed along the fringe of trees skirting the meadow. Through the tangle of branches, Ava could make out the beginnings of a dark stretch of water disappearing into the woods. "There's a lot of ponds in these parts," Bran Gallagher said. "And chalk streams. There's one runs right alongside the copse at Stainholme Abbey ruin."

Faye turned to Dan. "Hey, what if the murder victim was drowned? You could look for water in his lungs, right? I bet you could even pinpoint which pond he drowned in. That's what they'd do on CSI, right? We take water samples around here all the time, don't we, Bran? Maybe we could help with that?"

"It's a possibility," Dan stammered. "Looking for diatoms — microscopic animals in the organs and even clothes of victims of drowning has proved useful, but it's not always a hundred per cent reliable."

Ava cleared her throat with a loud, 'ahem.' "Thanks, Faye. We'll bear your offer of help in mind if it turns out the victim died by drowning."

As soon as Faye and Bran Gallagher moved away, Ava was tempted to tease Dan about his new admirer. Then she checked herself. Dan was a shy sort. Faye Wellings's obvious interest might give him a confidence boost.

"Are we looking at the actual crime scene?" she said, knowing that, like her, Dan could only speculate until the area had been processed. "What do you think happened here? Ewan Cameron stumbled on the farm robbers and they attacked him, then took his wallet and tried to destroy his car?" She frowned. "But what was he doing out in the woods late at night? Unless he was taking part in the robbery, but then why kill him?"

Ava and Dan donned the appropriate white suits and took a preliminary look at the car, a tired old Ford. The doors were unlocked. There was no glaring evidence that an act of violence had been committed in the vehicle. "Can't see any blood, but I suppose the killer could have cleaned up afterwards. Of course, we don't know how Cameron died yet. Plenty of ways to kill without spilling a drop of blood."

Ava bent to look inside the car, her eyes scanning the back and front seats. She became aware of Dan watching her nervously and reassured him. "Don't worry, I'm not going to touch anything." After a couple of minutes she straightened up and surveyed the area around the car instead, leaving the delicate work of searching for trace evidence to Dan. The case containing his equipment — an array of bottles and brushes, scissors, tweezers and jars — lay open on a plastic sheet spread out on the forest floor. A more detailed examination would follow once the vehicle was recovered and placed in storage. For now, Dan was looking for evidence that might be visible to his trained eye.

"Shout if you find anything interesting," Ava said. She stood in her oversized wellies and surveyed the immediate area. It was a short walk from where the car had been hidden to Ridgeway Farm where the theft had occurred. Ava poked her head through the car window and told Dan she was walking over to the farm to see what she could find out. Not about the robbery, that was part of a separate investigation, but given that Ewan Cameron's car had been found here, no one could rule out a possible link between the two. Ava pondered for a moment. Should she tell Saunders of her intention to visit the farm? He was in court, she concluded, and probably going to have his phone on mute all day.

A few acres of pastureland ran alongside the wood and Ava walked across, avoiding a pair of horses grazing there. Not far away she could see the outbuildings where the chemicals and equipment the thieves had got away with had likely been stored.

It turned out to be a pointless excursion. The farmer seemed more concerned about the theft than the fact that Cameron had been found dead not far from his land. Nor did he care that the victim's car had been dumped in the woods adjacent to his property. He'd seen nothing, heard nothing on the night of the robbery. No one had. No one ever does, he assured Ava. She trudged back over the field with the farmer's gloomy last words ringing in her ears.

"I knew it was only a matter of time until someone got killed by these thieves. Now maybe the bloody police will do something about it."

Chapter 5

Neal sat for a few minutes, looking at his phone and missing the sound of Ava's voice. He sipped his lukewarm tea and pulled a face. Jock Dodds had a lot of skills but making tea wasn't one of them. Had the conversation seemed strained to Ava? It had to him. He had been genuinely pleased to hear from her and he knew his voice had conveyed this. But he didn't know what he should have said. She'd called him about a case and he was glad she'd sought him out. She could have contacted the local force and asked them to send someone to break the news to Laura Cameron. Like him, Ava knew it was important to see how someone reacted to the news of a loved one's violent death. The motivation behind her call made solid sense from the point of view of the case she was investigating, but Neal found himself wanting to know if there had been more to it than that.

Since his walk up the Ben with Jock, Neal's low mood had begun to lift. He still had a picture in his mind of Maggie seemingly dying in his arms, but it was no longer a jarring, repetitive image. He was able to focus on the outcome. After all, the worst hadn't happened. Neal knew he should embrace that and let all the rest go. His thoughts turned to Laura Cameron and the sorrow that lay ahead for her when she learned of her husband's death. He finished his tea and set off, heavy-hearted.

The address Ava had given Neal led him to the door of a tenement block in Marchmont, a residential area south of the city centre. It was the sort of area Neal and his ex-wife Myrna might have ended up in had they stayed together. Archie would have grown up within sight of Arthur's Seat and with the Meadows as his playground. Neal sighed. Another life.

He rang the Camerons' bell and was admitted to a gloomy stairwell. Steps worn shiny with use led up to the fourth floor where a woman was already waiting by her door. "Mrs Cameron?" Neal asked. The woman nodded. He had explained who he was over the entry phone but not why he was calling. He wondered whether she suspected already. Her face gave no indication of her state of mind. Neal showed her his ID and she invited him in.

"Is it Ewan?" she asked.

"Yes."

"It's bad news, isn't it?"

Neal gave a nod. "I'm sorry to have to be the bearer of sad news, Mrs Cameron. Your husband's body was found yesterday morning in the Stromfordshire countryside."

"Stromfordshire?"

"Yes. Are you surprised to learn that your husband was so far from home?"

Laura Cameron nodded. Something was amiss. She was showing no outward signs of shock. Behind her tortoiseshell glasses, her eyes were not moist. She did emit a slight sigh.

"Would you like to sit down, Mrs Cameron?" Neal asked. "Can I get you something, a glass of water perhaps?"

She shook her head. "I'm sorry if I'm not reacting the way you'd expect me to, Inspector. My husband's been gone for nearly a week. I've run this scenario — along with many others — through my head scores of times since he failed to come home. When you've already imagined the worst, hearing the truth is almost a relief."

"I'm sorry for your loss," Neal said. He had geared himself up for an outburst of emotion and wasn't sure how to deal with this measured calm.

Laura Cameron sat down and invited Neal to do the same.

"There's also the fact that my husband has been absent in other ways for a long time now. Death is only one kind of separation, you know."

"Was your husband in the habit of disappearing for long periods of time?" Neal asked, gently.

"Not long periods. Days perhaps, never more than a week."

"Was he in any kind of trouble? Financial difficulties, perhaps?"

"Ewan hasn't worked for a while. He . . . had a sort of breakdown and lost his job. I'm a primary school teacher. Money's been a bit tight lately but we've got by."

Neal nodded, suspecting there was more to the story than Ewan losing his job. "I'm sorry to ask you this, Mrs Cameron, but were you and your husband having marital problems?"

Laura Cameron frowned. "We'd been . . . estranged, if that's the right word, for some time. To tell you the truth we didn't really communicate. Since his breakdown, Ewan's been spending nearly all of his time in the spare room, drawing. He went to art school and wanted to be an artist once, but we had a mortgage to pay — you know how it is."

Neal nodded faintly. He knew all about making sacrifices.

"Where did your husband go when he took off for a while? Did you ever ask him?"

"Of course. He just said that he'd been drinking heavily and crashed at one of his drinking buddies. I suppose he was an alcoholic, though we never really discussed it." There was a slight quiver in Laura Cameron's voice as she said this, but she maintained her composure. "I don't even know if it was just alcohol."

"Drugs?" Neal asked.

"Possibly. I don't really know. To tell the truth I was so busy working, I just kind of shut it all out. Was that terrible of me, Inspector? What must you think of me?"

"It doesn't matter what I think, Mrs Cameron. I know nothing about you or your husband and I'm not in a position to judge. Believe me, in this line of work you learn that people often have very complex reasons for the way they behave."

As Laura Cameron had not yet asked, Neal told her. "Your husband didn't die of natural causes, Mrs Cameron."

"Oh?" Laura said, suddenly less assured. "Was it an accident? Or was he murdered? It's alright, Inspector. I'm not going to fall apart when I hear the truth."

Later, describing Laura Cameron's apparent coldness to Ava, Neal told her that she had not, until that moment, come across as lacking in compassion. It was more that she had an air of resignation about her, as though she were accustomed to life knocking her back.

Neal cleared his throat. "I'm afraid I don't know. There will have to be a post-mortem examination. Do you have any idea why your husband would be in Stromfordshire, Mrs Cameron?" Neal waited, his gaze shifting to the coffee table, and an unopened box of tissues.

Laura looked suddenly guarded. "Ewan went to art college in Stromford. He lived there for three years. But as far as I know he hasn't been back since he graduated ten years ago."

A connection, then. Neal felt a tingle of excitement. "Could he have been visiting someone there? An old friend, perhaps?"

"Can you excuse me for a couple of minutes, Inspector?" Laura asked, standing up.

Neal nodded, wondering if she was going into another room to break down in private. He crossed to the triple bay window and looked out at the view. Marchmont was a pleasant, middle-class area. Its proximity to Edinburgh's universities meant that it was also popular with students. Jock had rented a room here as a student and he'd told Neal that the more permanent residents were unhappy at the number of homes now under multiple occupation.

Neal heard the sound of a flushing toilet, but Laura Cameron did not return immediately. He waited. When at last she came back, she was carrying a large photograph album, which she placed on the coffee table. Then, she sat on the sofa, close to Neal. He was aware of a trace of some vaguely familiar scent, of her leg next to his, long and slim in tight-fitting jeans.

Laura opened the album and pointed to a picture of two young women and two young men. One of the women was obviously a younger Laura. "Ewan was friends with another student at the art college, David Pine. David came to Edinburgh a couple of times, it's where he met my best friend, Rhona." She pointed to the other woman in the picture. "David and Rhona married after David graduated. Then, Ewan and David had a falling out and Rhona and I lost touch."

Neal wrote down the names. "What did your husband and Mr Pine fall out about? It must have been something pretty big if they never spoke again."

Laura shrugged. "I don't know. I asked Rhona but she didn't seem to know, and Ewan wouldn't tell me."

"Weren't you curious?"

"Of course, but Ewan got angry whenever I brought it up." She looked at Neal, a spark in her eye for the first time. "I'm sure a falling out between Ewan and David ten years ago wouldn't be an explanation for Ewan's death, if that's what you're thinking."

In fact this was exactly what had crossed Neal's mind. "Just trying to build up a picture of your husband, Mrs Cameron. It all helps to let us see the bigger picture. Some details might seem minor but they could be significant. This David and Rhona Pine, do you have contact details for them?"

Laura shook her head. "I don't even know if they still live in Stromford. Perhaps you could let me know if they do."

"Yes, as long as it's OK with them."

"Of course. Rhona and I were good friends once. Perhaps now that Ewan's gone . . ." Laura Cameron's voice trailed off. Perhaps she was realising that her focus ought to be on her dead husband. "We were childhood sweethearts. He did love me, he begged me to marry him." A pause. "And I did love him."

Did, Neal noted. He sensed that her use of the past tense arose not from suddenly being widowed, but referred to a time much more distant even than her marriage. He noticed her lips quivering.

Neal put down his pen, convinced that this was the moment when Laura Cameron was finally going to crack up. He was wrong. Apart from a bit of nervous hand-wringing, she kept it together. It struck him that there was an odd dichotomy about her utterances. One minute she claimed that she and her husband were leading almost separate lives, the next she insisted that they loved each other. Of course, the two weren't mutually exclusive, but Neal couldn't help feeling that there was something discordant in the way she described their relationship. Still, grief affected people in different ways.

He was about to ask if Laura would mind identifying her husband's body, when she asked, "Can I see him?"

"Yes. We need someone to make a positive identification," Neal said.

"Will I have to go to Stromford?"

"I'm sorry, but yes. The investigation into your husband's death will be carried out by the Stromfordshire police."

"By you?" She fiddled with the buttons on her oversized cardigan.

Neal caught a glimpse of her eyes behind her spectacles. They were the dark brown of old mahogany.

"I'm not sure," he answered truthfully. "My sergeant is working the case with another DI but I might be involved when I return to work."

"You're off duty now?" There was a trace of alarm in her tone.

"I'm on leave. My colleague called and asked if I would visit you. She thought it would be . . ."

". . . Useful to see how I reacted to the news of my husband's death? You can tell her how oddly I've behaved, Inspector Neal, how unlike the stereotypical bereaved wife."

Neal felt uncomfortable. She had summed up what he had been thinking. "I can arrange for someone to drive you down at your earliest convenience, Mrs Cameron." He handed her details of how to contact him.

"I'll have to contact my school and arrange a couple of days off work."

"Of course. I'll leave you to make the necessary arrangements."

It seemed peculiar not to be offering comfort to Laura Cameron. The normal conventions did not seem to apply, so Neal beat his retreat. Laura Cameron saw him out. He was certain she was watching him as he descended the four flights of stairs. As he exited, he heard her door bang shut. It sounded decisive.

Chapter 6

"Zak! Wake up!" Olivia Darby shook her son awake. Zak looked around the room, his eyes wide and fearful like a frightened animal.

"Time to get up, sweetheart. She looked at her son's peaky face and asked him if he was feeling alright. He said that he was, but she wasn't convinced. "Are you worrying about something? Is everything alright at school? You'd tell me, wouldn't you, if something was bothering you? It's not that murder, is it?"

Her son repeated that he was 'OK.'

Still anxious, she left him to get ready for school.

At breakfast, he seemed exhausted. He sat hunched over his bowl of porridge, looking like all the cares of the world were on his shoulders. Olivia knew better than to 'go on.'

At twenty to nine, Rowan Pine appeared in front of the house and waited by the garden gate. She did this every morning, unless it was wet, and then she'd come inside. Rowan was always the one waiting, Zak the one running around collecting his lunch and his PE kit at the last minute. This morning, though, Zak was out the door as soon as Rowan arrived. Was it Olivia's imagination or did Rowan look a little strained also? She was a pale child at the best of times, but this morning she looked like she was coming down with something. Olivia wondered whether she should call Rhona Pine and ask if there were any bugs doing the rounds. She hoped they weren't sickening for something. As she waved them off she told herself to stop worrying and get down to some work.

Olivia worked from home. Through a mixture of talent, hard work and determination, she'd managed to build up a small business. She was doing well, designing textiles, making cushions and other items. The inspiration for her designs came from nature and her friend Faye Wellings had been of invaluable help in introducing her to the flora and fauna of the Stromfordshire countryside. It gave Olivia a buzz to see her work for sale in the gift and craft shop on the Long Hill in Stromford, and know she could make her own way in the world. Of course it wasn't all arty work. Doing alterations and making up curtains were her bread and butter and they kept her busy. She enjoyed laying out the pretty material her clients brought to her on her huge kitchen table and turning them into something that would enhance their homes.

Olivia worked steadily for almost three hours. At noon, Belle started to become restless. "OK, Belle. Go get your lead and we'll take a walk in the woods." Belle padded off excitedly while Olivia tidied away her sewing things.

They took a shortcut across a frozen field. Brittle ice had formed over the furrows, and here and there Belle stopped to poke her nose through and lap at the cold water underneath.

Olivia's friend, Faye Wellings, was busy mending some bird boxes when Olivia tracked her down. "Good timing. I was just about to go back into the shack for lunch." The 'shack' was the big timbered hut where the rangers were based. It was warm inside, and they peeled off layers of clothing. Faye put the kettle on.

"I spoke with some of the police officers investigating the murder," Faye said, as she poured boiling water into a teapot and put a couple of mugs on the table. "Ham Bell said the whole place was swarming with cops. Couple of detectives from Stromford, forensics people, the lot."

Olivia raised her eyebrows. "There's no doubt it was murder, then?"

Faye shrugged. "Looks that way. Ham certainly seems to think so. Murder investigations are a bit out of his remit, though. He's more used to dealing with hare coursing and thefts of farm machinery. That's why they've called the big boys in — one of them is Ham's uncle, DI Reg Saunders."

"Poor man. How sad to end up in such a bleak spot. Let me know if you hear anything, won't you? I don't like the idea of a murderer on the loose with Zak and me alone in that cottage.

"Your cottage is a little isolated. Your nearest neighbours are the Pines, aren't they? I've heard they're a bit unfriendly."

"She's okay, a bit reserved. I don't really know him. They keep themselves to themselves. Zak's friendly with their eldest, Rowan — she's a nice kid. Anyway, look who's talking about being isolated. You live in the middle of nowhere too. What would you do if the mad axeman came calling?"

"I'd probably set him to work on some coppicing. Ham and Rosie's caravan is practically in my back garden, but you're all alone, Liv."

Olivia shrugged. "How's the build coming along?"

"It's coming along OK. They'd both like to spend more time on it but Ham's always so busy at work."

"It must be freezing in that caravan at this time of year."

"Rosie says it's surprisingly cosy. Especially with Ham to snuggle up to."

Rosie and Ham had been living in the caravan for the best part of a year while they built their dream house. Their ambition was to 'live off the grid.' Like a lot of the locals, Olivia thought they were both slightly bonkers. "Looks more like an archaeological dig than a new building."

Belle looked up suddenly, cocking an ear. Faye and Olivia exchanged uneasy glances.

"It's only Bran," Faye said, as the door opened and a man walked in dressed in faded jeans and a crumpled Fair Isle sweater. "All this talk about murder is making us jumpy. Anyway, time I got back to work." Faye waved at Bran. He waved back, but he was looking at Olivia.

"Hi, Bran," she said.

Bran nodded, suddenly awkward.

"I finished the last of the coppice work on the other side of the pond," he said to Faye. "I'll need your help with the fencing down by Lark's meadow this afternoon."

"Okay, boss," Faye answered. Bran and Faye were employed full-time, and there were a couple of others who worked part-time or came over from one of the other sites if they were needed. Bran was Irish by birth and had a captivating Irish accent. He had moved to Stromfordshire when he was twenty. He was fair-skinned and freckled, with ginger hair and an untrimmed ginger beard that gave him the look of a wild man.

Cold as it was outside, there was a sheen of sweat on his forehead from his recent labours. Olivia smelt his musky aroma of sweat and sawdust and the great outdoors. She remembered the previous month, when he had led her through a reel at a ceilidh in the village hall. After a few glasses of beer he'd at last plucked up the courage to ask her to dance with him. If only he'd known that she'd been holding her breath all night, waiting for him to do just that. They'd been seeing each other ever since, but hadn't told anyone, especially Zak. Bran sometimes stayed over at her cottage, arriving late in the evening after Zak was asleep and leaving in the early hours of the morning to avoid being seen by her son. Fortunately Zak was a sound sleeper and nothing short of an earthquake would cause him to stir once he'd dropped off. Olivia felt a little guilty at not telling Faye that she and Zak weren't always alone. In fact, Bran had been with her on the night of the murder. He had slipped away even earlier than usual to go for a run in the woods before work.

"I'd better be off," Olivia said, waving the leash at Belle, who was standing on her back legs, looking like she too had been waiting to dance with Bran.

"How's Zak?" he asked.

Safe subject, Olivia thought. "He's great. See you later, Bran."

Outside, Faye shook her head. "Honestly, I don't know who's more pathetic, you or him. You two are made for each other. Everyone can see it except you."

"Everyone?" Olivia was alarmed. She hated the thought of being the subject of village gossip.

"Well, you know what I mean — me and Ham and Rosie and . . ."

"Oh, right, everyone."

"He'd make a great dad for Zak," Faye said.

Olivia scowled. Her friend had overstepped the mark. "Zak's got me. He doesn't need anyone else."

"Well, if there is a psycho on the loose, I know I'd feel safer with a man like Bran under my roof. That's all I'm saying."

It was all Olivia allowed her to say. Mad at Faye for suggesting that she couldn't take care of Zak on her own when she had been doing just that since the day he was born, Olivia muttered, "See you later," and struck off across the field. Belle scurried behind her.

Chapter 7

A glowering grey sky hung over the railway station. Grey sleet, driven diagonally by a spiteful north wind, spat icy droplets onto platform four, where Ava was waiting for the ten thirty-five from Edinburgh. The train, inevitably, was running late. Fifteen minutes and counting. Sending the weather ahead of it, Ava was tempted to think, except that for weeks it had been freezing here too. She had driven to Pippinham from Stromford, there being no direct connection there with the route from the north. It was quicker to drive than change trains and she wanted the business of identifying the body over with as soon as possible.

At last the train lumbered into view and Ava waited as it slowed and came to a jolting halt on the platform. Laura Cameron was among the first to alight. She was wearing a navy down-filled parka with a fur-fringed hood and was holding a small, tartan suitcase, which she put on the ground as soon as she stepped down. She pulled up the handle, then stood, looking around her before her gaze fell on Ava quietly appraising her from behind the barrier.

"Laura Cameron?" Ava called. She had thought of bringing a sheet of paper with Laura's name on it to hold up, but it wasn't necessary. The station wasn't busy.

As she watched Laura making her way towards the barriers, Ava thought of her conversation with Neal the day before.

"She took the news of her husband's death very calmly," he'd said. "No tears, no histrionics. Yet I didn't get the impression she was a cold person. Just sort of resigned and accepting. Like she was used to disappointments." Ava fancied she could detect pity in his voice and wondered if Neal had been attracted to Laura Cameron. She thought that he had a penchant for vulnerable women. But as Laura approached, she seemed not vulnerable but, as Neal had said, strangely composed and self-contained.

She wheeled her suitcase through the barrier. "Sergeant Merry?"

"Yes." In the circumstances it seemed inappropriate to say she was pleased to meet her. "My car's parked in the car park. It's just outside the entrance."

"Is there somewhere I could grab a coffee first?" Laura asked. "There was no buffet car on the train because of a staff shortage and I'm gasping."

"Sure," Ava replied. "There's a little café just by the ticket office, where you can get a decent Americano." She knew because she'd just had one.

In the car, Laura sipped her coffee, looking out the window though there was nothing to see, only the high wall around the car park and the rain slashing against it. Laura seemed content to sit in silence, but Ava was biting back the questions on her lips.

"I suppose to bring me all this way, you must be pretty sure it's my husband's body you've found," Laura Cameron said, breaking the silence. "Strange, Ewan dying here, so far from home."

Not so strange, Ava thought. Neal had told her on the phone about Ewan Cameron's connection with Stromford. Only ten years ago, he'd spent the best part of three years at the art college there. Something had brought him back. Or someone.

"I'm sorry, Mrs Cameron. We are pretty sure the man we found is your husband."

Laura Cameron nodded.

"Inspector Neal said your husband went to college in Stromford?"

The look Laura Cameron gave her was hard to read, but it seemed to Ava that she was surprised Neal had spoken to her about his visit. As though passing on this information to a stranger represented a betrayal of her confidence.

"I've no idea why Ewan would come back here. He couldn't get away quickly enough after he graduated."

"Oh?" said Ava, "Why was that? Was he unhappy here?"

"My husband was the sort of person who wasn't particularly happy anywhere, Sergeant Merry. He was of a melancholy disposition."

It was a quaint, old-fashioned way of suggesting that Ewan Cameron might have been prone to depression. Ava waited, sensing Laura had more to say.

"He wasn't always like that, he'd been happy once."

She didn't say it but Ava had the distinct impression that Laura meant her husband's happiness preceded his marriage, or perhaps even his years at college.

Laura's hands were clasped around the empty coffee cup sitting on her lap. Not exactly a glass half-full sort of character, Ava thought. Then she reminded herself of the purpose of Laura Cameron's visit and felt ashamed.

"Are you ready?" she asked the woman, gently. Ava started up the car and drove out of the station almost directly into open countryside, wondering how a village in the middle of nowhere had a direct line to Edinburgh and

London when Stromford did not. Some people liked the fact that the town was off all the main routes. You really had to want to visit Stromford if you made it here. It was fortunate that the cathedral was a major attraction or the town might have died over the centuries.

"Did you come to visit your husband much when he was at college in Stromford, Mrs Cameron?"

Laura Cameron's reply surprised her. "Never."

"You were at school together, though, weren't you?"

Again, Laura gave Ava that hard-to-measure look. "DI Neal has obviously filled you in thoroughly."

"He didn't mention when you got married."

"We were childhood sweethearts, yes, but when we went to university we had an . . . arrangement. We both saw other people. We decided that if we still wanted each other afterwards, then we'd know we were meant to be together."

"So you had a kind of open relationship?" Ava asked.

"Yes."

"And did you see other people?"

She sighed. "I had a couple of relationships, just to amuse myself really. I was never in any doubt that Ewan was the one for me."

"This arrangement, whose idea was it? Was it your husband's?"

"I know what you're thinking, Sergeant Merry, that Ewan wanted to have his cake and eat it. But it wasn't like that. I had my freedom too."

Except you didn't want it. Ava and a boy she dated at school had made a similar arrangement. In her experience, few relationships survived the excitement of leaving your home town, going to university and meeting all kinds of new people.

"Did your husband date anyone seriously, that you're aware of?"

"No." Laura Cameron's reply was definitive.

"Inspector Neal told me about your friendship with David and Rhona Pine and Mr Cameron's falling out with David Pine. The Pines live in a village in the Stromfordshire countryside. Do you think your husband might have come here to see them?"

"How would I know? But I can't think of any other reason. Like I told Inspector Neal, I don't have a clue what Ewan and David fell out over. Ewan wouldn't talk about it."

So Laura and Ewan's marriage had been founded on a secret. Not a great recipe for a successful marriage. Ava would have insisted on knowing. They drove in silence for a bit and then Laura asked, "I suppose you'll be speaking with Rhona and David, won't you?"

"Yes. If Mr Cameron visited them during his time in Stromford, or if visiting them was the purpose of his trip here, they might be able to help with our investigation."

"Assisting the police with their enquiries. Isn't that just what you lot say when you suspect someone has something to do with the crime you're investigating?"

"No. That's a popular misconception." It was what Ava herself used to think before she became a police officer, and there was a grain of truth in the assumption. "Do you have any reason to believe Mr and Mrs Pine would want to harm your husband?"

"I haven't seen them for ten years. As far as I know Ewan hadn't either. Ten years is a long time to wait if you have a reason for wanting to kill someone, don't you think?"

No, Ava thought. Not in her experience. The past often bubbled up, even years later.

"You don't agree, Sergeant Merry?"

"Maybe. Some people have long memories — or are short on forgiveness. I wasn't suggesting that Mr and Mrs Pine are suspects, but they are a link to Mr Cameron and I think that warrants investigating." As should you, Ava thought.

When the car turned into the road leading to the hospital, Laura Cameron sniffed and Ava looked at her, wondering if at last she would show some sign of nerves. But as far as she could tell, the woman next to her was still in control of her emotions. Maybe she thinks there's still a possibility that it might not be him, Ava thought, pityingly. Everyone had a breaking point. She wondered if Laura Cameron would reach hers when faced with her husband's dead body, when hope was finally extinguished.

Ava was wrong. In the mortuary, the assistant pulled back the sheet covering Ewan Cameron's body, just enough to reveal his head and shoulders. "That's him," Laura said calmly.

"Take your time, Mrs Cameron. Are you sure?"

"I don't need any more time. That's my husband. That's Ewan." She turned away before the assistant replaced the sheet.

Ava tried to believe Neal's assertion that Laura Cameron was not a cold person. She took Laura's arm and guided her into the corridor. "Can I get you anything?" she asked.

"I don't think so."

"You must be hungry after your journey."

"No. Seeing my dead husband has dampened my appetite, but please go ahead and get something to eat if you're hungry, Sergeant Merry. Perhaps I'll buy a sandwich to eat on the train."

Ava was starving. She'd been up since six and had started the day with a five mile run before dropping her younger brother, Ollie, off at school. Since then she'd only had coffee and a handful of nuts and berries.

"I'm okay," she lied. "Mrs Cameron, what are your plans? Would you like me to book you a room for the night in a local hotel?"

Laura stared at her. "Actually, I'd rather go home. Could you arrange for a taxi to take me back to the station?"

"Already? Are you sure you feel like travelling after—?"

"Seeing my dead husband? Home's the only place I want to be. There's nothing for me here. How soon can Ewan's body be released? I need to arrange for it to be taken back to Edinburgh."

"I'm not sure," Ava admitted honestly. She knew it was likely to be some time.

"I have to get back to work tomorrow. I'm a primary school teacher. The children will be missing me. Will you, you know, let me know if there's any news?"

"Of course. Mrs Cameron, you are entitled to victim support. I could liaise with the force up there to arrange for something to be put in place for you in Edinburgh."

"No. I don't want anything like that. I'm not that sort of person."

Not what sort of person? Ava wondered. The kind who knew when to accept help when it was offered? Perhaps Laura Cameron was afraid of appearing needy.

"We may need to speak with you again soon."

"You can phone me, can't you?"

"I . . . yes, or someone could come up to Edinburgh."

"Isn't Inspector Neal still there?"

"He's returning soon."

"There is one thing you could do for me," Laura said. "Can you give Rhona Pine my contact details?"

"Of course."

"Wait. I'm not sure . . . perhaps you shouldn't. I'll let you know."

Ava was almost relieved to witness Laura's indecision. It proved that she was human after all. She glanced at her watch, wondering if she could enlist PJ as a taxi driver. She did not feel particularly thrilled at the prospect of driving Laura Cameron back to the station. Of course there were more questions she would like to ask but she had a feeling that despite her apparent equilibrium, Laura Cameron was hurting somewhere deep inside. Ava suspected that Laura was the kind of person who would wait until she was alone to grieve. She was beginning to believe, as Neal had, that it was not coldness but reserve that governed Laura's behaviour. She possessed a kind of quiet fortitude, born perhaps out of disappointment, as Neal conjectured, or perhaps something else. Maybe it was a Scottish thing, she thought, indulging in some uncharacteristic national stereotyping.

"My colleague, PC Jenkins, is free. I'll ask her to drive you back to the station."

"Thank you," Laura said quietly.

Ava drove them to the police station and hauled PJ out of the staffroom, where she was tucking into a giant Subway roll.

"I don't think she'll open up to you, but see if you can get her to talk about her husband and his student life in Stromford. I've got a feeling that she knows more than she's letting on about the reason why he fell out with David Pine ten years ago," Ava said. "Finish your lunch first," she added.

"There's another of these in the fridge if you're hungry," PJ said. "I got it for Steve but he's been called out. Possible domestic on the Foxgrove Estate."

"OMG, Peej. Never let me forget to tell you how much I love you," Ava said, her stomach rumbling. Then, in an afterthought, "Actually, take it for Mrs Cameron. I don't think she's eaten a thing today. And get her a coffee before you put her on the train."

PJ swept crumbs from her uniform and crossed to the fridge. She waved the sandwich enticingly under Ava's nose as she made for the door.

"Merry!" Saunders called over.

Ava had no idea he had been nearby. He had sent her to pick up Laura Cameron and take her to identify the body.

"Get your coat. We're going out to interview David and Rhona Pine. I got your text saying Laura Cameron made a positive ID."

He looked heavy and hungover, older than the last time she'd seen him. His clothes were creased, as though he'd spent the night in them, and he had a five o'clock shadow. If he was worrying about something, it was unlikely to be the case, Ava thought.

Outside in the car park, Saunders tossed her his car keys. "You drive. Wake me when we get there."

Ava had looked up the Pines' address as soon as Neal had told her about their connection with Ewan Cameron, so she had no need to ask where they were headed. Saunders belched loudly, souring the air. Then he settled back in the passenger seat and closed his eyes. Ava had never felt Neal's absence so keenly.

With Saunders asleep, there was no need for strained conversation during the forty minutes that it took to drive out to Stainholme village. More than once Ava had to slow almost to a standstill behind lumbering tractors or some other piece of hulking farm machinery. She was aware that theft of tractors and other heavy equipment by organised gangs was a growing problem out here in the sticks, but moving at twelve miles an hour on a narrow stretch of road where there was no possibility of overtaking made her feel like cheering them on.

The village itself was served only by narrow, winding roads. It consisted of a single main street with a school, church, village hall, village store and post office. Its homes were scattered and bounded by swathes of fields. The Pines lived in a barn conversion on the outskirts of the village. It was set back from the lane, half-hidden by a curving hedgerow. Ava admired it from a distance, liking the way that the winter sunshine through the trees cast tiger-striped shadows across its orange roof tiles. She gave Saunders a dig in the ribs. He snorted awake and looked at her irritably.

"You said to wake you when we got there," Ava said.

The door opened as they approached and a woman, who could only be Rhona Pine, stood before them with a sleepy baby cradled in her left arm and a half-empty bottle of formula milk in her right. Her eyes were ringed with dark circles, that trademark of all new parents. She had startlingly abundant red hair and her skin was pale and freckled. She wore jeans and a loose-fitting black jumper, with a soft pink muslin square draped over one shoulder.

DS Saunders showed her his badge. "Good afternoon. Is it alright if we come in?"

Rhona Pine nodded. Ava had phoned her to check that it was a convenient time to call.

"I'm Sergeant Ava Merry. I spoke with you earlier," she said.

Another nod. "Shaun's almost asleep. Do you mind if I put him down first?"

She led them into a light, airy sitting room with a large brick fireplace and a wood-burning stove giving out a welcome heat. Wide French doors gave a view of the garden and paddock land beyond, where a couple of ponies were grazing. How the other half live, Ava thought.

"Nice place," Saunders remarked.

"Bit minimalist, isn't it?" Ava said looking around. There wasn't much in the way of furniture, just a black leather sofa and two matching chairs, a huge plasma TV on the wall, a coffee table and a trio of wicker baskets arranged in a corner with a vase of flowers on top.

"Could do with a bit of plastering," Saunders said, referring to an exposed brickwork wall that Ava quite liked.

"So what do we know about the Pines?" Saunders asked.

"He's some kind of design consultant. Pretty successful if this place is anything to go by. She's a stay-at-home mum. They're both in their early thirties, three kids. Neither of them has form."

As she was speaking, Rhona Pine returned. She gave a polite cough as she entered the room. "Would you like tea or coffee?" Her accent reminded Ava of Neal's.

They both said no. A man appeared in the doorway. He hovered behind Rhona, looking protective.

"I'm David Pine." His voice and stance were assertive without being aggressive. "I understand this is about Ewan Cameron?"

Ava glanced at Saunders. He seemed content for her to ask the questions.

"Mr Cameron was a friend of yours, wasn't he?"

The Pines exchanged glances. They had probably rehearsed what to say, but not who was going to say it. David cleared his throat. "A long time ago. We were students together at the art college in Stromford, but Ewan went back to Edinburgh after he graduated. We lost touch, like you do."

"Did he contact you before coming to Stromford, or arrange to visit?" Ava went on. "Even if he was in Stromford on some business of his own, I'd expect him to look up his old friends."

David shook his head. "No. He didn't contact us or come to visit us. We didn't even know he was in Stromfordshire until you got in touch with us."

Rhona stared expressionlessly at the wooden floor. It seemed that she was content to let her husband speak for both of them.

"Mrs Pine? Were you surprised that Ewan Cameron didn't get in touch with you, since he was in town?" Rhona's pale face seemed to turn a shade paler, her freckles stood out like polka dots against her bleached skin. Ava's first thought was that she was afraid, but of what she had no idea.

"I . . . No. Perhaps he was intending to before . . . before . . ."

Before someone murdered him, thought Ava. To David Pine, she said, "Mr Pine, we are aware that you and Ewan

67

Cameron fell out in your last term at college." She waited a moment, giving David and Rhona time to digest this fact before asking her next, obvious question. "What did you fall out about, Mr Pine? We've spoken with Laura Cameron and she said her husband wouldn't tell her. It must have been something big if he couldn't even tell his wife about it."

Rhona Cameron suddenly looked animated. "You've seen Laura?"

"She was in Stromford yesterday. As the next of kin we asked her to identify her husband's body."

"Poor Laura," Rhona said. David put his arm around her and drew her to him.

Ava asked again.

The Pines looked at each other, then David sighed. "If you must know, Sergeant, I discovered that Ewan had slept with Rhona."

"Right. Was this before or after you were married?"

"Before," Rhona whispered.

Her husband's arm stayed firmly in place around her shoulder. "It only happened once."

Ava nodded. She could appreciate that David Pine might have fallen out with his best friend over something like that.

Rhona was beginning to look as though the only thing keeping her upright was her husband's support. David had provided a plausible explanation for the rift in his relationship with Ewan Cameron, but Ava couldn't help wondering if there was more to it.

Predictably, when questioned about their whereabouts at the time of Cameron's death, the Pines both claimed they were at home, Rhona asleep, David walking the floors with a colicky baby Shaun.

There was not much else for it but to thank the Pines for their time. Ava and Saunders made their way back to the car. Ava felt dispirited. David Pine had answered her questions willingly enough, but Ava had been struck by

Rhona's silence, her nervous demeanour. It was hard to believe that the Pines were not connected in some way to Ewan Cameron's death. Ava wished it was Jim Neal sitting next to her in the car. Then she would be voicing her thoughts, not keeping them to herself.

"Penny for them, Blondie," Saunders said, as if reading her mind.

"Just considering . . . scenarios," Ava replied.

"Worked it out yet?" His voice was mocking.

"There just don't seem to be that many possibilities. Unless the Pines are involved somehow."

"Yeah, well, if you ask me, Cameron's death had something to do with that raid on Ridgeway Farm. That's the angle I'm going to pursue. You and Jimmy-lad can follow a different angle if you can find one." Ava took her eye off the road to give him a questioning look.

"That's right, Scotty's back. Got in touch with DCI Lowe last night and said he'd be in this morning. Missed him, have you?"

Yes. Ava thought with a pang.

"I take it you won't miss old Reggie. Well, just for the record, the feeling's mutual."

* * *

The afternoon wore on. Time dragged while Ava reviewed her notes on Ewan Cameron's murder, did some research and drank so many cups of coffee she began to feel jittery. She took a white envelope from her handbag and slipped it into her drawer. Inside was a 'congratulations' card for PJ, who was sitting her detective constable's exam that afternoon. It was her second attempt and Ava had been coaching her for several weeks. If only her friend could conquer her nerves, she should do okay.

She hadn't really expected to find Neal sitting at his desk when she arrived back. Still, it was disappointing to see his room still empty every time she glanced across. He was probably in a briefing with DCI George Lowe. Ava put down her joy at Neal's return to relief that she would no longer be working so closely with Saunders, but there was more to it than that. How much more and what kind of more, she wasn't ready to acknowledge, so she pushed it to the back of her mind. Her relationship with Joel Agard was going well. He was a kind man, an attentive lover and she did have genuine feelings for him. It was just that she wasn't sure how deeply those feelings went, and she was afraid that Joel might be falling in love with her. Ava had no wish to hurt him. With a sigh, she pushed these thoughts to the back of her mind and tried to concentrate on her work.

Laura Cameron struck her as a strange character. Her apparent lack of emotion at the news of her husband's death or when seeing his body seemed at odds with her assertion about the love that had existed between them. Had. Somewhere along the line, their relationship had faltered. David Pine's claim that Ewan and Rhona had slept together hardly seemed enough reason for the break-up of their friendship. After all, David had forgiven Rhona and they had married soon afterwards. They had been expecting a child. Perhaps that had made the difference.

Laura Cameron claimed not to know the reason why her husband had fallen out with his best friend. Rhona had been *her* best friend, so how could she not have known? Why hadn't she insisted on Ewan telling her, since it meant that she couldn't see Rhona? It was all a bit unconvincing.

At three forty, Ava left her desk and went to the staffroom to make yet another coffee. As she waited for her cup to fill, she heard the sound of footsteps in the corridor outside. Ava felt a thrill of anticipation. When she turned around Jim Neal was standing in the doorway. "Jim!" Ava cried, before she could check herself. She was, after all, an impulsive sort of person.

"Ava." Jim Neal nodded. Then, incredibly, he smiled, pleased, it seemed at her apparent joy at seeing him. Ava held up a cup and Neal nodded again. "Earl Grey, please."

"Good to have you back, sir."

"Does that have anything to do with a certain Reg Saunders?"

"Not at all. I just prefer working with more enlightened men."

"You found him a bit old school, then?"

"Among other things," Ava said with uncharacteristic tact. "How's Maggie?"

"She's good. Actually, she'd like to see you. She wants to thank you."

"Thank me?" Ava was genuinely surprised.

"It was down to you that we discovered the identity of the killer in time." Ava was about to protest when Neal stopped her with a look. "I've been so wrapped up in myself since it happened that I haven't thanked you either. I'm sorry about that. I am deeply grateful for your intervention." He cleared his throat.

Ava could see that this was awkward for him. She handed him his tea and they both sat down. "My way wouldn't have worked," Ava said softly. "My instinct was to rush in, all guns blazing. If I'd done that—"

"Don't," Neal said. "There was no right way to play it. Let's just be thankful the outcome wasn't as bad as it could have been. Normally I'm in favour of reflecting, but . . . not in this case, not anymore."

"Okay," replied Ava, hesitantly. Relieved to move on, she asked, "Did DCI Lowe fill you in on the Cameron murder?"

"Yes, and I've spoken with Saunders. What intrigues me is the coincidence of Cameron being murdered in this particular part of the world, and so close to the Pines' home." He paused. "Have we organised a door-to-door around Stainholme village to see if anyone saw or heard anything the night Cameron was killed?"

"Yes, sir. There's also an appeal for more information going out on the local news this evening."

"Where's Ash at on the autopsy report?"

"He estimated time of death at between ten thirty and three in the morning."

"Cause of death?"

"Toxicology report hasn't come back yet but Ash believes he was drugged, then smothered."

Neal nodded. "The killer could be female if the victim was incapacitated first."

"Ash said the same thing. We're puzzled about Cameron's body being found so far from his car. It's a long way to drag a body, through the woods from Ridgeway to Stainholme. Why would you do that? We've considered the possibility that either Cameron or his killer were involved in the Ridgeway Farm robbery but that still doesn't account for Cameron's body turning up at the old abbey. Or the fact that Cameron's ID was found so near the farm. If he witnessed the crime, why kill him, drag him through the woods, then drop his wallet and driving licence so near his car? Would have been easier to torch the car with him in it."

Neal agreed. "That suggests to me that the farm robbery was a wholly separate incident and the car being left so near the scene of that crime simply coincidental. The killer could have driven out to the woods after dumping Cameron at the abbey, but why? It's tempting to believe it had something to do with the robbery, but I'm not convinced there's a connection. The whole thing seems like a bit of a botched job to me. I suspect the killer ran into some bad luck along the way and had to abandon his or her original plan."

"Wouldn't be the first one," Ava said. Chance was the one thing that even criminal masterminds couldn't factor into their plans.

"DI Saunders is going to concentrate on the farm robbery. He seems convinced that Cameron was either involved or fell foul of the gang in some way. That frees us up to focus on other avenues of investigation."

"Yes, sir!" Ava suppressed a joyful whoop. Neal evidently noticed her delight, for he gave her the ghost of a smile.

"Welcome back, sir."

Chapter 8

Laura Cameron stared at the unopened email in her inbox. She had longed for its arrival, and dreaded it too. Sergeant Merry had sent her Rhona's details, and without allowing time to reconsider, Laura had emailed her friend. As soon as Rhona's reply pinged its arrival in her inbox, it had stirred ambivalent feelings within her. She had never blamed Rhona for cutting her out of her life so abruptly, without warning or explanation. She had understood that Rhona's loyalty had been to her husband first and foremost. But it had hurt. More so because Laura suspected that, of all of them, she was the only one excluded from some hidden truth.

Ewan had changed over the course of his time at college in Stromford, but on the day when he had turned up on her doorstep in the pouring rain, begging her to marry him, he was once again the boy she had fallen in love with when she was just seventeen. It was as though fate had brought him back to her.

Weary suddenly of her indecisiveness, Laura opened the email. The two short paragraphs seemed inadequate compensation for ten years' lost friendship. Laura blinked away tears and moved to the window, drawing the curtains against the sleet and early evening darkness. Then she re-read the email from Rhona. Her friend was inviting her to come and stay with her and David and their three children in Stromford. This would have seemed less strange if Laura had seen Rhona in the past ten years. They had been good friends once, sharing a room in a draughty hall of residence at Edinburgh University. Rhona had married an Englishman, enduring the inexorable teasing of her Scottish friends. Laura had teased her less, because she and Rhona's husband David had once had a fling, before David and Rhona were really serious about each other. Rhona never found out and Laura sensed that David was always a little on edge when the three of them were together, in case it slipped out. Eventually, Laura had taken him aside and assured him that he had nothing to fear. After that, David seemed to relax more when they all met up, but ironically, Laura began to feel less comfortable.

Rhona and David had had children, two girls and most recently a baby boy. Laura sighed. She and Ewan had kept putting off parenthood. The last time she had pressed him to discuss it, Ewan had half-heartedly agreed that it must be now or never. Well, now it would be never.

In some ways, it made perfect sense for Laura and Rhona to resume their friendship. There had never been any acrimony between them, it had all been about Ewan and David. Rhona had started seeing David when he came up to Edinburgh with Ewan to celebrate the New Year. They had become a couple almost overnight. Laura remembered seeing them in a passionate embrace, standing on the stones marking the 'Heart of Midlothian,' as the bells of the Tron church struck midnight. After that, Rhona had divided her time between Edinburgh and Stromford, throwing away any chance of a decent degree. In Edinburgh, Laura had done very little other than studying.

It was Ewan who had suggested to Laura that they have a break in their relationship while they were at college. If they still felt they were destined to be together after they graduated, they would get married. Laura agreed. She had been reluctant at first, but she knew eighteen was too young to commit to one person, so *the arrangement* had begun. Over the next three years Laura had played the field and had her flings, but had met no one significant.

Laura sighed. Almost from the start of their arrangement, she had sensed a distance developing between them that had only widened as the years passed. She began to envisage a future in which Ewan no longer figured, until a day arrived when she discovered that she was no longer in love with him. Then, suddenly, in the last weeks of her final term, Ewan had argued with David and everything changed. He had come to her late one night and pleaded with her to marry him and, overwhelmed by the force of his passion, she had agreed, convincing herself that she still loved him after all.

Laura remembered how it had been in the beginning, when she was still at school. She had just been to a production of Macbeth at the Traverse Theatre in Edinburgh. Laura and her best friend had clambered onto the minibus first, followed by Ewan, while the rest of their group lingered in the theatre. At first Laura had thought Ewan was interested in her friend. They had had to wait a week for their first date, Laura was going away with her parents for the half term holiday. That week had been one of the happiest of her life.

For the first few months, they had excluded the rest of the world. Friends were neglected, some lost forever. In a few short weeks, Laura came to feel that she knew Ewan as well as she knew herself. She had clung to that belief through the empty years of her marriage, long after she began to doubt that she had any self-knowledge at all.

Her hand shook as it hovered over the keyboard. It was the thought of spending the long winter evenings alone that finally decided the matter. Laura emailed Rhona and accepted her invitation. The children at the primary school where she taught would miss her, but in her present state of mind Laura was convinced that her young charges would be better off with a supply teacher. Her head teacher was sympathetic when Laura asked for some time off. The rest was easy enough to organise.

* * *

Laura arrived on a cold January morning. David picked her up from the station, mumbled his condolences and kissed her on the cheek. As they walked across the station car park, they chatted about the weather. David and Rhona's elder daughter, Rowan, was waiting in the car with the newest addition to the family, four-month-old Shaun. Rowan chattered away throughout the journey, asking Laura questions, and telling her about the arrangements that had been made for her stay. Laura listened attentively and said all the right things. She glanced in the mirror a couple of times and saw David nodding approvingly.

As soon as the car pulled into the drive, Laura could see that Rhona had hardly changed from the girl she been almost a decade ago. She was standing there waiting to welcome them. Her hair was shorter, but still untamed and vibrantly red. Rhona called to David to leave the car in the drive. The car boot slammed loudly and Laura wondered if it meant David was angry. He brushed past them carrying Laura's suitcase. Rowan insisted on taking Laura's small backpack.

The Pines' younger daughter, Holly, appeared and the whole family accompanied Laura to her room, which was actually much more substantial.

"It's a granny flat," Rowan informed Laura. "Only we don't have any grannies so we use it for guests."

David placed Laura's suitcase on a chair. "Is here alright?"

"There's a walk-in wardrobe!" Rowan said, throwing open the door to show her.

"Downstairs everyone," Rhona ordered. "Let's leave Laura in peace to unpack and freshen up."

David and the girls retreated. Rhona took Laura's arm. "I'm so sorry about Ewan, Laura. I don't know what to say. We've had the police here asking questions but there wasn't much we could tell them." Rhona's words came in a rush. Then she said, "Make yourself at home. Come and go as you please. The girls won't bother you much. Holly will show off a bit at first but she'll soon settle down as she gets used to you being around. Don't feel you need to keep me company, either."

"It's good to see you, Rhone."

Rhona smiled. "Good to see you too, Laura. It's been way too long."

"You have a beautiful home," Laura observed, feeling a little awkward.

"House prices are better here than in Edinburgh," Rhona said, as though apologising for the luxury of her surroundings.

Shaun began to grizzle. "He's hungry. I'd better go and feed him. I'm still nursing him every so often."

"Feed him here while I unpack."

"You don't mind?"

"Of course not!"

Rhona sat on the bed and began loosening the top buttons of her shirt. She cradled Shaun on her left arm and lifted out a swollen breast. Shaun latched on and began feeding greedily. Laura watched, her unpacking forgotten.

"Do you regret not having children?" The directness of Rhona's question took Laura aback and Rhona corrected herself immediately. "I'm sorry, Laura. That was insensitive."

Laura shook her head. "No, it's all right. We'd almost made up our minds to have a child at last. Time was running out — faster than we knew, as it turned out. We couldn't make the decision lightly, so we put it off." Laura did not mention her own particular anxiety.

Rhona transferred Shaun to her right breast. "Everyone has fears about bringing a new life into the world. You just have to get on and do it." Rhona stroked Shaun's velvety scalp. "They atone for so much, don't you think?"

Laura thought 'atone' was rather a strange word to use in the context. She unpacked her cases and, for a while, the two women were silent. The easy banter they'd once shared had gone, but then it would have seemed inappropriate after their long estrangement and the circumstances surrounding their reunion. It was all very awkward.

"There we go," Rhona said, breaking the silence. She lifted the now satisfied child from her breast and laid him on the bed while she buttoned her shirt. "Do you feel as weird about this as I do?" she asked. "It used to be so natural, us being together like this. I don't quite know how to be with you anymore." She paused, and said softly, "I'm sorry I didn't answer your letters and emails."

"I'm sorry I wasn't more persistent about sending them. Let's just forget it. We both let circumstances and our relationships come between us. It's all water under the bridge, now that Ewan's gone. The present's all that counts now, Rhone."

This was not completely true, thought Laura. "Is it OK if I take a shower now?" Laura felt a sudden need to be alone.

"Of course. We'll be eating in an hour or so. I've made lasagne. It was always your favourite, remember?"

Laura smiled. Ten, eleven years ago, she thought. Things change.

As she was undressing Laura heard the sound of a car engine revving loudly. She crossed to the window and looked down at the drive. David was sitting at the wheel of the car. In front of him, the automatic garage door was rising slowly. Laura could see David's fingers drumming impatiently on the steering wheel. Suddenly he looked up and caught her eye. Then his eyes travelled downward. With a start, Laura realised that she was naked from the waist up, but for some reason she did not dip out of sight immediately. She lingered by the window, holding his gaze, enjoying the sensation of being looked at by a man again. The car revved and lurched forwards, stalling in front of the open garage door. Suddenly ashamed of her behaviour, Laura reached for a towel and ducked out of sight.

For several moments afterwards, she crouched on the floor, hugging her knees and experiencing a mixture of shame and disgust. She recalled the way their eyes had met, how David's eyes had travelled downwards, her own reluctance to move. She took a long, hot shower and then lingered in the granny flat, afraid to go downstairs. She remembered how uneasy David had been years ago when he feared that she might let slip to Rhona about their brief affair. As if things weren't likely to be awkward enough between them.

Rhona and David were making dinner when she came downstairs. Laura hovered in the kitchen doorway, watching them. David, busy chopping up carrots at the island, had his back to her, but Rhona saw her at once, and poured her a glass of prosecco.

"I'm only feeding Shaun myself a couple of times a day now, so I'm going to join you," she said, filling her own glass and clinking it against Laura's. "Here's to old friends," she said and raised her glass. The rhythmic sound of David's chopping was interrupted momentarily, then resumed. He muttered something about checking whether he'd switched the light off in the garage and squeezed past Laura and Rhona, not looking at either of them. Laura was awash with embarrassment and relief.

She and Rhona chattered as Rhona began preparing the vegetables that David had abandoned. "Can I help? I feel guilty watching you do everything," Laura said.

"It's all in hand. Why don't you keep the girls company for a bit? They're excited about having you here." She led Laura into what she described as the 'family room.' Rowan and Holly were dancing in front of a big TV, copying the movements of the dancers on the screen. Laura joined in for a couple of songs and then collapsed on the sofa.

Prosecco in hand, Laura watched the screen. People in medieval clothes, a mystical landscape, soporific music. Her eyelids drooped. The next thing she was aware of was Rhona shaking her awake.

"The girls tiptoed out when they saw you were asleep. They're upstairs washing their hands. It's time to eat."

They ate in the elegant dining room. David seemed to have recovered from his embarrassment and the children helped to dispel any awkwardness. They talked incessantly. Laura didn't mind, she was used to the chatter of youngsters in her classroom and it was strangely comforting. Besides, the children's presence meant that the conversation focused on safe territory and Laura was grateful for that.

After the meal, David insisted on clearing up, with the girls helping. Rhona and Laura moved to a cosy sitting room with a second bottle of prosecco. Suddenly, the past was all they seemed able to talk about. How they'd met, the good times they'd had in their university days, how much their lives had changed in the intervening years. Only one subject seemed to be taboo. Neither of them mentioned Ewan.

"Remember the time you drove your mini onto the beach, right up to the waves? You were a bit crazy in those days, Laura."

"You were driving!"

"No way!"

"I can't believe you don't remember that. You were the crazy one, Rhone. I was always the quiet one, remember?"

"Oh my God, you're right! I remember now. You grabbed the wheel at the last minute to steer us away from the sea."

"Memory's a tricky thing. The past isn't as fixed as we think it is. We're constantly reinventing it, adding to it. Sometimes I wonder if we can rely on our memories at all," Laura said. Her words had a strange effect on Rhona. She seemed suddenly uneasy. Laura felt a little edgy herself, remembering her fling with David and the incident at the bedroom window. Perhaps Rhona was worried she'd ask her why David and Ewan had fallen out. Surely now that Ewan was dead they could finally talk about it? Laura risked a question.

"I missed you, Rhone. It was so strange you and David cutting ties like that. Ewan wouldn't tell me what he and David had fallen out about. It must have been something big . . ."

Rhona had a faraway look in her eyes. Still not the right time, then, Laura thought, sipping her wine. By now she was feeling quite drunk. She yawned. "You have a beautiful family. The girls are great and Shaun's so sweet."

"I'm lucky. Everything's worked out so well. Better than I deserved."

Rhona spoke so softly that Laura had to lean forward to hear. Rhona had changed after all, Laura thought. She had been the confident one, the mad one, the one who took risks and had a good time while Laura slogged away at getting a good degree. And now this house, the children. Ten years ago Laura would never have guessed that this was the way her friend would be living. She'd pictured Rhona travelling the world, or having a great job in PR or marketing, anything but this cosy domesticity. It seemed so at odds with Rhona's former spirited self.

"I know what you're thinking," Rhona said, as if reading Laura's thoughts. She swept an arm around her. "All of this. It isn't — wasn't me."

Laura didn't bother to protest. It was a long time since she'd had so much to drink and the room was beginning to spin.

"It's atonement." Rhona used the word again, speaking almost too quietly to be heard. Drunk as she was, Laura picked up on the word. Before she could ask Rhona what she meant, David appeared as if out of nowhere and took up the empty bottle of prosecco.

He gave the bottle a shake. "I see you two have taken up your old habits." To his wife, he said, "It's time for Shaun's feed, darling. Why don't you go to bed and I'll bring his bottle up?" Laura watched as he helped Rhona out of her chair and propelled her towards the door. Rather unnecessary, she thought. She doubted Rhona was so drunk that she could not manage to get out of the chair and walk to the door by herself. If Shaun was being bottle-fed, David could have done that himself. Obviously David was trying to bring the evening to a close. She couldn't think why. Rhona hadn't said anything embarrassing, had she? She tried to remember, but the alcohol was playing havoc with her mind. Something about atonement, that was it.

From the stairs, Laura could hear the sound of raised voices. She crept upstairs and shuffled haltingly across the landing to their bedroom door and strained to hear what was being said. All she could catch was the odd word. "I told you not to drink too much while she's here," David said. "I wasn't going to say anything," Rhona replied. The voices faded. There was the sound of the en suite door closing, then silence

Laura went back downstairs and sat for a while longer, wondering if David would return, but he didn't. She was glad. Without the children around as a distraction, the awkwardness between them would have surfaced again. It seemed strange, being left alone on her first night. No one had said goodnight to her. Laura could see a strip of light shining from under the kitchen door. Would David or

Rhona come back downstairs to turn it off, check that the outside doors were locked? Since Ewan's death, Laura had acquired a new set of rituals, the checks that Ewan used to carry out last thing at night. It had been comforting to lie in the darkness listening to the sound of the house being secured for the night, and then hearing Ewan's footsteps on the stairs.

* * *

Laura woke at two in the morning from a restless sleep. Her mouth was parched and her head ached dully. She had forgotten to bring a glass of water upstairs with her.

She went downstairs. The kitchen door was ajar, the light on. She had closed the door and turned the light off herself. Laura hesitated. Was it David or Rhona? Her raging thirst propelled her on.

Rhona looked up and smiled when she entered the kitchen. "Thirsty? Fancy a cup of tea? Don't worry about making a noise, my lot would sleep through a hurricane."

Nevertheless, Laura closed the door softly behind her. "Ewan was practically an insomniac."

Rhona didn't comment. Laura was becoming used to the idea that any mention of her late husband was met with silence. Right at that moment she didn't feel like confronting Rhona over it.

"Here you go." As well as a cup of tea, Rhona handed over a couple of paracetamol and a glass of water. She took a couple of pills too, saying, "How sad are we? We used to be able to drink the lads under the table."

But Rhona did not seem to want to linger. The awkwardness between them was back. They took their drinks upstairs and parted on the landing. Before going to her room, Laura tiptoed over to the girls' room and peeked inside. The room was bathed in the soft orange glow of a night light and she could hear the children's rhythmic breathing. Rowan stirred suddenly and muttered something in her sleep. Laura thought she caught the words 'ghost' and 'murder.'

* * *

David hardly spoke at breakfast. He ate his toast and drank his tea half-concealed behind the *Times* newspaper, while Rowan and Holly darted about preparing for school. Rhona and the baby were not yet awake. Holly insisted on making tea and toast for Laura.

At eight fifteen, David said, "Excuse me, Laura. I have to drop the kids at school, then I've an important meeting with a client at nine thirty. Make yourself a decent cup of tea, no need to drink Holly's dishwater. Rhona should be down shortly."

"Holly's tea is fine." His abruptness and ill humour irritated Laura. Was this all down to his embarrassment at seeing her naked at the window the day before? Laura remembered the way David's eyes had travelled downwards, lingering, and the sudden illicit pleasure that she had experienced at being appreciated by a man again. She smiled, enjoying his discomfort.

David had enjoyed being with her once. In their second year at university in Edinburgh, Rhona and she had shared a flat above a newsagent. One weekend Rhona was away visiting her parents in Glasgow and Ewan was in Stromford. On the Friday, David had turned up unexpectedly and he and Laura went to a Chinese restaurant on Lothian Road. The house wine was cheap, and afterwards they drank too much in a pub in the Grassmarket and were in high spirits by the time they made their way back to Forrest Road. David had a crazy notion about climbing Salisbury Crags, but he settled for climbing the stairs to the flat and having sex with Laura. They had sex a few more times that weekend until David was struck by a fit of conscience. He told her that he was head over heels in love with Rhona, and begged Laura not to tell her.

Laura made some tea and took a cup upstairs for Rhona. She knocked softly on the bedroom door, wary of waking the baby, and left the tea on Rhona's bedside table. She could hear the shower running in the en suite. Rhona was singing. Shaun was asleep in a cot next to the king-sized bed. Laura watched him for a few moments, marvelling at the sight of his tiny, perfect fingers. A faint whiff of ammonia came from under the covers. Laura tiptoed out and crossed the landing. She passed the door to another room, which stood ajar. Curious, Laura looked inside. She saw a ruffled duvet, as though someone had slept on top of the covers. A pair of worn leather brogues that David had been wearing when he picked Laura up from the station, were lying upturned on the floor at the foot of the bed, as though they had been kicked off carelessly.

Laura felt embarrassed. She had a feeling that Rhona wouldn't wish her to know that she and David had slept in separate bedrooms. Closing the door behind her, Laura went back downstairs to the kitchen. She made another drink, coffee this time, and looked at the crossword in the paper. It was a beautiful morning, sunny, frosty, and sharp. Compared to her own house in Marchmont, it seemed very quiet. Unaccustomed to such silence she turned the radio on and fiddled with the settings until she found a station playing music she liked.

Time ticked by. Rhona finally appeared, holding a gurgling, smiling Shaun. Rhona handed her son over and Laura kissed the baby's velvety crown.

"I'm sorry . . ." she began.

"Don't be. I don't mind what time you get up."

Laura looked up.

"I heard you earlier. I know what you're thinking, but it's not the case. We don't often sleep in separate rooms. Sometimes we bed-hop so one of us can get a decent night's sleep — not easy with a baby in the house."

"It's none of my business, Rhona." Laura suddenly remembered the peculiar word her friend had used to describe her present life, her perfect family. Was sleeping apart from her husband part of her 'atonement' too?

Rhona suggested a shopping trip to Stromford. She and David had been invited to a birthday party in the village hall, for someone called Hammond Bell, who was married to a friend of Rhona's. Rhona wanted something to wear and she had decided that Laura should get something new and come to the party. As practically the whole village was going, one more would not be noticed. And, she insisted, it would help lift Laura's mood. Laura thought it a bit insensitive of Rhona to put it like that, as though Laura had not been bereaved but merely needed a bit of cheering up.

Rhona drove them into Stromford and parked in a multi-storey car park in the city's main shopping area. As they drove past the historic Uphill part of town where the cathedral dominated the view, Laura wished she could go there instead of to the shops. She had no religious leanings but she wanted the peace she imagined she might find in the cathedral's ancient cloisters.

With a complete lack of tact, Rhona began telling Laura that a man had fallen to his death from the cathedral roof just before Christmas. "Actually, it turned out it was murder." Then she stopped. "I'm so sorry, Laura. I keep saying the wrong thing, don't I?"

Yes, you do, Laura thought, but all she said was, "Don't worry about it. I can't expect everyone to treat me with kid gloves."

Laura really wasn't in the mood for shopping. She pushed Shaun in his buggy and waited patiently while Rhona spent ages in various changing rooms trying on an array of dresses. Unable to generate any enthusiasm for her own outfit, she let Rhona select a modest shift dress for her, bottle green, of a soft, clingy material. Looking at herself in the mirror, Laura was surprised to see the dress bring a spark into her eyes. She bought the dress, ignoring Rhona's smug smile. And because she was suddenly grateful to Rhona for lifting her spirits after all, she insisted on buying Rowan and Holly a book each, and a teddy bear for Shaun.

Later, though, wearing the green dress and some jewellery borrowed from Rhona, she felt her mood begin to deflate. "Maybe I won't come after all. I'll only spoil things for you two if I am miserable. Ewan hasn't been dead a week yet. It seems somehow inappropriate to be going to a party and I really don't feel much like it."

Rhona dismissed her fears. "Come anyway. It's not such a long way to the village hall. You could always come back early if you're feeling overwhelmed."

Laura caved.

* * *

She felt out of place at the party. Rhona was thoughtful at first, introducing her to her friends and drawing her into conversations, but after a few glasses of wine she became less attentive, and Laura found herself alone. She sat at one of the tables, listening to the music, watching people dance and thinking about Ewan. She didn't notice the man who sat down next to her until he spoke.

"I saw you come in with David and Rhona Pine. Are you a friend of theirs?" Laura twisted round. His smile seemed genuine but Laura sensed that he was nervous. "I'm Gabe North, I'm an architect. I did some work for Ham and Rosie Bell."

"The eco house? Rhona told me about it. I thought they were doing it all themselves."

"They consulted me for some advice on the plans. I have a particular interest in environmentally-friendly projects."

"I'm Laura Cameron. I'm staying with David and Rhona." *And my husband's just been murdered.* Should she tell him? How?

But there was no need to wait. Gabe North said, "I'm sorry. Your surname . . . I should have realised. I'm so sorry about your husband."

Laura nodded and there was an awkward silence. The music in the background had been popular when she and Ewan started dating at school. She felt her eyes well up, her throat constrict, and she turned away from Gabe North. She felt Ewan's loss most keenly when she thought of those early days.

"It must be hard for David too," North said. "As I remember, he and your husband were inseparable at college."

"You knew Ewan?"

"I didn't really know him or David well. We moved in different circles and were studying different courses. Occasionally our paths would cross, at social events, mostly, like tonight. Ham and Rosie invited me, Rhona is friendly with Rosie, that sort of thing."

"Actually, my husband and David hadn't spoken for years, since college in fact. They had a falling out. You didn't like them, did you?"

North looked at her in surprise. "What makes you say that?"

Laura didn't answer. The truth was she didn't know. It had been a sudden intuition. But then, Ewan hadn't been particularly likeable. She shrugged. "Ewan could be arrogant. Not everyone took to him."

"You're right," North said. "I won't lie. I didn't particularly like them." His honesty was unexpected, and Laura wasn't sure whether she liked it.

"Any particular reason?" she asked.

North fidgeted with his beer glass and looked around as though checking that no one was within earshot. "There was a girl, Stephanie Woodson. I'd been seeing her for a couple of weeks and she told me she was doing some life modelling for a student at the art college. She wouldn't tell me who it was. Steph was a single parent with a nine-year-old daughter, and she needed all the extra money she could get. Then, one day I saw her with Ewan Cameron and I just knew."

Laura tried to think if she had ever heard Ewan or David mention a woman called Steph. Most of the time they had talked freely about the people they were seeing, but Laura couldn't recall a Steph. "So you disliked Ewan because he might have been seeing your girlfriend of a couple of weeks?" Laura could not keep a mocking tone from her voice.

Gabe's expression darkened. "I didn't give a shit about that."

"Why then?"

Gabe cast a furtive look over his shoulder. He leaned towards her and, keeping his voice low, said, "Steph disappeared."

"Disappeared?"

"She went missing."

"With her daughter?"

"No. I was babysitting for her the night she disappeared. Steph went out, telling me she was going to a friend's hen night. I never saw her again."

"Oh." It took a moment for the penny to drop. "Hold on a minute. Are you saying you think Ewan, or David — or both of them — had something to do with this Steph's disappearance?"

"Maybe. I don't know." North seemed suddenly edgy. He nibbled at a fingernail, then hid his hand under the table. "Your husband never mentioned anyone called Steph?"

"Not that I remember."

"Did he tell you he was questioned by the police about her disappearance? He and David both were."

"No. Is that really true?"

"Yes. They denied knowing Steph, and they gave each other an alibi. David's wife claimed she'd been with them the evening Steph disappeared. They all claimed they'd been at David and Ewan's flat, drinking and watching movies."

"Well, they probably were. You don't believe that though, obviously." Laura felt suddenly angered by North's insinuations. A thought occurred to her. "Were you questioned?"

"Yes, I was questioned. Despite the fact that I spent the night looking after Steph's daughter."

"Did she turn up, or did the police find her eventually?"

"No."

Laura shivered. "What happened to her daughter?"

"I don't know. She went to live with relatives, I think. I didn't keep in touch. No one would have wanted me to, given that I was a suspect in her mother's disappearance." North's tone was understandably bitter. Understandable, that is, if he were innocent.

Watching his nervous mannerisms and sensing his unease, Laura couldn't help wondering. She was suddenly suspicious. "Why are you telling me this?" North stared at his bitten-down nails. "You knew exactly who I was when you approached me, didn't you?"

His face said it all. Suddenly it was all too much for her. "You're crazy!" Laura stood up abruptly, and swayed slightly from the wine she'd drunk earlier. North reached out an arm to steady her, but she shrugged him off. She moved quickly away from him, back to the throng of partygoers.

She looked around for Rhona, but it was David who found her. He gripped her by the arm. "Where's Rhona?" Laura yelled above the din of music and voices. David shrugged, gripping her arm so tightly that Laura imagined blood vessels exploding under his touch. "David! Let go. You're hurting me."

"Sorry. Come on, let's dance."

"No, I don't want to." But David pushed her onto the dance floor and, afraid of attracting attention, Laura began to jiggle.

"Did you enjoy your conversation with Mr North?"

"Who?"

"Gabriel North. Looked like you two were having a nice, cosy chat. What did he say to you?"

Laura pretended she was drunker than she was. "Nothing much. We talked about Edinburgh mostly. He knows the city quite well."

"Looked like your discussion got a bit heated. Was he bothering you?"

"Oh no. It was just a . . . difference of opinion."

David nodded. Laura had the impression he wanted to say more, but the music slowed and couples moved together. They stepped apart. Rhona appeared from nowhere and David took her in his arms. Laura edged away but she was aware of David's gaze following her across the hall as she escaped to the Ladies.

A barmaid followed her out. "Scuse me. You know that man you was talking to before? He left this for you." It was a folded sheet of paper with Gabe North's contact details written in red ink. The barmaid gave her a wink. "Reckon you're in with a chance there, duck. Lucky you. He's hot — for an older bloke."

Was he? Laura told herself she hadn't noticed, but, back in the hall, gazing over at the table where she and North had been, now occupied by another couple, she felt a sense of loss.

David and Rhona's babysitter phoned to say that Holly had had another nightmare and wouldn't settle. David left the party, encouraging Laura and Rhona to stay. After midnight, they returned to the house to find it in darkness. Laura was relieved not to have to face David again that night.

* * *

The following day she couldn't get Gabe North out of her mind. She hadn't thought she had paid much attention to what he looked like, but now she found that she could recall his features in some detail. He wasn't particularly tall but was broad, evidently someone who worked out regularly and he had close-cropped, almost spiky fair hair. Nothing at all like Ewan, who had been tall and unhealthily thin, weedy almost, with thick, brown hair and hooded eyelids.

She had crushed North's note into her purse, and now looked at it as she sipped a cup of coffee in the kitchen after breakfast. David and the girls had left. Rhona and Shaun were still asleep. She picked up her phone and was about to call Gabe when the kitchen door creaked. David walked over to the island and raked in a drawer, extracting a plastic card. "Forgot my parking pass. Were you about to phone someone? Don't mind me."

"Oh, no, I was just wondering whether to make an appointment at a hairdresser's in Stromford. The number's engaged. I'll try later."

"See you later," David said, slipping the card into his pocket. Laura watched from the window. He pointed his keys at his car and the headlights flashed a silent greeting. Laura watched him hesitate a moment by the door before he opened it. Laura remembered how he had looked at her, standing naked at the bedroom window the day she arrived, and how she had lingered, appreciating his gaze. She shuddered. This time the memory gave her no pleasure.

Chapter 9

Rowan Pine spotted Zak Darby waiting outside the village hall and pedalled vigorously across the car park to join him. It was Saturday morning. At school the day before, she had whispered in his ear, "We need to talk somewhere private. It's about *you know what.*" So they'd arranged to meet in the village. They could tell their parents they were going to the mobile library that parked at the village hall once a fortnight. Since the murder, kids in the area had been put on a tighter rein.

Rowan skidded to a stop next to Zak and they pushed their bikes into the small playground adjacent to the village hall. It was for little kids really, but it was too cold a day for parents to be out with toddlers, so they sat on the swings.

"You'll never believe what's happened," Rowan said. "The dead man. His name's Ewan Cameron and his wife is staying at our house!"

Zak went pale, and stared at her. "What are you talking about, Rowan?"

"It's true. She was a friend of Mum's and Dad's years ago, and the murdered man was too."

Zak clutched at his throat.

"What's wrong, Zak? Is it your asthma?"

Zak whipped out his new inhaler and took a puff. When his breathing had steadied he looked at Rowan. "Are you kidding me?"

"No, it's true. Come round and meet her. Her name's Laura. She's nice."

"No," Zak said quickly. "I don't want to meet her."

Rowan shrugged. "Up to you. Weird, though, isn't it?"

Zak ignored the question. He said, "My mum's been talking to your mum. She said your mum told her you were having nightmares. Are they about what we saw?"

"I keep dreaming about it. What if he'd caught us, Zak?"

"He didn't, did he? It's stupid worrying about something that never happened."

"I can't help having nightmares."

"You haven't told them have you, about us going out at night like that?"

"No. I'm not stupid. I said I couldn't remember. I'll make something up, but I won't tell them. Promise." She crossed little fingers with Zak. Then, "What if he saw us, though?"

"He couldn't have. It was too dark in the woods. We couldn't see *his* face, could we?"

"What if he comes to my house?" Rowan said.

Zak looked shocked. "Why would he do that? He doesn't know you were in the woods that night. I've just told you that."

"No, not for me. For *her*."

Zak stood up and took hold of the swing. He pushed it so hard that he had to jump out of the way as it swung back at him. "Don't say that," he said fiercely. "Nothing's going to happen if you just keep quiet about the whole thing." He took hold of Rowan's swing and twisted the chains around tightly, then let them go, sending Rowan into a dizzying spin. Usually she laughed and shrieked when he did that, but today she felt scared. What was wrong with Zak? Why was he behaving like this?

As the swing came to a halt, Zak leaned close to Rowan. "If you tell anyone, I won't be your best friend any more, okay?"

She stared at him for a moment. "Okay I won't," she agreed. She'd been tempted to tell her mum, but Zak's behaviour was freaking her out. She swore she wouldn't again, this time on her baby brother's life, and Zak seemed to relax. All the same, Rowan thought it was a big secret to keep, and she wasn't happy about it.

* * *

After saying goodbye to Rowan and choosing a couple of books at the mobile library, Zak pedalled home. He was surprised to see a car parked in the road outside his house. They didn't often get visitors. Zak wheeled his bike around to the back of the house and locked it in the small shed in the garden. He could hear his mother's girlish laughter as he pushed open the back door into the kitchen. His mother's laugh was followed by a deep, male one and Zak stopped dead. Male visitors were almost unheard of in the Darby household. He left his shoes by the back door and crept into the hall. His mother and her visitor were in the living room. He wanted to stand and listen unseen, but his mother always seemed to know when he was in the house.

"Zak! Is that you, love? Come and say hello to Mr Gallagher."

Zak shuffled into the room.

"Hey there, Zak. How's it going?" Mr Gallagher asked in his deep, strange voice. He was Irish, his mother had told him, like Eoin Colfer, the man who wrote those Artemis Fowl books Zak liked to read. It wasn't the first time they'd met, but Mr Gallagher had never been to their house before.

"Why don't you call me Bran?" the man said.

Zak tried to look him in the eye, but found he couldn't. He looked at his mother nervously.

"Bran's just been fitting a new lock on the front door," his mum said. "He was worried about us living out here on our own after what happened at Stainholme Abbey. You know — the murder." His mother's voice dropped when she said those last words.

"He didn't need to. I can look after you, Mum," Zak said, shooting a defiant look at Bran.

"Sure you can, Zak," Bran Gallagher said. "But you're at school during the day and your mum's here all alone. We wouldn't want anything to happen to her, would we?"

Zak stared at the floor, sullenly.

The smiles between his mother and Bran Gallagher made Zak explode with rage. "Tell him to leave, mum!" he blurted out before he could stop himself.

"Zak! That's rude. Apologise to Bran."

Zak stared at Gallagher, dismayed. A mocking smile played on Gallagher's lips — or so it seemed to Zak. "No!" Zak said, and ran out the room.

His mother called him back, then he heard her apologising to Gallagher. Gallagher said, "It's alright, Liv. The boy's just used to having you to himself, that's all. I'll nip off now. Is it alright if I come back later?"

Listening from the top of the stairs, Zak felt his heart miss a beat. He heard his mother answer, "Yes, I'd like that."

Zak went into his bedroom and closed the door. He kept thinking, "He's coming back. Mum likes him and he's coming back."

* * *

A barrage of excited squeals sounded from the room outside Jim Neal's office. PJ was surrounded by a group of other officers, all slapping her on the back and calling out their congratulations. Neal smiled. He was pleased she had passed the exam. He liked PJ, more so now that she no longer fancied him and was able to address him without becoming a stuttering, blushing wreck. She would be a good addition to the team. The fact that PJ and Ava were good friends was an added bonus. There was no change in PJ's rank, but now she was a detective constable Neal could assign more professional tasks to her. And, of course, she'd be out of uniform which opened up other possibilities. Neal got up and made his way out to congratulate PJ.

"Well done, *Detective* Constable!" he said warmly. "And welcome to the team." A beaming PJ thanked him and invited him along to her celebratory drink in the Crown after work. Neal nodded. He would go along for an hour, just to show his face. He always turned down invitations to birthday drinks and the like, using his son Archie as an excuse, partly because he wasn't keen on socialising and partly because he feared losing control under the influence and behaving unprofessionally. There were some who believed that socialising with the team helped with bonding and teamwork, but Neal wasn't one of those. Too many times he'd seen senior colleagues lose respect because of their drunken antics.

"When you've finished celebrating, I'd like to see both of you in my office," he said, nodding at Ava and PJ. They followed him in.

"Ava, I'd like you to bring PJ up to speed on the Cameron case. I know she's been involved peripherally but now that she's a detective . . ." He paused, letting PJ savour the word, "we can make more use of her."

"Yes, sir," Ava replied, clearly pleased at the prospect of working more closely with her friend.

"As you know, DI Saunders is helping Hammond Bell with his investigation into the theft of chemicals and machinery from Ridgeway Farm. Given that this theft occurred the same night and in such close proximity to where Ewan Cameron's car was found, we can't rule out that the cases are linked. Cameron might have had the misfortune to have been in the wrong place at the wrong time. He might have witnessed someone or something that put him at risk, or he might have been killed for an entirely different reason. We need to start looking for patterns."

PJ kept nodding solemnly. "We'll get them, sir," she said earnestly.

Neal suppressed a smile and Ava snorted.

"What is it? What did I say?" PJ said.

"Five minutes in the job and you're already sounding like a TV detective," said Ava. PJ reddened. "Never mind, Peej. It won't be long before you're a jaded old pro like us."

"Speak for yourself," Neal retorted. He was taken aback when they stared at him. He wasn't known for being flippant.

"Find out as much as you can about David and Rhona Pine's past history, DC Jenkins, and Ewan and Laura Cameron's too. Find out who Cameron and Pine associated with at the art college and arrange for anyone who remembers them well to be interviewed. Oh, and while you're at it, see if you can find out why Ewan Cameron lost his job in Edinburgh. Laura Cameron mentioned something about a breakdown when I spoke to her up there but I'd like to hear what his former employer has to say. And see what you can find out about everyone's movements in the past couple of months. Have the Pines been out of Stromford lately? How many times has Ewan Cameron been here? Check credit card statements and whatever else you can think of to get a clearer picture of what they've been doing and where they've been going."

"A friend of my mum's taught at the art college years ago, sir. Should I speak with her?" PJ asked. Of the three of them, PJ was the only one who was Stromford born and bred. Her presence on the investigation would be a plus in more ways than one, Neal realised.

"Absolutely. That's just the sort of thing that can be really useful to an investigation. Just be careful that you don't reveal any more than you have to. We don't want our hard work compromised by gossip."

As Neal spoke, PJ wrote busily in her notebook, nodding as she did so. Now she looked up and beamed at Neal. "Yes, sir!"

"One more thing, Detective Constable," Neal said. "No need to do everything on your own. There's a whole team of people out there who can assist." He indicated their colleagues in the workroom. "Make sure you tap into their skills and expertise as well."

"I'll get right on it, sir. Thanks for your confidence in me. I won't let you down."

When PJ left, she seemed to take the life out of the room with her and for a few moments, Neal and Ava sat in deflated silence. "I'm so pleased for her. She's a gem, isn't she, sir? She's going to make a great detective," Ava said. Her own personality and enthusiasm soon filled the vacuum PJ had left. Neal felt a sudden need to assert his authority.

"I hope so. The last thing we need is another loose cannon on the team." As soon as the words were out of his mouth, he regretted them. He was referring to Ava's 'lone wolf' behaviour on their first case together, when she'd gone behind his back in pursuit of her own agenda. In their more recent case, she had proved herself capable of working cooperatively, of respecting his authority and decisions in a crisis. He was being petty firing this kind of criticism her way. He could tell his words had stung. Neal saw her struggle not to make some sarcastic retort. He felt admiration for his sergeant and shame for his own behaviour. But he didn't apologise. Why did it always have to be this way between them? One step forwards, two steps back. Neal sighed. What was it his gran used to say? "One step at a time makes for good walking." Not at this rate, he thought, sourly.

"Grab your coat," Neal said, looking at his watch. "One of our PCs on a door-to-door trawl of Stainholme village reported that a neighbour heard kids' voices at gone midnight in the lane at the back of Olivia Darby's cottage the night Cameron died. Faye Wellings mentioned Darby, as I recall. It's probably not relevant but I've arranged to speak with Olivia Darby and while we're in Stainholme, we can call on the Pines again."

* * *

Ava kept him waiting. Hands in his pockets, Neal stood by his car in the station car park. A frisky wind was blowing, stirring in Neal a sense of open spaces, vacant lots, sea salt and memories of all the times he'd walked the streets of Edinburgh with Myrna, their coats flapping and the cold stinging their faces. He'd spent a lot of time waiting for Myrna in his teenage years. Once he had thought he would have been prepared to wait forever if she'd have him. Then she fell pregnant with Archie and it was her turn to wait. She bided her time until she had given birth to their son and then she was gone, off to pursue her singing career. Myrna had been Neal's first love. After she'd left, he'd idealised her for a long time, until one day he'd accepted that if she had stayed, things would never have worked between them. It had been some time now since Neal had thought of Myrna with more than a faint stirring of nostalgia.

Ava appeared out of nowhere and asked if he wanted her to drive. Neal shook his head. He resisted asking her where she'd been and didn't look at his watch. They had a forty-minute drive ahead of them and Neal guessed that Ava wouldn't be in the mood for talking. He was wrong. It seemed that it wasn't in her nature to bear a grudge — but of course, he knew that. Still, she stuck strictly to business.

"Olivia Darby is Faye Wellings's friend, isn't she? She lives alone with her young son. Do you think it was her kid the neighbour heard? Not many kids that age would be out at that time of the night, would they?"

Neal thought of Archie. His son was afraid of the dark and slept with a night light in his bedroom. "No. Unless he waited until his mum was asleep, then gave her the slip. Can't think what he'd be getting up to. Someone was with him. A friend, perhaps? The neighbour claimed she could hear two voices, both of them kids, so unless they were accompanied by an unspeaking adult, there's a good chance they were up to some mischief."

"Not necessarily," Ava replied rather too quickly. "Ollie sneaked out after curfew once to see if he could spot some comet or other. Or was it a planet? He was only about ten at the time. Maybe you should ask Archie what he gets up to when you're asleep."

Neal wasn't sure if this was a retaliatory dig. He let it go.

They arrived at Stainholme village just as a large delivery lorry was reversing into the street from a side road running alongside the village shop. Neal drummed impatiently on the steering wheel.

"For god's sake, Merry, jump out and direct him. How he ever got an HGV licence, I don't know."

Ava did as instructed and there was a further delay as the grateful driver wound down his window and engaged her in conversation. Ava glanced over at Neal and then smiled at the driver. *Two can play at that game*, Neal thought and gave two impatient beeps on the horn. Ava waved the driver off and strolled back to the car, scowling at Neal.

* * *

In response to Ava's knock on the door to Olivia Darby's cottage, the door opened a crack and a woman's face peered out over the security chain. "Oliva Darby?" Ava said.

"Yes." Ignoring Ava she looked at Neal. "Are you Inspector Neal?"

"Yes. And this is Sergeant Merry. Would it be alright if we came inside? This shouldn't take long."

Olivia slid the chain off and opened the door. She led them into a long, low-ceilinged kitchen with exposed timbers and a flagstone floor. An old-fashioned mangle rested on one of the kitchen tops. Pots and pans and kitchen utensils, as well as some items with no clear purpose hung from hooks on the whitewashed walls. There was a milk churn and a well bucket containing dried flowers, brass weighing scales and a copper kettle. Yet it managed to be tasteful rather than cluttered. Neal would have been surprised if there had been anything other than an Aga in the kitchen.

"Wow!" Ava said. "You've got some pretty cool bits and bobs in here, haven't you?"

Olivia smiled. "I'm afraid I've got a bit of an obsession with antique kitchen paraphernalia — well, antiques in general, really. They're all around the house."

"Where do you get them from?" Ava asked. Neal wondered where this was leading. He had been to Ava's cottage and knew that her taste in décor was nothing like this. Was she thinking of branching out? More likely she was just making conversation to put Olivia Darby at her ease.

"Oh, you know, boot sales, junk shops, that kind of thing. I'm pretty handy at restoring things too." She pointed at the rustic-looking kitchen table painted a duck-egg blue. "Bought that for ten quid from a charity furniture shop, stripped it down and painted it. D'you like it?"

"I love it. It's such a pretty colour. I paid a bloody fortune for my table. It must be great to be so creative."

"Thank you. But something tells me you haven't come here to admire my kitchen."

"You're aware that a man's body was discovered not far from here, at Stainholme Abbey ruin last Monday morning?" Neal said. It wasn't really a question. Olivia Darby would have to have been living on another planet for the past few days not to have heard about a murder that occurred practically on her doorstep."

"Yes. Poor man. I take it you haven't arrested anyone yet, or you wouldn't be here asking questions. How can I help you?" She sounded genuinely surprised to be on their radar.

"We had a call from one of your neighbours — a Mrs Jean Bryce?"

Olivia made a face. "Yes. Jean's my nearest neighbour. She lives just down the lane and her garden backs onto ours. What did she have to say? I expect it was something about Zak. She's always complaining about him and his friends making too much noise when they're in the garden. She confiscated his football when he accidentally kicked it over the hedge a couple of weeks ago. Don't tell me she's suggesting Zak had something to do with the murder?"

Neal smiled. He rather liked Olivia Darby's forthrightness. "Not exactly. Apparently she's something of an insomniac and was lying awake at two in the morning last Monday, reading, when she heard some voices coming from the lane outside her house. She thought one of them sounded like Zak and that the other voice might have been a girl's."

"Oh. That's impossible. Zak was tucked up in bed asleep. It couldn't have been him. In fact, I'm having a hard time believing any child that age would be out at that time of the night."

"Mrs Darby," intervened Ava. "Could Zak have slipped out without you hearing him?"

"Absolutely not. Do either of you have children?" Neal nodded. "Then you'll know how unlikely that is. Parents sleep with one ear open."

"But it is a possibility, isn't it?" Ava persisted. "Unless you were awake all night he could have crept out while you were asleep."

Olivia shook her head. "No. I told you, I would have heard something."

She was unlikely to be moved on the issue so Neal changed tack slightly. "What about Zak's friends?" he asked. "Can you think of any girls he's particularly friendly with who might have been in the lane that night?"

"Only Rowan Pine." Neal and Ava exchanged a look. "But what kind of parent lets their kids go strolling down country lanes in the middle of the night? Not the Pines, I'm sure." Olivia deliberated a moment. "Except maybe travellers. You could speak to Ham Bell about that. I know he has problems with poachers from time to time. And there was that business with the theft at Ridgeway Farm."

Neal nodded. "If you could find a minute to ask Zak, please? It might be better coming from you as his parent."

"I'll ask him but I'm not sure I like the idea of it. He's already a bit off at the moment."

"Off?" Neal asked.

"I think this whole murder thing's got him spooked. And he's not the only one. His friend, Rowan, Rhona and David Pine's eldest daughter, has been having nightmares ever since it happened."

Neal glanced at Ava, wondering if she was thinking the same thing.

"Jean Bryce is always complaining about something, Inspector, and she probably sleeps a lot more soundly than she claims to. I think you're wasting your time with this line of enquiry."

Neal decided to wrap things up. "Thanks for your time, Mrs Darby."

Olivia saw them to the door. "That's a good lock you've got on there," Neal observed. "Have you had it fitted recently?"

"Yes. Bran Gallagher did it for me. He was concerned about me being here by myself with Zak."

"I've met Mr Gallagher. He's one of the rangers, isn't he?" Ava remarked.

Olivia Darby's face lit up. "He's a good man, Bran. It's a shame that Zak's taken a sudden dislike to him, he used to like him well enough. I think he might be jealous. He's had me all to himself since his dad left. Zak walked in when Bran was here fitting the lock and I think he read a bit too much into the situation."

On the way back to the car, Neal said to Ava, "I take it we were of the same mind back there when Mrs Darby mentioned that Zak was friends with the Pines' daughter?"

Ava nodded. "All roads lead back to the Pines. Rowan Pine could be the girl Mrs Bryce heard in the lane that night."

"Yes, assuming Mrs Bryce really did hear something. Next stop, the Pines — and Laura Cameron."

"Yeah. Is it just me or is it kind of strange that she's staying with two people who are potential suspects in her husband's murder?" Ava said. She shrugged. "I suppose she probably doesn't look on them the same way we do. What I do find extremely odd is that she was obviously really close to Rhona once, and gave up that friendship so readily. It was their husbands who fell out, as far as I can gather, not them. It's a bit pathetic that the women let that ruin their friendship. I know what I'd say if my partner tried to stop me seeing my best mate."

Neal could well imagine. "Well, there was also geography," he pointed out.

"Huh? Oh, you mean they were separated by distance, the Pines down here, the Camerons in Scotland? Yeah, but even so . . ."

Ava was a confident, assertive person. It wasn't easy for her to accept weakness in others. It wasn't that she lacked empathy, Neal knew, just that it made her angry to think that there were people who exploited vulnerable individuals. Her brother Ollie had been bullied at his last school and Ava was encouraging him to take up martial arts training. Ava was a strong-minded woman who would accept nothing less than complete equality in a relationship. It was a trait he admired in her. Myrna had been strong-minded too. He'd never blamed or judged her for walking away from a life she didn't want.

"She struck me as being a person who doesn't seem very sure of herself," Ava continued. "She told you Ewan Cameron begged her to marry him, which suggests to me that he preyed on her passive nature. Maybe she would be a different person today if she'd never agreed to marry him. Anyway, she did want to be in the area until we release her husband's body. I warned her that's not likely to be any time soon."

As they belted themselves in, Neal wondered if Ava was still dating Dr Agard. He didn't have the courage to ask, so he kept pondering it all the way to the Pines' converted barn. She hadn't mentioned him, but Neal had hardly been back a day. He'd have to find some casual way of finding out without asking her directly. Not that it was any concern of his. Yet . . .

"You've just passed the turn-off, sir."

"Shit!" Neal took a left into the village hall car park. He drove out the other side and took the turning Ava pointed to. Another bloody dirt track. Didn't people believe in proper roads in these parts? It was like stepping back in time.

Finally the Pines' property came into view. "Nice place," he said. "He's some kind of consultant. Must pay well. She doesn't work, does she?"

"Stay-at-home mum," Ava replied non-judgementally. "They've got three kids. Youngest's only three or four months old, I think. Rather her than me."

Ava was in her mid-twenties and clearly not feeling broody. Sometimes Neal felt that the half dozen or so years between them was a real chasm. He couldn't imagine his life without his son, but sometimes he wondered what he would be doing now if he hadn't become a father when he was barely out of his teens. His friend Jock Dodds was the same age as him and had had a fair few relationships. He was fond of Maggie, Neal knew, and nothing would make Neal happier than for the two of them to get together. Maggie was eight years younger than Jock and she was a bit flighty. God knows, he'd dropped enough hints on Jock's behalf, but Maggie never revealed what she felt about Jock. He couldn't be expected to wait forever. The trouble was, Neal thought, they were perfect for each other.

"You coming, sir?"

Neal realised that Ava was already out of the car and he was still strapped in. He made a bit of a show of looking for something in his jacket pocket, then got out of the car. A shiny MPV was parked outside a double garage which looked as though it was a converted stables. A beige Porsche was parked alongside it. "Nice," Ava commented as she passed it. Her remark suggested no hint of envy. Ava wasn't a flash car kind of person, Neal knew. She owned a modest Ford Escort and he'd overheard her telling PJ once that she wasn't interested in cars. What *was* Ava interested in? Should he know more about her? Did he want to? Jock had teased him about working with a looker like Ava — Archie had shown him a picture on his phone — and seeming to know so little about her. "We're colleagues, that's all," Neal had assured his friend. *So what?* Jock's shrug had seemed to say.

Ava rang the Pines' doorbell. Neal cleared his throat. He was finding it difficult to concentrate today, but that was a positive sign. Before his week in Scotland, his thoughts had run on a loop between Maggie's injury and their blues and twos dash to Stromford central. It was refreshing to find that he could be distracted by random thoughts again.

To Neal's surprise it was Laura Cameron who answered the door. "Rhona's just putting the baby down for a nap and David's working in his study. I'll give him a shout."

But there was no need, for David appeared in the hall at that moment and led them into an open-plan kitchen that contrasted sharply with Olivia Darby's. It was all clean lines and high-tech gadgets and one wall was made entirely of glass, giving the illusion that the kitchen was part of the countryside outside.

"We designed the whole place ourselves — with the help of an architect, of course."

"It's awesome," Ava said. She had made a similar comment on her previous visit with Saunders.

David smiled, obviously pleased. "I thought it would be easier if we all sat around the table," he said. When Rhona arrived, she offered them drinks and when everyone declined, she sat down next to Laura. To Neal it felt as though they had come for a dinner party. David placed his hands on the table, palms up, and said, "Let the interrogation begin." He leaned back and folded his arms across his chest.

His slightly sardonic tone irritated Neal. "Hardly an interrogation, Mr Pine. My sergeant and I would just like to run some questions by you."

Next to him, Ava turned over a page in her notebook and crossed her legs, wriggling in her seat as she did so. "Don't mind me," she said. "I'll just jot down a few notes as we go along." She smiled at the assembled group.

Neal admired how she had neatly asserted their authority over David without seeming to. "Excuse me if my next question causes you distress, Mrs Cameron," he began. "We are aware that your husband and Mr Pine fell out ten years ago. When questioned about this by Sergeant Merry, Mr Pine alleged that it had been because he'd discovered that Mr Cameron had slept with his fiancée, now Mrs Pine. Were you aware of this?"

"Inspector! I hardly think you should be asking Laura such a question at a time like this," David said.

"For god's sake, David. I knew all about that at the time," Laura said calmly.

Rhona stared at her open-mouthed. "How?"

"Oh come on, Rhona. It was bloody obvious. You flirted with him relentlessly. He probably did it to get you off his back."

"You aren't angry?" Rhona said, glancing nervously at David. He had uncrossed his arms and was leaning forward, arms outstretched in front of him.

"It was during the time of our arrangement, remember? You must do. We told each other about our affairs. The minute Ewan asked me to marry him we both turned a page on all that sleeping around. And out of us all, David was the one with the biggest grievance. He and Rhona didn't have the kind of arrangement Ewan and I had." Then Laura gasped. I'm sorry, David. I didn't mean for that to sound like you had a reason to murder Ewan." David gave a tight-lipped smile.

"You never forgave Ewan Cameron his affair with your wife?" Neal asked David Pine.

"No. He betrayed our friendship," David mumbled.

Neal noticed Laura give David a sardonic look and wondered what it meant. David went on. "Doesn't mean I wanted to kill him, for heavens' sake. Surely I'd have bumped him off years ago if that had been my inclination."

Neal nodded. "But you forgave Rhona?"

"I loved Rhona. She was expecting our child."

Throughout this exchange, Rhona had been gazing down at the polished surface of the kitchen table. She seemed absent, as though her mind were elsewhere. Only at the mention of their child, did her face show a flicker of interest.

"Mrs Pine? Are you alright?" Ava asked.

"I just don't see why we're bringing all this up now. It has no relevance to Ewan's death. I don't understand the need for all these questions about the past. Surely whatever happened in the past has been—"

David interrupted. "They're just doing their job, Rhona. Don't upset yourself."

Neal wanted to ask Rhona what she had been about to say. She appeared to be unravelling in front of them, and by the looks of him, David was working himself into a temper. Only Laura Cameron seemed unaffected. Her expression was inscrutable.

David said, "Seems to me that you'd be far better off out in the field — literally — than sitting around a table hinting to innocent people that they've done something evil."

Then Ava pitched in. "Mr and Mrs Pine. We've just been speaking with Olivia Darby. She's a friend of yours, isn't she?" Rhona nodded. "Mrs Darby's neighbour thinks she heard children's voices in the lane beside her cottage sometime after midnight on Monday. She thinks one of the voices belonged to Zak and that the other voice sounded like a girl's. Olivia Darby's just been telling us that Rowan is friends with Zak. Has she mentioned any late night adventures to you?"

The Pines exchanged puzzled glances. Neal wondered if they were genuine.

"Both our girls were fast asleep at that time of night," David said. He gave a mocking laugh. "Are our children suspects now, Sergeant?"

Ava smiled, humouring him. "No, it's just that if they were out at that time, they might have seen or heard something."

David was irate again. "Look, do you have to keep worrying my wife like this? She's been suffering from post-natal depression and this kind of thing isn't helpful."

It was Laura Cameron's turn to express surprise. "You didn't mention anything, Rhone. How bad is it?" She leaned over and touched her friend's hand.

So she could, after all, express emotion, thought Neal.

"I'm all right. It's not that bad. The medication's working."

Ava apologised. "I'm sorry for any upset. It's just that in a murder investigation we can't afford to be too considerate of people's feelings. Our priority has to be finding out who took another person's life."

Neal was pleased with Ava's response. He added, "I expect that finding out who killed Mr Cameron is important to everyone in this room."

Neal saw Laura nudge Rhona. "Did you want to say something, Mrs Cameron?"

Laura hesitated. "I . . . I just wondered if there was any point in mentioning Rowan's nightmares." She looked at Rhona.

"Ah, yes. Mrs Darby mentioned those. The first one occurred the night after Mr Cameron's death, didn't it?"

"So what?" David Pine said scornfully. "Ewan's murder has been the talk of the village. The kids have probably been scaring one another silly over it at school. It's no wonder if she's having nightmares about it."

Neal studied the Pines through narrowed eyes. "I'd be grateful if you'd ask Rowan about it anyway. Probably better coming from you than us."

David Pine's face was puce and Rhona looked worried. Laura Cameron stared down at the table.

Finally David said, "We'll speak with our daughter — for all the good it will do." He looked at his watch. "If there's nothing else, I have work to do."

Neal nodded. "That's all for now."

David stood up immediately and made for the door. Rhona muttered something about the baby crying and went upstairs. It was left to Laura to see Neal and Ava to the door.

"Are you alright staying here with Mr and Mrs Pine?" Ava asked.

"Why wouldn't I be? Unlike you, I'm certain that David and Rhona had nothing to do with Ewan's death. I know they might be suspects, given David and Ewan's past history, but I know them and I know they aren't capable of harming anyone."

Neal said nothing.

* * *

It was late morning now and once Neal and Ava turned back onto the main road to Stromford, the countryside around them unfolded for miles in all directions. Acres of farmland, sporadic woodland, gentle hills, all resting under a troubled sky.

"Looks like rain," Ava commented.

Neal glanced in the rear-view mirror and glimpsed the pewter clouds massing over the retreating Wolds. "Should outrun it," he replied.

"Did you get the impression that they're all hiding something?" Ava asked.

"I got the impression that the Pines were wary. And did you see the look Laura gave David when he mentioned that Ewan had betrayed their friendship? It all but screamed 'hypocrite.' I wouldn't be surprised if those two have a history as well. I suspect there was more behind the rift between Ewan and David than simple sexual jealousy. And I think we're going to have the devil of a time finding out what, unless we stumble upon something."

Unfortunately, stumbling upon something was not a valid strategy in investigative police work.

Chapter 10

Laura was wondering whether to go into Stromford for a couple of hours. She might bump into Gabe North. She could take the bus to town and arrive around lunchtime when he would be more likely to be out of the office. Except she didn't really want to leave things to chance. She picked up her phone.

Laura had fingered the folded note with North's contact details until it was creased and almost illegible. Not that it would matter. She had already memorised them.

After the two detectives departed, she had sat alone in the kitchen for a while. David's study door had slammed shut. Rhona was still upstairs seeing to Shaun. Laura had the feeling that she would be left to her own devices for a while.

"I was hoping you'd call," Gabe said. His voice sounded strained, raised against the din of some background noise, traffic perhaps. "Can you meet me?"

"I don't know if I should."

"Then why are you calling?" A pause. "In an hour then? Can you manage that? There's a Café Nero on the top end of the High Street."

A longer pause. "Alright."

"Good. See you then."

Laura's anxiety felt like it was constricting her throat. Should she call back? Say that she'd never meant to agree to the meeting, that she'd felt pressured into it? But Gabe had not pressed. As usual, she had been passive, too eager to do what somebody else wanted, too happy to drift. Laura gave a sigh. She would meet him. Rhona and David would probably be relieved if she went out for a bit.

She knocked on Rhona's bedroom door and found her lying on her bed, Shaun asleep by her side. "I have a headache," Rhona said. It was a poor excuse. When Laura explained that she wanted to go to Stromford, Rhona immediately offered her car.

Driving into town, Laura questioned her feelings about Ewan's death. She didn't understand them. Why was she feeling so little emotion? Surely she should be overwhelmed with sorrow. Then again, people did speak of being numb with grief. Perhaps that was it. She wondered what others thought of her when they were confronted by her apparent *sang froid*. Obviously they would think that she had not loved her husband — but she had. Once. Things change.

Laura also wondered about David's revelation that Rhona suffered from post-natal depression. It surprised her that Rhona hadn't told her. Laura hoped that all the upset had not made her friend's condition worse.

She reached the outskirts of Stromford too early for her rendezvous with Gabe North. After parking the car in a multi-storey in the centre of town, Laura drifted around town, killing time. The city's mood seemed as sombre as her own. When she was tired of window-shopping, she sat in a tearoom on the Long Hill drinking hot chocolate and eavesdropping on a conversation between two elderly women at a nearby table. One of them was saying that she was disappointed with what the city had become. "Isn't it annoying when you want to take a trip down memory lane and nothing's the same anymore?"

Her words echoed in Laura's mind. For her, nothing would ever be the same again. With a jolt, she realised that Ewan was not just off on one of his benders. This time he was gone for good. She wondered if her lack of emotion arose from the frequency of his absences — both physical and emotional. The truth was he had turned increasingly inwards after their hasty wedding. The drinking had started almost immediately and alcohol made Ewan morose. Once, when she dared to ask him why he drank, he had stared at her as if he expected her to know the answer. For a while, she had worried that it was something to do with her, and that he regretted the marriage. Later, she became convinced that this was only partly the truth. Ewan was consumed with self-loathing. He spent hours hidden away in the spare room, supposedly drawing or painting but never seeming to produce anything. He had had so much talent, so much promise, it was as though he was deliberately squandering his gift. Punishing himself. Laura sat bolt upright. She was reminded of Rhona saying the word 'atonement.' It struck her that both her husband and her friend had given up on the lives they were meant to lead. She thought of Ewan, pleading with her to marry him and wondered for the first time if he had been begging, not for her love, but for the punishment he felt he deserved.

She arrived at the café early and made her way to a secluded table with a mug of coffee and a pain au chocolat. She saw Gabe striding along the pavement dressed in a long dark coat, the tails billowing out, revealing a flash of burgundy lining with every step. He was looking straight ahead. It did not seem to occur to him to look in the window. He caught sight of her, signalled a 'hello,' and proceeded to the counter to buy a drink before sliding into the seat opposite her.

"Glad you could make it," he said. Laura inclined her head. "I'm sorry I left the party so abruptly the other night but I noticed David Pine watching us and I didn't want him to make a scene."

Laura wrapped her hands around her mug and hugged it to her chest. "Why would he make a scene?"

Gabe ignored the question. "Did he say anything to you after I left?" Laura touched the bruise on her arm where David had gripped it so tightly.

"He asked what we were talking about." She noticed a flicker of alarm cross Gabe's face and reassured him. "I didn't tell him anything. I pretended to be tipsy."

"Doesn't it strike you as strange, him wanting to know?"

"Not really. You made it plain that there was no love lost between you. If anything, he was probably looking out for me. I don't know. I'm not sure why I've come here, really. I told you I don't believe my husband or my friends had anything to do with your girlfriend's disappearance. You aren't going to convince me otherwise."

"I'd like to try," Gabe said softly.

Laura felt a flash of anger. "You're full of crap, and I don't have to sit here and listen to it."

"That's true, you don't. If the past is sacred and immutable for you, then just go and carry on as before."

"The past isn't just fixed for me, Mr North, it's fixed for everyone."

"Only if you shut off your mind to different interpretations of it."

"Full of crap," Laura reiterated. Her shoulders ached with tension. Her hands trembled as she returned her mug to the table. The coffee was too strong, too bitter and she hadn't really wanted it after the hot chocolate.

Whatever she had just told Gabe North, she understood that she badly needed to re-examine the past ten years.

"Wherever they were the night Steph disappeared, your husband and friends were not at their flat as they claimed to the police," Gabe said.

"How could you possibly know that?"

"I know because I was there that evening."

"I thought you said you were babysitting Steph's daughter?"

"I . . . left her for a couple of hours. She was asleep. I didn't think any harm could come to her." Gabe looked ashamed. "I was young and stupid and I'm not proud of it."

"So there's a gap big enough to drive a lorry through in your alibi for the night Steph disappeared? And you're accusing my husband and friends of something unthinkable, when from where I'm sitting it could just as easily have been you? That's bloody laughable!" Her voice was becoming shrill and Gabe looked alarmed. "What's wrong? Scared somebody'll hear me and start asking questions?"

"Calm down, Laura." When he spoke her name she stared at him, her anger subsiding. "Hear me out at least, then do what you think best."

"What were you doing at David and Ewan's flat when they weren't there?"

"I broke in."

This was so unexpected it had to be true. "Why would you do that?"

"Again, it's not something I'm proud of. I thought Steph was sleeping with Ewan and I wanted to catch them at it. I suppose I was jealous."

"That's pathetic and sad."

"I totally agree. But it does prove — to me at any rate — that all three of them lied about their whereabouts that night."

"But you couldn't tell the police that because then you'd be destroying your own alibi."

"That's right."

"Why should I believe you? I mean why are you so intent on bringing all this up now? I get that Steph was your girlfriend and that you don't know what became of her, but why now?"

"I've never stopped wondering what happened to Steph. But eventually, for my own peace of mind, I had to let it go. I probably wouldn't have brought it all up again if it hadn't been for . . ." Gabe seemed to check himself. His gaze was turned towards the baristas busy behind the counter with their noisy, hissing machines.

"Hadn't been for what?" Laura prompted. She was becoming impatient.

"Steph's daughter, Tess. She tracked me down a few weeks ago. She remembered me as the man who used to babysit for her and tell her stories. She remembered my name even though she was only a child when her mother disappeared."

Laura gasped. "Wait. Was this before or after Ewan's death?"

"Before. She didn't know your husband, or the Pines. The timing was coincidental. She begged me to help her find out the truth about what happened to her mother. I refused at first, but . . . well, I suppose I felt a certain responsibility." Laura eyed Gabe with distrust. "I know. It's all a bit of a mess. And I know it seems oddly coincidental Ewan's turning up here just after Tess contacted me, but it is what it is."

Laura leaned towards him. "Did Tess make contact with Ewan? Did she lure him down here? So that she could get her revenge . . . or kill him?"

Gabe seemed genuinely surprised. "That's not . . . No! And she didn't ask me to kill him either."

Laura's head reeled. She again had the suspicion that the people around her all seemed to know something she didn't. Ten years ago they had left her out, and she was still excluded now.

Another, more disturbing thought worried away at the back of her mind. Ewan had talked openly about all of his sexual partners, and assured her that none of them had meant anything. When they'd taken up their relationship again, they'd even joked with each other about their affairs. But not once had Ewan ever mentioned Steph.

Gabe North was looking at her, frowning, and Laura realised that she had been silent for some time.

"Are you afraid of me?" he asked.

Laura shook her head.

"How well did you know your husband, Mrs Cameron?"

"I . . . I knew him as well as I knew myself. We grew up together. Don't shake your head like that. You're going to say people change or that no one ever truly knows another person . . ."

Suddenly she could take no more. She excused herself and went to the Ladies. She sat down in a cubicle, shaking with frustration and anger. Fuck their fucking arrangement. Fuck the three years they had spent apart. Could a person change utterly in that amount of time? The truth was, Laura knew very little about Ewan's time in Stromford. She hadn't been part of that life.

Laura became aware that she was sobbing uncontrollably. A voice outside the cubicle said, "Mrs Cameron? Is that you? Are you all right? A Mr North asked me to check on you. He said you looked unwell when you left him."

"Tell him to go to hell!" Laura said. "Tell him to leave me alone!" Inside her head there was another voice. *Tell him I don't want to look any deeper. Damn him and his questions and insinuations.*

A pause. "Mrs Cameron? Are you all right?"

Laura laughed hysterically. "Do I sound all right?"

"Should I call someone?"

Laura realised that the do-gooder outside wasn't going to give up easily. With a sigh, she unlocked the door and stepped out. "Thank you for your concern," she said. The woman peered at her through rimless glasses, her eyes avid with ill-disguised curiosity. "I'm all right now." Before the woman could question her, Laura barged past her back into the coffee shop. She saw Gabe North seated where she'd left him, fingers to his mouth. Biting his nails down to the quick, no doubt. He made to stand as Laura strode over to him. Did he think that she was going to walk right past his table and storm out of the café? Laura threw herself into the chair opposite him.

"The truth is, Mr North, I haven't been completely honest with myself and that's a hard thing to admit." Gabe North looked surprised. "Ewan was different after our three years apart. Of course he was. I was too. People do a lot of growing up at that stage in their life."

"How was he different?"

"Well, for one thing he was anxious for us to be married as soon as possible. I was surprised because I'd felt us drifting apart and I was ready to be let off the commitment hook. When we met in the Easter holidays during his last term at Stromford, I had suspected he was too. Then all of a sudden he was back in Edinburgh and desperate to pick up where we'd left off."

Gabe looked flushed. "Security. He needed to feel safe again. To convince himself that he was still the person he thought he was. Being accepted and loved by you was proof that he could be good. He was adrift morally and you were an anchor. Marriage stopped him having to confront the enormity of what he'd done. In some ways it could be viewed as—"

"What, his punishment? His chance for *atonement*?" His insinuations were hurtful and unsettling. Laura was reminded yet again of Rhona speaking about atonement. "You mean he'd fucked up and marrying me was his chance for redemption? Marriage to me would be shit but not as shit as admitting to his crime — whatever that was — and going to prison!" Heads turned in their direction and Laura realised that she was shouting. She glared around angrily. One of the faces belonged to the 'do-gooder' from the Ladies.

"That's not what I said. Come on, let's get out of here." In a loud voice, Gabe addressed the gawpers. "Show's over, folks."

Outside, Laura allowed Gabe to steer her down some steep steps leading to the river. A narrowboat scythed through the water, leaving swans and ducks bobbing behind it. Laura felt exhausted. She leaned over the railing, wishing she could jump over and land on the narrowboat's deck and just follow the river wherever it took her. She had spent the last ten years of her life floundering in the wake of Ewan's moods, why not let herself be borne away by a gentler current?

After a few moments, Gabe said, "I'm sorry. I got carried away and I upset you. I keep forgetting that Ewan Cameron was your husband. I can't just land my suspicions on you and expect you to embrace them wholeheartedly. All I ask is that you spend some time looking back on the past ten years. Try and reflect on your time with Ewan and see things the way I do."

Laura felt exhausted. "Sure. Revise my marriage, my life, practically all of the past ten years, just like that. That's a big ask. What if I don't like this new version? What if it shows me that for all those years I was living a lie? How am I supposed to come to terms with a thing like that?"

"You'll find a way. The truth is cathartic. You didn't need to meet me again, but something made you contact me. You're already halfway there."

"How do you even know she's dead? I mean, they never found a body, right?"

"She wouldn't have abandoned Tess."

"Oh," said Laura. "No, I suppose not."

"The police were hopeless. When they couldn't pin her disappearance on me they just gave up. Lack of evidence, they said. The case went cold."

"The detectives looking into Ewan's death seem competent enough," Laura said, picturing the brooding inspector and his effortlessly beautiful sergeant. "Maybe I should speak with them about Steph. Not because I think my husband and my friends were involved. The opposite, in fact. To prove to you that I'm right. I'm sorry for Steph's daughter. It must be heart-breaking for her not to know what happened to her mother." Gabe looked alarmed at her suggestion, Laura noticed. "What is it? Are you afraid of what else they might discover? If I tell them you left Tess alone for a couple of hours? You say you went to David and Ewan's flat, but how can you prove it?"

"I was afraid to tell the truth about that back then, but I'm not now. I'd go and confess this minute if I thought it would do any good, but it won't. The police will only waste more time focusing on me instead of investigating what they need to."

"I don't see how I can help you, Gabe," she said.

"There must be something you can uncover while you are staying with the Pines. You knew Rhona well once, didn't you? Maybe you can make her talk to you."

Again, that certainty, persisting in the face of all Laura's denials, that Ewan and her friends were involved in Steph's disappearance.

Laura sighed. "I'll see what I can find out. Brace yourself for disappointment, Gabe." Turning from him, she gazed across the river to the busy market square where lunchtime shoppers were darting to and fro. If she were back home in Edinburgh, she too would be preoccupied with work and all those mundane tasks that make for an unexamined life. Laura had long suspected that her busy life was a way to distract her from her relationship with Ewan. She had allowed the years to tick by unscrutinised, unfelt. She had never asked herself if she was happy.

Standing by the side of the river with Gabe North, she felt a familiar emotion, loneliness. It had been her constant, sometimes her only companion throughout most of her marriage to Ewan.

"I have to get back to work. Can I expect to hear from you again?"

"Maybe," Laura answered, her eyes on the stretch of river no longer furrowed by the retreating narrowboat. She was aware of Gabe North nodding soberly, and of the sound of his feet on the steps, but she kept her eyes on the water, marvelling at how the swans were content to glide on its now calm surface, the narrowboat's turbulence already forgotten.

Chapter 11

Ava's dislike of Reg Saunders didn't spring simply from the fact that he was old school in his attitudes. She could forgive the fact that he was more interested in her body than her mind. After all, she'd come across plenty of women who shared that very view of men. No, her dislike of him sprang from nothing more rational than a prickly feeling that she felt whenever she was in his company. It came down to the fact that she simply didn't trust him. And in Ava's book, trust was everything when it came to relationships, in her work and her personal life.

She wasn't in the best of moods, therefore, when she approached Saunders for an update on the theft of chemicals from Ridgeway Farm on the night Ewan Cameron met his untimely end. His smile was lascivious when she greeted him with a reluctant, "Good morning."

"At least pretend you mean it, Blondie," Saunders said, just managing to keep his eyes on her face. "If you're after info on the Ridgeway theft, I don't have a lot for you. Josh Martin, the owner, might as well have advertised his stock of chemicals in the Courier and invited thieves to help themselves."

"His security was a bit lax then, was it?" Ava said.

"Try *non-existent*. He kept his supplies of pesticides and fertilisers in an outbuilding out of view of the farmhouse. No security lighting, alarms or cameras. He did have a padlock on the door but the windows were unsecured. The thieves entered via one of them. Didn't even need to smash the glass."

"Any evidence left on site? Footprints? Discarded materials?" Ava asked hopefully.

Saunders shook his head. "Nada. We do know they drove across a couple of fields to access the farm. Left tracks behind but they used a transit van, common make, no identifiable features. They knew what they were doing all right. Magpie Farm is a couple of miles west of Ridgeway but Gordon Perkins has state of the art security. No one in their right mind would target his stores over the Martins'."

"How much did they get away with?"

"Five grand's worth of chemicals, but Martin also had ten grand's worth of tools and equipment stored in the same outbuilding. They took the lot."

"I'm assuming there were no identification markings on any of it?"

Saunders merely gave her a look.

"So. Ewan Cameron. Do you think there's a connection? Or was it just coincidence that he died the same night? Murder's a big step up from theft."

Saunders pursed his lips and gave a non-committal grunt. "Not if you're desperate or if you don't give a shit about the value of a human life. If the thieves weren't local opportunists, the alternative would be an organised gang of some sort, and Stromford's got its share of low-life scumbags." Ava suspected that he was alluding to the recent influx of Eastern European migrants to Stromford, to whom any rise in criminal activity was routinely attributed, justifiably or otherwise. She was aware of Saunders waiting for her to comment, but she let his remark go unchallenged. Like most bigots, he was careful not to express his views outright. Nowadays people like him made use of suggestion and innuendo.

"I suppose it's too much to hope that there were any witnesses?" she said.

"Way too much. Unless you count a couple of nags in the paddock behind the outbuildings."

"Cameron's car was found close to Ridgeway Farm — practically on the doorstep. If he'd witnessed something, the thieves could easily have killed him and dumped his body a distance up the road at the abbey ruin, but why would they bother? It would have taken them out of their way. Why not just leave him in the car?"

Reg shrugged. He looked bored. "They bumped him off and dumped him. Why look further than that?"

"Well, thanks anyway."

"My pleasure, Blondie."

Ava winced. She winced again when Saunders noticed and smirked. She retreated hastily.

* * *

"Honestly, Peej, Reg Saunders gives me the creeps."

"Huh?" said PJ, "Oh, yeah, Reg Saunders. He's a lech. Tried it on with me at the Christmas party a few years back. I told him where to go. I wouldn't have thought he'd have the nerve to take you on, though."

"I'll take that as a compliment." Ava was five six and slim, but not skinny. Her body was muscled from years of exercise and martial arts training. At the station she had a reputation for being able to take care of herself.

"He calls me Blondie," she told PJ. "I could probably report him for that if I could even be bothered."

"He has a nickname for most people. He tends to keep them slightly below insulting. He calls DI Neal 'Scotty.' As in 'Beam me up.'"

"I know, I know," Ava said. "I hear you were here till eight last night. You know, there's no need to burn yourself out just because you're a detective now. Remember what Neal said about sharing tasks with the rest of the team?"

"I didn't even notice the time," PJ said. "I got so caught up in what I was doing."

"What have you got so far?" Ava asked.

"I decided to start with David Pine and Ewan Cameron, so I contacted my mum's friend, Julia — you know, the one I said used to teach at the art college? She remembered them. They were both good students. Ewan was the talented one, the one she thought would make it as an artist. David had a good head for business, apparently. He's been pretty successful, hasn't he?" Ava nodded. "They were friends all through art college. Julia was surprised to hear they'd fallen out."

"Did she give you any sort of impression of what kind of people they were?"

"Sorry. She just said they were typical students."

Ava felt a little sorry for PJ. She was trying so hard. Ava hoped she had more to offer than this.

"I did go down to the college and request a list of students who were there at the same time as Pine and Cameron. I've been looking through, seeing if any of the names are in our system or if any of them are still in the area. A couple of their classmates have form. Drugs, alcohol-related incidents, other fairly minor stuff. There was one thing that's probably not relevant. Pine and Cameron were both questioned in relation to the disappearance of a young mother in 2004. A suspect in the case who was later cleared pointed the finger at them but they had alibis and there was no evidence to link them with the woman." She shrugged. "Probably nothing."

Ava whistled softly. "That's not nothing, Peej. It's certainly worth following up. I don't suppose you noticed who the investigating officers were, did you?" She waited while PJ checked the database.

"You'll never guess. Your friend and mine, DI Saunders, was one of them. He interviewed Cameron and Pine and also a Rhona Wilson. The future Mrs Rhona Pine, I'm guessing."

"That's odd," Ava remarked.

PJ looked at her quizzically.

"Saunders didn't say anything about having come across the Pines before. Still, it was ten years ago, maybe he just forgot. Good find, though, Peej. High five!"

"High five!" They slapped palms, just as Neal appeared. He raised an eyebrow and Ava explained.

"Pull out the case file, it may be relevant," Neal instructed PJ. "DS Merry will look it over with you. If anything shouts out to you, let me know. How are you getting on with the other stuff I asked you to look into?" Neal perched on a corner of PJ's desk and Ava smiled. Not so long ago PJ would have swooned if Neal had paid her this much attention. Now she was in a happy relationship with Steve Bryce, and she hardly seemed to notice.

"Nothing from their credit checks yet. I've asked Mateusz to check out their profiles on Facebook and other social networking sites."

"Mateusz?"

"Mateusz Wyrzyk. Young Polish guy. He started when you were on leave, sir. Good with computers."

Neal nodded.

"I phoned Ewan Cameron's most recent employer. Seems he never fulfilled his promise as an artist. Ended up drifting from job to job. He was dismissed from his most recent job for his frequent absences. His manager hinted that there might have been an issue with drugs or alcohol but when I questioned her she said it was only a hunch based on Cameron's behaviour and appearance."

"Did Laura Cameron mention any sort of addiction when you spoke with her in Edinburgh?" Ava asked Neal.

"She mentioned that he drank. As far as drugs go, I got the impression she didn't want to know.

"She never mentioned it to me. Maybe she was worried we'd take the death of a drug addict or an alcoholic less seriously?"

Neal's only response was, "Hmm."

"Are people always this uncooperative?" asked PJ.

"They tend to be selective about what they choose to divulge," Ava commented. "I have a feeling that Laura Cameron hasn't been very forthcoming at all about her relationship with her husband. One minute she's all 'I loved him from the start,' and the next it's 'actually we'd grown apart and I didn't really give a toss about him.' Does anyone else get that impression?"

"I suspect she found her husband as baffling as we do," Neal said. "Understanding Ewan Cameron's state of mind could be the key to discovering why he was killed."

"Oh, I almost forgot," PJ said. "Dan Cardew called about half an hour ago. He wanted to speak to either one of you."

"I'll go down and see him," Ava said.

Neal nodded, already making for his office.

Ava found the shy SOCO in the forensics department. It was situated in the basement and Ava often wondered how its denizens put up with their subterranean working environment. She thought she'd go crazy not seeing daylight all day. Dan tended to bumble a bit in her presence, which might have made conversation awkward were it not for Ava's easy-going manner and her ability to make people feel valued. And Dan's enthusiasm for his work tended to make him forget his shyness once he got into it.

Ava greeted Dan cheerfully. "PJ said you might have something for us."

Dan led her over to his workspace, where Ava recognised some of the items that had been retrieved from around Ewan Cameron's body. Sealed in a transparent evidence bag with an identifying label, was the blue inhaler case that she'd picked up in the woods.

"DNA and other lab tests haven't come back yet," Dan explained unnecessarily. Nowadays this kind of work had to be outsourced, everything was cost-driven, even murder investigations. "I've run some basic tests on Mr Cameron's clothing and the items that were recovered from his person."

Ava nodded, looking over the scant personal possessions. There was a wristwatch, a couple of pens, some loose change and an Edinburgh library card. No wallet, no mobile phone, no wedding ring. Some of these had been recovered near the car, along with Cameron's driving licence, and were lying on a separate part of the table. She waited for Dan to fill her in.

"When a body is dragged along the ground, sometimes you find particles deposited on the clothing. I analysed the soil samples I collected from the folds in Mr Cameron's trousers and compared these to soil samples taken from the site where his car was found."

Ava nodded, interested.

Dan lifted up two separate bags each containing soil particulates. "They were quite different," he said. "I'll spare you the technical details. Essentially it's unlikely that Mr Cameron was killed where his car was found. It's still a mystery why he and the car were so far apart, though."

Ava thanked Dan. There was little that was new in the information, but it did make it seem less likely that Cameron's death and the robbery at Ridgeway Farm were linked. As she walked up from Dan's subterranean chamber, light spilled through the glass doors at the top, throwing a brilliant light onto the last few steps.

Ava gave a wry smile.

Chapter 12

"I'm sorry I was out so long today, Rhone." Rhona was taking a fruit cake out of the oven and Laura stood at the kitchen door, watching. Shaun was gurgling contentedly in his carrycot, and David was still at work. The girls' voices drifted through from the sitting room where they were engaged in some game or other. It was early evening and the kitchen was warm and cosy. It seemed a good time to talk.

"Have you eaten?" Rhona asked. "I've made a cake. The children have had their tea. I thought we could eat later when the girls have gone to bed. David's going to be late."

"The cake smells wonderful. I'd love a piece. Shall I make a cup of tea?" Laura put the kettle on while Rhona tipped the cake onto a cooling tray. As she waited for the water to boil, Laura gazed abstractedly at a pot of rosemary on the windowsill. The herbs reminded her suddenly of Ewan, of a sketch he had made of her window box in Edinburgh, full of scraggly herbs that refused to die. She'd thought the sketch quite lovely and Ewan had offered to have it framed for her birthday. It was on the kitchen wall above her fridge.

Laura had little appetite but knew she ought to eat. She watched as Rhona cut two generous slices of fruitcake and put them on plates.

Rhona took a bite, saying, "I like it like this, hot and straight from the oven. Let yours cool down if you prefer."

Well, it's now or never, Laura thought. Watching her friend closely, she asked, "Rhona, do you remember our last year at uni when you were travelling down to Stromford every other weekend to see David?"

"When I should have been studying for finals, you mean? You used to make me feel guilty staying behind to work."

Laura smiled. Her heart beat faster as she asked her next question. "Was Ewan seeing someone at that time? A woman quite a bit older than him, with a child? I think her name was Steph."

Rhona's full five seconds of silence spoke volumes. "Steph? No. The name doesn't sound familiar."

"Think hard, Rhona. It's kind of important."

Rhona looked unsure. Strange to think that they had told each other everything once. Or so Laura had believed. "Why, Laura? You know I was never comfortable about your so-called arrangement. Rhona pushed aside her plate, as though the cake was suddenly distasteful.

"I'm just, well, curious, that's all. Now that Ewan's . . . gone, I kind of resent those years apart, the time he spent with other women. I feel I want to claw those years back, you know? There'll be no more future so I want more of the past." Then, suddenly tired of tiptoeing around it, Laura blurted out, "I know what happened to her."

Rhona stared at her. Her expression was puzzled and fearful. "What do you mean?" she asked.

"I know she disappeared," Laura said. She saw Rhona's fear recede. What had she expected Laura to say? Now, more than ever, Laura was convinced that she had been left out. They knew something. As she studied Rhona's reactions, she felt sure her friend was trying to assess just how much she needed to say. Laura had no intention of making it easy for her.

Neither of them spoke. Rhona glanced over at her son who had dozed off, his head slumping forward at an awkward angle. She reached out to him, then her arm dropped to her side.

Laura broke the silence. "It must have been harrowing for you. Being questioned by the police after Steph went missing, I mean. As though you were suspects." Laura's voice dropped to a whisper. "Was she . . . special to him? You know — not like the others. Did he . . . care about her?" She'd wanted to ask if Ewan had loved Steph but the word stuck in her throat. Rhona wouldn't meet her eye. "Don't tell me you don't remember this Steph. I know you do."

Rhona's eyes darted about as though she had been backed into a corner. Finally she looked up and Laura recoiled, alarmed at the malice in her narrowed eyes.

"Yes, I remember Steph. Ewan was besotted with her." Spite had hardened Rhona's features. "There. Happy now?"

Besotted. "So she wasn't like the others? She *was* special?"

They heard the crunching of tyres on gravel. Rhona's expression conveyed a warning. "That's David, he's back early. Probably best not to mention our conversation. He was so sensitive about it all at the time. No point stirring up old ghosts." Rhona hurried out of the door.

Laura fixed her eyes on the pot of rosemary again. There was something unsettling about Rhona's desire to hide their discussion from David. Her fingers touched the bruise on her arm where David had gripped her at the party the other night. It was still tender. His eagerness to know what Gabe North had been saying to her was also unsettling. Laura shivered. Had it been wise to come and stay with Rhona and David after so many years of not speaking to them? Did she really know her friends anymore? Laura was beginning to feel that David and Rhona were strangers to her.

Laura did not believe that David and Ewan had fallen out for the reason she'd been given. She was being denied some knowledge about the past. She envied David and Rhona. Even if the knowledge they shared was dreadful, it bound them together tightly.

She made no mention of Steph in David's presence.

Later, at the children's bedtime, Rowan burst into tears. She had been having nightmares every night since Ewan died, and her teacher had told Rhona that she'd been upset at school a couple of times and wouldn't say what was troubling her.

"She asked if everything was alright at home," Rhona explained to Laura. "I mentioned that you were staying with us and told her that it was your husband who was found at the old abbey. But the nightmares started before you arrived. I don't understand what's upsetting her."

"You don't think what the police suggested might be true, do you? That Rowan and her friend Zak might have been out the night Ewan was murdered? What if they saw something and they're too frightened to tell?"

But as before, Rhona would have none of it. She had questioned her daughter about it, Laura knew, but how did she know whether Rowan was telling the truth when she said she had been in bed all that night? It was a mistake to think that children could not lie convincingly. Laura had learned that much in her years as a teacher. Often it was about the biggest, darkest secrets that they lied the most convincingly.

Unwilling to let Rhona off the hook, Laura waited until the children were asleep and David was in his study. Then she resumed their earlier conversation. "What do you think happened to Steph?"

Rhona was sipping wine. The crystal glass glinted in the light from a candle in a storm jar on the coffee table. Rhona gave a deep sigh. "Oh, Laura. Why do you have to keep going on about her? You're the one Ewan wanted in the end. He married you, didn't he?" There was no kindness or reassurance in her tone, but rather weariness and a hint of rancour. "Surely he told you, didn't he?"

"He never mentioned her at all," Laura said without thinking.

"So who did? Was it that Gabe North you were talking to at Ham's birthday party?"

Laura realised her mistake and tried to backtrack. "No, not him. Ewan must have mentioned Steph some time, or maybe I saw her name written down somewhere." She realised that her palms were sweating, and resisted the urge to wipe them on her jeans.

Rhona sighed again. She looked at Laura, and this time her eyes were full of pity. "Ewan told David he loved Steph more than life itself."

Laura's head reeled. She tried to swallow but her mouth was dry. She had already guessed, but it still hit her with the force of a runaway train.

"I'm sorry," Rhona said, the pity gone. "But you did ask."

"So what was I? His second choice? Because Steph disappeared?" Rhona didn't answer. "That's it then, isn't it? I'm right."

"What do you want me to tell you, Laura?"

Laura snapped back. "The truth would be nice for a change. Why did you all tell the police that you didn't know Steph?"

"Just . . . Let it go, please, Laura," Rhona said. "It won't bring you any peace and there's really nothing else to tell. They had a relationship for a time and then Steph vanished. End of story."

Laura could tell she was uneasy again. Rhona kept looking at the door, as though afraid that David might walk in at any moment. It was in Laura's mind to say that she would speak to him, only Rhona's obvious disquiet restrained her.

Laura's eyes narrowed. "I think you know what happened to Steph. I think you've all been lying about something and I want to know what it is."

"Please, Laura. So much has happened since then. David and I have brought three wonderful children into the world. That's got to count for something, hasn't it?"

There it was again — an idea of *atonement*. Were Rhona's children supposed to compensate for something ugly in her past? She wondered if she should do as Rhona suggested and let it go, but then she remembered Gabe's plea. Laura was inclined to be passive and accepting. She had wondered, of course she had, why Ewan had practically begged her to marry him. But then she had closed her eyes to the fact that Ewan had become a stranger to her. Did she have the right to deny Steph's daughter access to the truth that she herself had failed to seek?

* * *

Olivia Darby dropped her son Zak off at school, waited a few minutes until he was out of sight and then reversed the car, driving back the way she'd come. She'd told Zak she was going to Stromford, and she was — only not immediately. First she had to meet someone. There was a continental market in town and she wanted to pick up a few treats. It was a journey she often made, usually alone or with Faye or another female friend. This morning she was going with Bran Gallagher. He had a day off work and they had arranged to spend it in Stromford, looking around the market and having lunch together. It was a sort of date, she supposed, even though they were meeting during the day. She had waved Zak off at the school gates, feeling deceitful. She had mentioned the market to him and promised to bring back some of those pastries he really liked from the French stall. She had not told him she was going with Bran.

The way Zak had reacted to Bran mystified her. True, it had just been the two of them for a long time, but Zak himself had recently suggested that she try Internet dating. Olivia suspected that his friend, Rowan Pine, had been behind that particular idea. Still, it had pleased her to think that Zak would be amenable to having a man around the house. As long as it wasn't Bran, it seemed. When she had questioned him about it, Zak had clammed up. He had muttered a kind of apology the following morning and said that he didn't think Bran was the right sort of person for her. This had made Oliva smile. She wondered what kind of man her son had in mind. Someone like Bran, she would have thought, until the outburst. She hoped Zak could be persuaded to come round. She couldn't imagine having a relationship with someone her son disliked, but then again, she could not allow Zak to dictate her choice of partner. She sighed. Bringing up a child was a challenging business, and bringing up a child alone even more so. Wouldn't it be nice to have someone else to share the responsibility! But not just any old someone. Olivia was falling in love.

The realisation had crept up on her gradually. She recalled her first encounter with Faye Wellings's big, ginger-bearded colleague. She had been intimidated by his sheer bulk and had even taken a step back, as if she'd seen a large, hairy animal. Bran later told her he was used to reactions like this. "By the time I turned fifteen I was over six feet tall and my teachers looked nervous when I walked into the classroom. Everyone called me Hägar, as in the Horrible."

As she turned the car towards Bran's place, she caught sight of Rhona Pine waving to her from her car parked up outside the village hall. Olivia pulled up alongside her.

"Have you got a minute?" Rhona asked, her hand on the door handle. Before Olivia could reply, she slid into the passenger seat beside her. "I wanted to talk to you about something." Rhona didn't seem to notice Olivia's glance at her watch. They'd last spoken a few days ago at Hammond Bell's birthday party in the village hall. Rhona had winked at her, whispering, "That Bran's a real hunk."

But now Rhona had other things on her mind. "We had a visit from the police the other day, asking if Rowan had been out in the middle of the night — the night of the murder. They said your neighbour claimed to have heard Zak and a girl in the lane outside her cottage. We told them it was rubbish, of course. There's no way our kids would be able to slip out at that time of night without us knowing." She looked at Olivia, and added, "Is there?"

Olivia shook her head. "Of course not." She couldn't resist a gentle probe. "It must be hard on you and David, all this. You knew the man who died, didn't you?"

Rhona fiddled with the fringe of her scarf. "He was a friend of David's when they were at the art college in Stromford, but we hadn't seen or heard from him in years. Now half the village probably thinks we bumped him off." Her voice had a bitter edge to it.

Olivia, who had been thinking just that, said, "Of course they don't, Rhona." Rhona gave a thin smile and reached for the car door as Laura said, "That was his wife — widow I mean, who was with you at Ham's birthday party the other night, wasn't it?"

"Laura, yes. She and I were good friends years ago so I invited her to stay while the police investigate her husband's murder. I talked her into going to the party."

"It was a good night, wasn't it?"

"Yes. Kind of overshadowed by events for us, though."

"Oh, yes. Sorry, Rhona." She felt embarrassed by her lack of tact. "By the way, how are Rowan's nightmares?"

"She's been having them every night since it happened. I'm a bit concerned. Her teachers mentioned she's been upset at school too." She shrugged. "I suppose it's a passing phase. How's Zak? He hasn't been over much lately."

"Zak's fine. Showing signs of becoming a stroppy teenager already." She didn't mention Zak's outburst over Bran. Everybody probably knew by now that she and Bran Gallaher were an item, but she didn't feel like discussing it with Rhona Pine. Especially since every moment she spent with Rhona meant less time with Bran. She admonished herself for poking her nose into Rhona's business when she had no wish to share her own.

"I won't keep you any longer," Rhona said. "I just wanted to know if you were of the same mind as us on that business with the police." She was outside the car now, fiddling with her scarf again. She seemed edgy, jittery almost, but who wouldn't be in the circumstances? Olivia pulled away from the kerb, conscious of Rhona watching her from the pavement. Just before turning at the junction, she glanced in her rear-view mirror and saw Rhona still standing where she'd left her. She wondered if she should suggest to Zak that he see less of Rowan Pine. The Pines couldn't be discounted as suspects. Who else in the village could have a motive for killing him? The Pines were the only people who knew him. Ham had told Faye Wellings that whoever carried out the raid on Ridgeway Farm might have killed Ewan Cameron. Olivia shuddered at the thought of a killer in their midst.

Chapter 13

"Whichever way you look at it, it wasn't a rigorous investigation," Ava said.

Neal couldn't disagree with that. It depressed him to think that officers he knew, colleagues, had done such shoddy work. If it made him depressed, it made Ava livid.

"It's shameful, that's what it is!"

He sensed that Ava's anger was directed at DI Saunders. As if she'd needed any more cause to dislike him. Neal wasn't a fan of Saunders either. He'd worked a couple of cases with him before Ava's time and found him to be sloppy and untrustworthy. Not the sort of person you'd trust to have your back in a crisis.

He nodded. "Reg is old school." Reg was also clever. He knew how far to push it. The report in front of Neal showed a deplorable lack of good judgement and respect for others as well as a lack of thoroughness, yet it couldn't be called corrupt. Saunders had got away with it.

Ava was still sounding off. "I know Reg Saunders wasn't the SIO on the case, sir, but even so, he could have done a better job." She threw her hands in the air. "He might as well have said she deserved whatever happened to her."

Neal let her finish her rant, then he said, "All right, Sergeant. You're preaching to the converted, you know."

"Yes, sir. Sorry, sir. We should reopen the case, sir. No one ever found out what happened to Stephanie. And she had a daughter. Goodness only knows what happened to her."

"The report tells us what happened to her. She went to live with her mother's cousin, a pharmacist in Pippinham."

On his first case with Ava, Neal had learned that she was passionate about injustice or violence against women, and sexual violence in particular. She'd never confided the reason and he hadn't asked, piecing together the meagre scraps of information she let slip about her past life. She had dropped out of university, and Neal suspected something had happened there that caused her to abandon her studies. He hoped she would tell him when she was ready, but Neal appreciated that might never happen.

Neal also recognised that Ava's eagerness to reopen the case was not only based on her outrage at the shoddy way it was handled. They both knew that it might have direct relevance to Ewan Cameron's murder. "There are questions that need answers," he said softly.

Ava closed her eyes for a moment. "Maybe the real reason for Pine and Cameron's tiff had something to do with Stephanie."

Neal picked up his phone. "Reg, do you think you could come down to my office for a minute? There's something I'd like to discuss with you concerning the Cameron case. Okay. See you in ten." He turned to Ava. "Keep your cool and let me do the talking. Agreed?"

Ava took a couple of deep breaths. "Of course, sir."

Neal and Ava discussed the case. There were few suspects.

"David and Rhona Pine, obviously," Ava said. "They wouldn't be the first husband and wife to give each other a false alibi. Pine and Cameron were best mates and shared a flat together after their first year at college."

Neal nodded. "What else?"

"Not a lot so far. PJ's managed to track down some of their fellow students at the time, but although some of them remember Pine and Cameron they don't have much to say about them. No scandals, unfortunately, so there's nothing for us to run with. And no one seems to remember Stephanie. She wasn't a student so it's unlikely they would, I suppose."

"Hmm. Laura Cameron said her husband was a bit of a loner at home in Edinburgh. She did mention that he disappeared for days at a time. It's possible he had a problem with drugs or alcohol. I've been in touch with the local police and asked them to look into that for me." He scribbled a reminder to himself. "We need to trace Stephanie's daughter, of course. I don't see why she'd have a grievance against Ewan Cameron, but we can't rule out her involvement."

"So our suspect list consists of David and Rhona Pine — the thieves who made off with a stash of chemicals — and a nineteen-year-old girl who's probably never even heard of Ewan Cameron," Ava said, glibly. "Of course we could include Zak Darby and Rowan Pine as they were allegedly roaming about on the night of the murder. And what about the whole rest of Stainholme village while we're at it?"

Neal's smile was forced. At that moment, Saunders finally made his appearance. Neal greeted him and Ava and Saunders exchanged perfunctory nods.

Neal noted that Saunders's eye had gone straight to the file open on his desk.

"Ah, I see you've been reviewing the Woodson case. Is that what you wanted to speak with me about?"

Neal nodded.

"Well, you're barking up the wrong tree with that one, Jim. It has nothing to do with the present investigation."

"Well, there is a common element," Neal commented dryly.

For some reason, Saunders looked at Ava before turning his gaze to Neal. "Ewan Cameron?"

"And David Pine. They were both questioned after Stephanie Woodson's disappearance. Along with this . . ." Neal rifled through the pages of the document. "Gabriel North. Why didn't you mention any of this before, Reg?"

"Like I said, it's not relevant. It's bloody obvious that Cameron was in the wrong place at the wrong time and got in the way of the Ridgeway Farm robbery. That's what should be the focus of this investigation, not an old case involving some missing slag who probably ran off to escape the responsibility of bringing up a kid on her own."

Neal didn't need to see how Ava responded to this. "Nevertheless," he said, "Stephanie Woodson's disappearance cannot be discounted as a significant element in the Cameron enquiry. Surely you can see that?"

Saunders gave an exaggerated sigh.

"The notes state that Stephanie's disappearance was reported by Gabriel North, who was babysitting for her the night she didn't come home. She told him she was meeting a female friend. The name she gave North turned out to be false," Neal said.

"He'd only just met her. He was a naïve kid from a nice background, ten years her junior. Steph was a looker. He probably thought he'd died and gone to heaven when she showed an interest in him. All she wanted was a free babysitter."

"North was your main suspect?"

"That's right. Claimed he was at home with the kid all night. We only had his word for it that Steph went out that evening. She wasn't seen anywhere around town."

"So she'd invented a story about seeing a female friend who didn't actually exist. North seemed to think that she was with Cameron and Pine. Why was that?"

Saunders shrugged. "Who knows? He claimed he'd seen Cameron talking with Steph earlier in the day and jumped to conclusions. We spoke with Pine and Cameron and they had an alibi. They were home all evening with Pine's then girlfriend, the future Mrs Pine."

"There's no mention anywhere of a warrant to search their flat," Neal said.

"It wasn't considered necessary. It was obvious the kids were telling the truth. There wasn't a scrap of evidence to link them to her. All we had were North's suspicions."

"Stephanie's daughter was eight years old at the time. Was she able to provide any information about North being with her that night?"

"She remembered him reading her a bedtime story. Nothing else. Except waking up the next morning and asking where her mother was. North was there when she woke up but he could easily have slipped out in the night when she was asleep. Or killed Steph in her own home for that matter. Remember we only have his word for it that Steph went out with a friend. He could have been with her, or she could have gone out earlier and returned to her place after North put the kid to bed."

Neal frowned. "Forensics found nothing amiss in Stephanie Woodson's home. If she came to harm, it's unlikely to have been there unless her killer was very, very careful."

"There's no evidence she came to any harm. If you ask me, she just got tired of the kid and fucked off." Saunders turned to Ava, "Pardon my French. She was behind with her rent, too." He looked at Neal. "Steph Woodson was probably on the game. Women like her disappear all the time, Jim, that's the truth of it. A lot of the time no one even misses them."

Neal gathered that, in Reg Saunders's book, 'women like her' weren't worth missing.

"She had a daughter," Ava said. "I expect she missed her mother."

"Yeah, well. I reckon the kid was better off without a mother like that."

Before Ava could reply, Neal said, "Ava, find out where Tess Woodson is now and arrange for us to talk to her."

"Yes, sir."

Ava hesitated, but Neal wasn't dismissing her. Turning to Saunders, he said, "Thanks, Reg. We'll take it from here. Keep us up to speed on your enquiries into the farm robbery."

Saunders grunted, plainly riled at Neal's refusal to forget the Stephanie Woodson investigation. "Re-examine the case all you like, but you won't find anything in there to account for Cameron's murder. Waste of time if you ask me." He went out, slamming the door.

"Just as well we're not asking you," Neal muttered. He seldom made remarks like this in front of a junior officer. He was annoyed with himself, but the sight of Ava's beaming smile was worth it.

"I'll get right on that, sir," she said.

Neal called her back. "How is your brother?" he asked.

Ava looked surprised. "He's good, sir."

"And his friend, the one who helped with the Gray Mitchell case?"

"George? He's good too, sir. Leon Warrior's kind of taken him under his wing. I think he felt he owed it to his partner. Apparently he's thinking of volunteering at a shelter for gay kids. Gray would have been pleased."

"Thank Ollie and his friend for me, will you, Ava? I got so swept up in all the business with Maggie I forgot to mention it."

"That's understandable. How is Maggie?"

"Getting there, as my old mum would have said," Neal said.

"I'd be happy to have a drink with her sometime. You know, give her a chance to talk about it, if you think that'd help."

"I think she'd like that. I know she doesn't want to talk about it with her friends, but I think she'd open up to you. Considering you all but saved her life."

"The paramedics saved her life."

Neal nodded. He began shuffling the documents from the file. He wasn't very good at small talk and though he didn't want Ava to leave, he could think of nothing more to say to keep her in the room.

"Right then, I'll get on," Ava said. "You've got my contact details."

Neal looked up, startled.

"For Maggie," Ava clarified.

"Ah, yes. I'll let her know and leave it up to her to call you."

Chapter 14

Laura met Gabe North outside the cathedral. They walked to a residential street in the Uphill area. North lived in a semi-detached house with a square bay window, its red wooden door half-hidden behind an overgrown conifer. He showed Laura into a sitting room overlooking a long garden and asked if she would like a drink. While he was in the kitchen preparing coffee, there was a knock at the door and a moment later, Laura heard the sound of hushed voices in the hallway.

Gabe came into the room, accompanied by a brittle-looking young woman. "Laura, I'd like you to meet—"

"Tess Woodson." Laura completed the introduction.

Tess hovered in the doorway, her face half-concealed behind wisps of long hair. She looked self-conscious. Laura's directness had clearly unnerved her, and Laura felt instantly sorry for her predicament. It was Gabe she was angry at, not this thin young girl who had been dealt such a poor hand so early in her life.

"I thought it was time the two of you met," Gabe said. His expression was uncertain, as hesitant as his young visitor.

Laura wondered how Tess felt about meeting the wife of the man she probably believed killed her mother. She wanted to tell Tess that Ewan had had nothing to do with Steph's disappearance. The trouble was that she was no longer sure. She said nothing and Tess too was silent.

Gabe muttered something about coffee and steered Tess to an armchair. Then he retreated from the room. Perhaps he thought the two of them would have a lot to talk about.

To fill the awkward silence, Laura asked, "Do you remember my husband, Tess?"

The girl shook her head. She was sitting with her back to the French window, the stark winter garden a fitting backdrop to her air of misery. The feeble light from outside threw a shadow across her face and Laura shivered. She felt as though she was looking at a ghost. In a way she was, for this fragile girl was probably all that was left of Steph.

Gabe returned and handed each of them a mug of coffee.

"I'm sorry for springing Tess on you without warning, Laura. I just thought you might feel more engaged if you met her." He turned to Tess. "As I said, Laura never met your mother and her husband never told her that he knew her. This is all new to her, too. Laura, I know we're asking a lot of you. I understand that the shock of your husband's death is still raw. I can only guess what pain my interference and suspicions must be causing you."

He droned on.

Laura looked over at Tess, wishing she could see her face more clearly. She walked over to her and looked into her face. What she saw made the room spin.

Laura would have fallen over if Tess hadn't jumped up and steadied her. She and Gabe helped Laura to a chair and Gabe made her lean forward with her head between her knees until she began to recover.

"Are you okay?" Gabe asked.

Kneeling on the floor at his side, Tess was looking up at her, frowning. "I'm fine. Sorry, I just felt a bit faint, that's all. Do you look like your mother?"

Tess looked at Gabe. Didn't she speak to anyone but him?

Again, it was Gabe who answered. "Yes. Steph was . . . Tess is her mother's exact double."

"I recognise you," Laura said. "Your face is familiar. I've seen it before."

"How? When?" Tess gasped.

Her eyes reminded Laura of the characters in the manga books that Ewan had read. They were huge and wondering and shone with unshed tears. Laura spoke in a whisper. "In his drawings. He drew her face — your face — all the time."

"Are you sure?" asked Gabe.

"Yes."

"Then this proves that Ewan did know Steph." He drove a fist into his palm. "I knew he was lying and now we can prove it."

Laura wondered what he meant by that 'We.'

Ewan had turned the spare room in their flat into his studio. Before his disappearance he had all but moved in there. Laura had seldom ventured inside, but one day she had gone in to look for something and had come across a folder full of drawings. They all showed the same face: Steph's, or Tess's face. Of course she had wondered about the woman, and why Ewan drew her over and over.

"Perhaps it proves that Ewan knew your mother, Tess, but it doesn't mean that he harmed her, or that he was responsible for her disappearance," Laura said. Turning to Gabe, she added, "Rhona admitted to me that Ewan knew Stephanie. That he was . . . obsessed by her."

Gabe gave her a look of astonishment. "She told you that? She and David denied it ten years ago."

"She might still deny it. It would be my word against hers if we went to the police. And, she's terrified that

David might find out she told me. He's always hovering about, listening to our conversations, especially when we've had a drink. Like he's afraid that Rhona will let something slip."

"If we can show the police that Ewan drew Steph, it would prove that he knew her, whatever the Pines might say. These drawings, do you have them somewhere safe?" Gabe asked.

Laura didn't answer. "No," she said at last. "Ewan destroyed all his artwork before he left for Stromford. He cut up or shredded everything."

A small part of her felt triumphant at the disappointment on their faces. How dare they accuse Ewan of killing Stephanie Woodson? But a bigger part of her felt pity. And something more. Laura was no longer in denial. She had to know. And like her, Tess Woodson was a victim of a conspiracy of silence. She reached for the girl's hand and said, "I'm sorry."

Gabe paced the room. "Think, Laura. Is it possible that something could have survived? A drawing you've missed, or a photograph even?"

"I haven't looked through all of Ewan's things yet. So it's possible there's a picture of Tess — I mean Steph — somewhere in my flat." She half expected Gabe to bundle them into his car and drive up to Edinburgh with them.

"What about David and Rhona's house? Perhaps they have a picture somewhere."

He was going to ask her to search their house. Laura was about to object when she caught sight of Tess's pinched, hopeful face. "I'll look," she said. She was aware of a shifting of allegiance from the people she'd known ten years ago and the man she'd lived with, to the ones in this room. Gabe and Tess were pinning all their hopes on her. It should have felt like a betrayal, but instead it felt liberating.

"I'll help you," Gabe said.

"How can you possibly do that?"

"Offer to babysit for David and Rhona one night so that they can go out together. Call me when they've gone and I'll come round. We can both look."

Laura considered this. She would feel better about going through David and Rhona's things if she didn't have to do it alone.

"Okay."

Gabe smiled, and Laura noticed for the first time how attractive he was. He was very different to Ewan. Ewan had been dark, and Gabe was fair. His unassuming manner suggested composure rather than weakness. Laura felt self-conscious. It was days since she'd taken any trouble with her appearance. Her hair was a mess and her clothes were crumpled from being stuffed hastily into her suitcase.

"I . . . I still think it's a waste of time, and it doesn't prove Ewan . . ." Laura paused, aware that Tess was hanging on her every word. "I mean, all it proves is that Ewan knew Steph, not that . . ."

Tess took her hand. Laura could feel the bones beneath the cool flesh. Tess had little more substance than the pictures of her vanished mother. If Gabe's suspicions were right, Ewan had wronged them both.

Tess left soon afterwards. Gabe began to apologise as soon as she had gone.

"Don't keep saying you're sorry," Laura told him. "You have every right to want to know what happened to Steph. If my husband was involved, then I'll have to accept it — even the unthinkable." She paused. "How did you get over Steph's disappearance? I mean, has it plagued you all these years to the extent of ruining your life?"

He frowned and looked past her out through the French windows. A wind had begun to blow, animating the stark branches of the trees. Gabe swept back a tuft of hair that had fallen over his brow.

"For a long time I thought about her every day. I couldn't believe that the police gave up looking for her so quickly. It was like they didn't care. I was given a load of statistics about the number of people that go missing every year. I still don't understand why they would think *she'd run away from her responsibilities.* She loved Tess and took good care of her." He sighed. "But, yes, I moved on. I'd only known Steph for a couple of weeks before she disappeared. I wasn't in love with her. I thought I was at the time, but you know, young love . . . I was angry for a long time because I'd been suspected of harming her, but the worst was the not knowing. I couldn't refuse Tess when she reached out to me. I'm doing this for her. I hope you understand that."

"Yes, I believe you," Laura said. "I'll suggest the babysitting thing to Rhona and let you know what happens." A sudden movement in the garden caught her eye. A squirrel darted up a tree trunk to help itself to nuts from a swaying bird feeder. Laura was aware that Gabe too, was watching its antics and a few moments passed in distracted silence. "I should go," she said at last. She could tell that Gabe North wanted her to stay, and she wondered what she would do if he were to ask her. She stood up. He brought her coat and held it out for her in an outdated, chivalrous gesture.

* * *

Laura had left Rhona at home with Shaun, who was unwell with one of those mysterious viruses that often afflict babies and young children. She had taken the bus to Stromford and now she walked down the Long Hill, intending to buy some books for the girls before making for the bus station. On the way, she made a diversion to the art college. It had been incorporated into the university but was still housed in a late Victorian red-brick building on a street off the top end of the High Street. She had never visited Ewan during his three years in Stromford, and she was curious to see where he had spent that part of his life.

Laura sank down on a wall opposite the grimy façade. Why had Ewan never told her about Steph? There was no longer any doubt that he had loved her. Rhona had told her as much and there were the drawings, hundreds of them, all of Steph. When Ewan withdrew, had he been shutting out the world, or just his wife? Or retreating from himself? If Gabe were right and Ewan had been responsible for Steph's disappearance, or even for her death — there, she'd said it — had he been consumed by guilt? Had he decided to visit Rhona and David because Steph's disappearance was their business too? Laura confronted what had been at the back of her mind ever since her first meeting with Gabe North. Rhona and David were complicit in whatever it was that Ewan had done. Was it something so terrible, so threatening to David and Rhona's present way of life that they had been compelled to deal with Ewan's guilt by killing him?

For a while Laura sat on the wall, beset by memories and imaginings. She watched the students scurrying past. They looked so young, so incapable of anything but going about the business of enjoying their lives. Rhona had used the word 'atonement,' referring to her perfect little family. Was it possible to right a wrong by subsequently living a good life? Ewan's punishment had been to marry his childhood sweetheart and condemn them both to a loveless marriage. She wondered if he or David, or Rhona, had given any thought to her when they decided to 'atone' for whatever they had done to Steph.

Chapter 15

Ava was feeling uncharacteristically nervous. Maggie Neal had texted her to ask if they could meet for a drink. She had meant it when she told Neal that she would be happy to meet his sister. It was just that she hadn't expected her to get in touch so quickly.

So here she was, standing in the freezing cold outside their arranged meeting-place, a bar of Maggie's choosing in the Swanpool. This was an area of the city that was abuzz with bars and cafes and restaurants, all overlooking a broad stretch of water where the river Strom swelled into a mini-lake, somewhat pretentiously known as the Marina. Across the water the university buildings dominated the view and because it was only a short walk away, Swanpool was a popular haunt of students.

She spotted Maggie walking down the steps from the bridge over the Strom and gave her a wave. Maggie waved back. She was wearing a red leather jacket and a short tartan skirt with leggings and black patent ankle boots. She'd straightened her unruly red hair and it made her look more sophisticated. Around her neck, and covering her scar, she'd wound a black cashmere scarf. Ava noticed how fragile she looked. She couldn't help remembering the terrible sight of Maggie lying in her brother's arms, bleeding to death, or so it had seemed at the time. She swallowed, hoping she wasn't going to embarrass them both by crying.

"Maggie! Good to see you. You look great."

"Thanks, Ava."

There was a slightly awkward pause. Ava had met Maggie only once before and they didn't really know each other well. Sensing that she would have to take the lead, Ava nodded towards the closest bar. Loud music pounded from within and a throng of young people blocked the entrance. From all directions, people seemed to be converging on the waterfront. The revellers were making an early start.

Maggie hung back. "Actually, do you mind if we go somewhere quieter? I'd forgotten how noisy it is here and my throat's still not up to shouting."

Ava nodded readily. She had thought this was a strange choice of venue for a quiet chat. Perhaps Maggie had wanted to be part of a vibrant, life-affirming environment, then realised she couldn't cope. They walked away from the river, heading in the direction of the Long Hill. Ava sneaked a sidelong glance at Maggie, wondering if the crowds and the liveliness of the riverside reminded her of the Christmas market where her assault had taken place.

"I know a cosy little bistro on Pebble Lane just past the Roman Arch. Would that do?" she asked.

Maggie smiled. "Romano's? It's one of Jimmy's favourite places to eat."

Useful to know, Ava thought. She must avoid it when she was out with Joel. The waitress showed them to a table upstairs where it was quiet, and went to fetch a bottle of wine.

"So, did Jimmy put you up to this?"

Ava considered fibbing, then thought better of it. "Well, sort of. He's worried about you. But I've been looking for an excuse to get to know you better."

"He wants to know if I'm really okay or just putting on a brave face for his benefit."

"I suppose so. Can you blame him?"

Maggie gave a little laugh. Then she sighed. "Jimmy's over-protective of me. You knew we were quite young when our mother died?"

Ava shook her head. She knew virtually nothing about Jim Neal's personal life and circumstances. She leaned forward, eager to know more.

"No, I don't suppose he's told you much about his past. He keeps things to himself. Mum died of cancer when Jimmy was fifteen and I was nine. Our dad was always a heavy drinker but after Mum died he became an alcoholic. It wasn't grief so much as the fact that she wasn't there to hold him back anymore." Maggie paused as the waitress brought their wine. "When things got really bad, Jimmy went to stay with his friend Jock Dodds and his family. I moved in with Mum's sister, Auntie Jean. She didn't have room for both of us and Jimmy and Jock were like brothers. We lived one street away from each other and saw each other at school and whenever else we wanted to, so it wasn't that bad."

Ava gave a sympathetic nod.

"I got on well with Auntie Jean. Everything was going well at school, then when I was sixteen — just — I met this man. He was quite a bit older than me."

Ava raised her eyebrows.

"Twenty-two years actually. He was thirty-eight." Ava opened her mouth but Maggie said, "I know, I know. Jimmy said it all at the time, but I was incredibly stubborn. Anyway, I didn't think he had any right to comment since he became a father at nineteen."

Ava wondered if she should tell Maggie not to say any more about her brother. It felt almost wrong to be finding out so much.

"Anyway, to cut a long story short, I moved in with Stu. Jimmy was furious. He practically accused Stu of being a paedophile. We didn't talk for months. Stu and I were together for just over a year."

"How did it end?" Ava asked.

"In tears, not surprisingly. I found out he was seeing a fifteen-year-old girl behind my back. So Jimmy had been right, of course. And I'd wasted a year of my life. I didn't even get a job or go to college or anything. Stu was well off and liked me being," she coughed, "available."

Ava frowned. She despised sexual predators, particularly those who targeted young girls.

"I went off to London for a bit but that didn't work out either, so I came to Stromford to stay with Jimmy. Sometimes he acts like he's my father as well as Archie's. I guess he wants to make up for what he sees as not having looked out for me better when I was younger. So you can appreciate that this . . ." Maggie loosened the scarf at her throat to reveal the livid scar across her neck, "was very hard for him to take."

Ava nodded slowly. "Yes, I sort of get that." She'd had a hunch that her DI was attracted to vulnerable women. Was his sister at the root of it? She wondered if Neal had ever physically confronted this man, Stu.

As if she'd read her mind, Maggie said, "Don't breathe a word of this, but when Jimmy found out, he gave Stu a thrashing. Jock had to pull him off."

Ava was digesting this when Maggie said, "No doubt he's never mentioned Myrna either."

Myrna? Was she Archie's mother? Ava held her breath.

"She and Jimmy were childhood sweethearts. They started going out when they were sixteen. They were nineteen when Myrna got pregnant. She wanted to have an abortion. She had a place to study music at university and she wanted to train to be an opera singer — she had a great voice. She's becoming quite well-known now — Myrna MacDonald?"

Ava shook her head. She would be going straight to Google later. "Sorry, I don't really know much about opera. Ollie likes Gilbert and Sullivan. He's always singing funny songs from *HMS Pinafore* and stuff. What's that one about the Ruler of the Queen's Navy who's never been to sea?" She began to hum.

Maggie laughed. "Myrna was great fun. Really full of life, but she was also kind of flighty and . . . and mercurial. It would have killed her to be stuck at home with a baby. Jimmy persuaded her to carry on with the pregnancy and promised he'd take complete responsibility for their child."

"Wow."

"Yeah. It's not that he was anti-abortion or anything. He just said he was intending to become a father at some point in his life, so why not then? He thought he knew exactly what he'd be getting himself into." Maggie shook her head. "Of course, no one knows what being a parent involves until they have a kid. To his credit, Jimmy embraced it from the start."

"Was that why their relationship ended?"

"Yes, but I'm pretty sure they would have split up anyway."

"Oh?"

"I mean, we're all kind of still growing at that age, aren't we? Trying on different personas to see which one fits. Not Jimmy, though. He wasn't always as staid and serious as he is now, but he always seemed older than his years. I think he just found his true self sooner than most of us and stuck with it. Myrna was a chameleon, always changing. She would have driven Jimmy crazy eventually, even though I think that's what attracted him in the first place. He used to say that there was much more to her beneath the surface, and maybe there was, but however hard you scratched, you'd still be hard pushed to define the real Myrna."

"Oh," Ava said again. She was having difficulty imagining the Jim Neal she knew being attracted to the sort of woman Maggie was describing.

The waitress brought their food. As she picked up her knife and fork, Ava realised how effectively Maggie had deflected attention away from herself, and steered the conversation to her brother. Suddenly Ava felt she had been duped. She stabbed a piece of chicken with her fork and said, "So, how are you feeling, really?"

"I'm fine, really I am. My throat's still a bit raw and my voice sounds like it belongs to someone else, but I had a lucky escape and I'm focusing on how great it is to still be here. The more people keep asking me how I *really* feel, the more pissed off I get." Maggie's voice, soft at first, had risen until heads began to turn in their direction.

Ava touched her arm. "Last month I nearly killed someone. I really wasn't feeling that bad about it because I acted in self-defence and he didn't die, but they made me see a counsellor anyway. Maybe if he had died I would have felt differently. Working out how you feel about something is not always straightforward. You need time to process what happened to you. I know my experience was nothing like yours, I didn't almost die." Ava paused. "I did once though, so I do know how it feels." Ava hadn't meant to tell Maggie this. She'd never shared it with anyone, not even her parents.

Maggie gave her a look, beseeching her to continue.

"It was when I was a student. I made friends with another girl, called Sophie. She'd had a very difficult childhood. She was sexually abused by her uncle for six years. He was her mother's brother and had stepped in as a kind of father figure after Sophie's dad died. It was the usual story. He was a well-respected professional and when Sophie told her mum about the abuse, she didn't believe her. Worse still, Sophie found out that her mother was in a relationship with the uncle."

Maggie gasped. "That's terrible! What happened?"

"She ran away when she was fifteen and went into a women's refuge. She was lucky enough to be befriended by an older woman there who'd escaped from an abusive relationship, and they moved into a flat together. They sort of helped each other."

Ava ate another piece of chicken. It tasted of nothing. She washed it down with a slug of wine. "I'm sorry to say this story doesn't have a happy ending. Sophie got herself together enough to get to university. Then she got a call about her friend, the woman she'd met at the refuge. The woman's husband had tracked her down and killed her. As you can imagine, Sophie was distraught. She . . . well, she took some pills. When she didn't show up for lectures I raised the alarm. I went to her room with the warden of the residence where she was living and when she unlocked the door with the master key, we found Sophie. She was still alive but she died of liver failure a couple of days later."

Ava thought of that last time she'd seen Sophie, so still and so dead. She pushed her plate away, her appetite suddenly gone.

"You went after her uncle, didn't you?" Maggie whispered.

"Yes. I confronted him, and Sophie's mother." She winced at the memory. "They were a formidable pair, wouldn't admit to a single thing. They told me Sophie was a twisted little liar who'd hated her mother and been jealous of her uncle. When I told them I was going to the police to get justice for Sophie, the uncle went berserk."

"He attacked you?"

"Yes. And I wasn't a martial arts expert in those days. He had his hands around my throat and I'm convinced he would have killed me if Sophie's mother hadn't suddenly come to her senses and picked up a breadknife."

"Oh my God!"

"She stabbed him in the back."

"She killed him?" asked Maggie.

"No. She punctured a lung, but he survived. I thought I was going to die," Ava said. "The way his eyes looked when his hands were round my throat. There was no emotion in them, know what I mean?"

"Shit."

"Yeah." Ava shrugged. She put down her knife and fork and leaned back in her chair.

Maggie stared out of the window, then she asked, "Is that why you gave up your studies?"

"Yes, but not for the reason you might think. It wasn't that I was traumatised by what happened to me. I just felt that it was a bit of an indulgence to be spending my time reading books when there was so much injustice out there in the world. Sounds naff, I know, but the whole experience of being a victim just made me want to fight back. I never wanted to find myself in a vulnerable position again, so I took up karate, kick-boxing, the lot, and applied to the police because I wanted to help people like Sophie and her friend." A pause. "That's how *I* dealt with my near-death experience."

Maggie nodded slowly.

"Don't lock what happened to you away in a box, Maggie. That box will just sit there and you'll become more and more afraid of what's inside. I think that's what happened to Sophie, eventually. Her friend's death made her believe there was no escaping the past."

"Your job puts you in danger all the time. How do you cope with that?"

"Because I know I can. Physically, and more importantly, up here." Ava tapped her head.

"And emotionally? How do you know you're not just doing a dangerous job because you haven't really confronted what happened to you? All this keep-fit business that Jimmy says is an obsession with you, isn't that just a form of denial, of running away, even?"

Maggie's question caught Ava off guard. "We all find our ways of coping," she answered, but her tone was less assured than before. "Anyway, we're supposed to be talking about you."

Maggie gave a strange smile. It was almost smug. "I said I was fine, Ava, and I am. Seems to me like you're the one who needs to look inside the box."

Ava sighed. She had set out to get Maggie to open up about her experience, but somehow Maggie had turned the conversation around and Ava had said none of the things she'd intended to say. Instead, she had revealed a whole lot more about herself than she felt comfortable sharing. She'd also learned a lot about Jim Neal without even asking. It was perplexing. She looked at Maggie Neal and thought her statement about feeling fine might just be the truth.

"I'm assuming that our conversation this evening is confidential?" Ava said. "Your brother is a very private man at work. I don't think he'd be too pleased that you've told me all about Myrna."

"Of course," Maggie answered. "And thanks for the advice, Ava. You can tell Jimmy I'm fine and that I've already made an appointment to see a counsellor. They found me one before I left hospital. I just hadn't got around to mentioning it to him."

"Oh," Ava said, yet again.

Maggie gave her a warm smile. "Let's get together again soon. I think it's so cool that we get along so well." She reached over and patted Ava's arm. "I have a feeling we're going to be just like sisters. Now, tell me all about this Dr Agard you're seeing."

* * *

"Gabe North still lives in Stromford. And I've got an address for Tess Woodson! PJ shouted.

"Good morning to you too." Ava wasn't feeling her best.

PJ looked her up and down. "Saw your car in the car park this morning. Did you stay over at Joel's?" She made it sound like an accusation.

"No. I had dinner with Maggie Neal and drank too much, so I had to leave the car and take a taxi home. I got another taxi in with Ollie this morning."

"How is it going with Joel?"

"Okay." Ava said, aware of sounding unenthusiastic.

"Not *the* one, then?"

"Probably not." Ava moved to her desk. She didn't feel like confiding in PJ. She'd done too much confiding the evening before. The truth was, Joel had dumped her. It was something new for Ava, and while she wasn't upset — they'd only had a handful of dates — her ego had taken a bit of a knock. Joel was a smart guy. He'd probably worked out that she wasn't interested in a long-term relationship with him and had cut his losses. She'd tell PJ soon enough. After last night she was still feeling a bit exposed emotionally.

"Inspector Neal wants to see you," PJ said.

"Where is he?" Ava had already noticed that his office was empty.

"With George Lowe. He should be back any minute now."

By the time Ava had grabbed a coffee, Neal was waiting for her. Entering his office, she felt nervous. There was no particular reason why she'd never talked about her traumatic experience. She'd only told Maggie because she thought it would encourage Maggie to open up and confide in her. Now she understood that Maggie was much savvier than she'd thought. She hoped Maggie had kept her word and not told her brother.

"Maggie seems to have enjoyed herself last night," Neal said, cheerily by his standards. "Thanks for speaking with her, Ava. It turns out she'd already arranged to have some counselling, but I'm grateful to you nevertheless."

"I enjoyed her company," Ava said, realising that she meant it.

"Good. Right then. Let's get down to business. Did PJ mention she'd got addresses for Gabe North and Tess Woodson?"

"Yes, sir."

"I've contacted North and arranged for him to come in this morning. He'll be here in half an hour. I'd like you to sit in on the interview. He's not a suspect as such but it will be useful to find out what he knows about Ewan Cameron and the Pines."

"What about Stephanie's daughter?"

"I've asked PJ to contact her and arrange for us to visit. Did she say if she'd managed to organise that yet?"

Ava shook her head.

* * *

Gabe North turned up ten minutes early. PJ showed him into an interview room and made him a cup of tea. By the time Ava and Neal joined him he was fidgeting in his seat and glancing at his watch.

"I'm sorry if we're keeping you from your work, Mr North. We'll try to keep this as brief as possible. I'm Inspector Jim Neal and this is my colleague, Sergeant Ava Merry. We're investigating the murder of Mr Ewan Cameron. I believe you once knew Mr Cameron and his friends Rhona and David Pine?"

"We weren't friends. I was at the art college at the same time as Cameron and Pine, that's all. I saw them around."

"You were all questioned ten years ago about the disappearance of a young woman by the name of Stephanie Woodson. You were a suspect, as you were probably the last person to see Miss Woodson alive. You told the investigating officer that you believed Cameron had something to do with her disappearance. On what did you base your accusation?"

"Does your report mention that I was the one who reported Steph missing?"

"Yes it does."

"There's something I didn't mention at the time. I'd like to mention it now."

Ava and Neal exchanged glances.

"I went to Pine and Cameron's flat the night Steph disappeared. I thought Steph would be there with Cameron. I believed she was having an affair with him. I was a stupid, jealous kid and I expected to find them in bed together. I didn't mention this to the police at the time because I was supposed to be babysitting Steph's daughter, Tess, and I left her alone for a couple of hours. Not only that, but the babysitting was my alibi. I'm not proud of leaving a young child alone. All I can say is I didn't really appreciate what a responsibility it was at the time. I thought she'd be all right as she was sleeping."

Neal nodded. "Why did you think Cameron was involved in Stephanie Woodson's disappearance? Our records of the investigation show that he was questioned and claimed not to have known her personally. No one else who was questioned could recall seeing them together."

"I . . . he . . . I don't have any proof. It was just a feeling. She told me she'd posed nude for him a couple of times and I saw them talking together in the street once, so I assumed they knew each other."

"And you were in a relationship with her?"

North coloured. "I thought I was, but with the benefit of experience and hindsight, I can see now that she was merely using me."

"Were you in a sexual relationship with her?"

"We had sex on one occasion. After that Steph made a lot of excuses to avoid having sex with me." He looked down at his hands.

Ava noticed that his nails were bitten to the quick. "How long had you been in a relationship with Stephanie before she disappeared?" she asked him.

"About four weeks. And I did a lot more babysitting than lovemaking in that time. I was rather naïve for my age, Sergeant."

Ava couldn't help thinking of Reg Saunders's observation that North must have thought he'd died and gone to heaven when Stephanie Woodson had paid him some attention. Annoyingly, he was probably right. Gabe North had matured into a confident enough individual and he was not bad to look at. Only his nail-biting habit hinted at the nervous young man he'd once been.

"I'm still having trouble understanding why you'd think Ewan Cameron might have harmed Stephanie."

"But his alibi . . . all of their alibis . . ."

"We only have your word for it that there was no one at their flat the evening you called there. And the police didn't even know that at the time, because you chose not to tell them."

"You see? That's another reason why I didn't bring it up sooner," North said. "I suppose I'm now a suspect in Ewan Cameron's murder investigation?"

"It would help if you can tell us what you were doing the night he was murdered," said Neal.

"I was at home. Alone. Working on a project. I'm an architect." He held his wrists out. "Might as well arrest me now."

Neal ignored the gesture. "Tell me what you know about Ewan Cameron. You must have known him better than you say to have formed the opinion that he was capable of murder. That is what you think, isn't it?"

"Yes." North stared again at his hands, looking abject.

For pity's sake, grow a pair. Ava was beginning to feel impatient with North's fecklessness. She said, "So, apart from the fact that you were jealous of him because he drew your girlfriend without her clothes on, you have nothing to support your opinion?"

"They weren't at the flat. Ask them where they all really were that evening."

"We'll do that. Thanks for your time, Mr North. We'll be in touch," Neal said.

North stood up uncertainly. "Are you going to reopen Steph's case?"

Ava looked at Neal. He had that tight-lipped, frowning expression on his face.

"I'll see you out, Mr North," she said, and walked to the door.

After North's departure, Neal called Ava and PJ into his office. He filled PJ in on the interview, he asked for their opinions.

"Well, he has a motive for killing Cameron, don't you think?" Ava said. "He obviously resented Cameron's 'relationship' with Stephanie and he still has strong feelings about it, I reckon. Then again, why would he wait this long? Unless he's recently made some sort of discovery that's got him all riled up again."

"Maybe he killed Stephanie too," PJ chipped in.

Neal and Ava looked at her, encouraging her to continue.

"Well, he could have been angry at her for cheating on him with Ewan Cameron. We only have his word for it that Steph went out at all that evening. What if she stayed at home, they rowed over Cameron and North lost control?"

Ava added, "The original investigators considered that a possibility, but there was no evidence to back it up. Saunders and his then partner did search Stephanie's flat and forensics failed to find anything. Pity they didn't search the flat Ewan Cameron and David Pine shared." She added, "The investigation wasn't exactly thorough." She turned to Neal. "You heard what DI Saunders said, sir. He had a pretty low opinion of Stephanie and was content to believe she simply abandoned her child. He could have acted on Gabe's suspicions about Cameron but he didn't. He simply accepted the alibi the Pines gave him. I appreciate the lack of evidence but . . ."

"We need more information on Stephanie Woodson. PJ, find out what you can. Contact her old school, any friends or relatives you can track down, anyone who remembers her. Ava, we'll speak with Stephanie's daughter, Tess, and Stephanie's sister."

"I've just had a thought," PJ said. "Mr North said that Stephanie posed as a nude model for Mr Cameron. Do you think any of his drawings might have survived? It would prove that Cameron knew Stephanie, wouldn't it?"

Ava was glad Neal didn't point out that even though Steph had modelled for Cameron, she still might not have known him personally.

"By all means look into it, DC Jenkins," Neal said.

* * *

Tess Woodson lived in a busy market town around twenty miles from Stromford. Only a few weeks ago the fields on either side of the road would have been blanketed with snow. The big thaw had uncovered another, less beautiful monochromatic landscape. Or so it seemed to Ava, looking out of the car at a flaccid, colourless sky drooping over fields of grey and black.

Her companion's mood seemed to have darkened along with the landscape and the weather. Neal had fallen silent as soon as they left Stromford. Ava wondered absently if he suffered from seasonal affective disorder. She had yet to work with him in the spring and summer months. She imagined him sitting next to her dressed in shorts and a sleeveless Hawaiian shirt, a pair of Ray-bans perched on his aquiline nose. Would he be smiling? Or perhaps it would take more than a bit of sunshine to cheer him up. According to Maggie he had not always been so serious. Then, at a busy roundabout, a white van cut in front of them from the outside lane. Ava cursed the driver loud and long, and Neal laughed.

The satnav led them to a street of fifties' semis on the outskirts of Pippinham. After a longish wait, a smartly-dressed woman answered the door. Tess's aunt was still wearing her outdoor coat and had clearly just returned from work.

"Would either of you like a drink?" she asked. They declined and followed her down the hallway. She pushed a door open with her foot, saying, "Tess is in the sitting room."

Aunt and niece both had the slender gracefulness of ballet dancers. Their deep-set eyes gleamed with intelligence. Ava wondered if people mistook them for mother and daughter. Tess seemed very shy. She was, Ava knew, eighteen or nineteen, but she seemed younger.

"Are you here about my mother?" Tess asked.

Neal nodded at Ava.

"Yes and no," Ava began. "We're investigating the death of a man by the name of Ewan Cameron. You might have heard about it on the news? His body was found in the Stromfordshire lime woods area last week."

Tess nodded. "I don't see how I can help you with that."

"On the night your mother disappeared, she left you at home with a man called Gabriel North. He was her boyfriend at the time and according to him, your mother went out that night with some friends. Mr North believed that your mother was with Ewan Cameron that evening. He also thinks that Mr Cameron might have been involved somehow in your mother's disappearance."

"This isn't news to us, Sergeant." Eloise Woodson was holding a tortoiseshell cat. She sat down next to her niece, stroking the animal, which purred loudly.

"I know," Ava said, momentarily distracted by the cat. It was a dead ringer for her own Camden. "But we're examining the possibility that there might be some sort of link between the two cases."

"I suppose that's sensible, although there's the question of the length of time between them," said Eloise. "What do you think, Tess?"

Tess shrugged. "I think if the police had shown more interest ten years ago we'd know by now what became of my mother."

Eloise placed a hand on her niece's arm. She said, "Officers, my sister was not altogether conventional but there is one thing I can tell you with absolute certainty. She loved Tess and she would never have abandoned her, no matter what the circumstances were." She went on, "By 'unconventional' I simply mean that she wasn't bothered about what other people thought of her. She wanted to sample everything life had to offer — sex, drugs, motherhood, the lot."

Ava glanced at Tess to see her reaction. Tess's expression revealed nothing.

Ava said, "Your sister was quite young when Tess was born, wasn't she?"

"Twenty. But she was a wonderful mother. Her devotion to Tess was never in question."

Ava looked at Neal. He gave no hint of what he was thinking. Ava thought that Eloise was protesting too much.

"She was a great mum," Tess said, her eyes shining with tears. "She read to me all the time, played with me, took me places. I felt loved."

Ava didn't have the heart to mention the fact that Tess had been placed in the care of a man her mother hardly knew. Aunt and niece were practically clinging to one another. Neglected, the cat leapt from Eloise's lap and carefully stretched each leg before crossing to Ava and winding itself around her ankles.

"Do you have any memory of your mother mentioning Ewan Cameron's name, Tess?" Ava asked.

"No. I remember Gabe North. He babysat for me a couple of times and gave me a copy of *Anne of Green Gables*. l still have it."

"Have you had any reason to contact Mr North recently?"

"No."

The response came too fast. Ava and Neal's eyes met. "How about you, Mrs Woodson? Have you had any contact with Mr North since your sister's disappearance?"

"Of course not. Why would I? He was a suspect. I was sure the police would arrest him. I still don't really know why they didn't, given there seemed to be no one else involved. I've always suspected he concocted that story about Ewan Cameron to deflect suspicion from himself. Have you questioned him about that poor man's murder yet?"

Ava was reluctant to admit that until a day ago, they had been unaware of Gabriel North's existence.

Neal intervened. "Mr Cameron shared a flat with a friend by the name of David Pine. Is that name familiar to you? Or Rhona Sinclair, who became Mrs Rhona Pine?"

"Sorry, no. I was only eight. I don't remember a lot except missing my mum."

"My father spent five years trying to find Stephanie," Eloise told them. "He walked the streets showing people her picture. He went to every town in Stromfordshire and beyond. He even went to London. He died five years ago, never knowing what happened to her. My mother died the year after. I'm not saying it killed them but . . . well . . ." She gave Ava and Neal a desolate look. Then, her features hardened. "It's a terrible thing to say, but I'm glad this Ewan Cameron murder has reignited interest in what happened to my sister. I never believed the police carried out a proper investigation at the time."

"Me too," Tess said. "You are going to reopen Mum's case, aren't you?"

Ava cleared her throat but it was Neal who answered. "Our primary concern is to find Mr Cameron's killer. If the investigation throws up any new insights into your mother's disappearance, we'll follow them up. That's all I can say for the present. I'm sorry, but I don't want to give you false hope."

He stood up and Ava followed suit. The tortoiseshell cat was first over the threshold into the front garden.

"Your cat reminds me of my own," Ava remarked. "Same markings. He's lovely."

"She." Eloise corrected her. "Tortoiseshell cats are almost without exception female."

Ava stared at her. "Seriously?"

Eloise stared right back. "Yes. Seriously. Isn't there anything you detectives can get right?"

This sudden hostility took Ava by surprise. It was almost as surprising as learning that her beloved Camden was a girl.

Back in the car, Neal asked Ava for her thoughts.

"Outlandish as it sounds, I can't help thinking that those two might just have a motive for killing Cameron. They're desperate to refocus police time and resources on Stephanie's disappearance. Maybe they enticed him down here somehow—"

Neal cut her off. "Intriguing idea, if a little far-fetched. I do think Tess is hiding something from us, though. She denied having been in touch with North, but I got the impression she was lying."

"Yeah, me too. North didn't mention Tess either, except when he talked about babysitting her ten years ago. I wonder what motive either or both of them would have for concealing that they'd met recently?"

They lapsed into silence for a while. Then Neal asked, "You really had no idea Camden was female?"

Was he grinning? "I swear. I mean there's nothing there, but I just assumed he'd had his 'bits' removed. He

173

— she — was a stray, so I had no way of knowing for sure."

Neal leaned back and laughed. That was twice in one afternoon.

Ava glanced at him. Maybe he was coming down with something.

* * *

"There's been a big development on the robbery at Ridgeway Farm," PJ informed Ava and Neal upon their return. "Hammond Bell got a tip-off about a hare-coursing incident out at Pikefield this morning. He chased a number of the perps and managed to arrest one of them with the help of a local farmer who was out on his quad bike and ran him into a ditch. PC Bell questioned him in the local nick and he claimed he was out poaching on the night of the farm robbery. He had some information that he was willing to share in exchange for leniency."

Neal whistled. "Go on," he said.

"His name is Shane Doyle. It's not the first time he's been involved in this kind of thing. He's got two priors for hare coursing and illegal gambling. Ham told him he'd make some calls, see what could be done in exchange for the information. But Doyle seemed quite happy to spill without any definite promises." PJ looked down at her notes. "He claims to have witnessed three white males loading barrels into the back of a white transit van. He was a bit vague about the time — after midnight, he thought." She paused again, unable to contain her excitement. "Now this is the best bit. Doyle recognised them! They're regulars at the pub where he and his mates show their hare coursing films." Ava smiled, and PJ continued. "He gave Ham their names and Ham passed the info onto Reg Saunders. He and a couple of PCs have just driven out to a place they rent in Holdenfield with a warrant to search the premises for stolen goods."

"Excellent. Do you know if Ham asked Doyle whether he'd seen or heard anyone else out and about that night? Or if he'd come across Ewan Cameron's car?"

PJ looked sheepish. "Sorry, sir. I didn't think to ask."

Neal nodded. Turning to Ava, he said, "Call Bell now and see if he can get anything more out of Doyle. If he can tell us anything, this could be a real breakthrough. I'll be in my office."

Through his open door he heard Ava consoling the crestfallen PJ. "Don't worry, Peej. You can't always think of everything."

"I'm such a doofus. It was the obvious thing to ask about, wasn't it?"

Neal didn't catch Ava's reply. A couple of minutes later he heard her speaking on the phone. Then, mid-call, she strode across to Neal's office. "PC Bell is still holding Doyle. He wants to know if we'd like to question him ourselves." Neal gave her the thumbs up.

* * *

An hour later, Bell brought Doyle in. Doyle agreed to an informal interview without legal representation.

"So," Neal began. "Tell us what you saw that night."

Doyle reiterated his story about seeing the gang loading barrels into the back of a van. He even gave them part of the registration, as he remembered it, though Neal doubted that Doyle's recall was a hundred per cent reliable. Doyle was in his mid-thirties, short and slight, with black hair that was turning grey at the temples. He looked as though he spent much of his life outdoors, for his ruddy complexion was prematurely wrinkled. Neal thought of a word from long ago: tinker. It was what his Irish grandparents had called the travellers who passed through their village every year.

"And what else did you see that night?" Neal asked.

"I saw another car," Doyle said softly, looking at Ava. "It was parked by the woods on the other side of Ridgeway Farm. Near the old abbey."

"Do you know what time that was?"

Doyle shook his wrists to show that he didn't wear a watch. "Between midnight and three, I reckon."

"Were you close enough to see anyone in the car? Did you see anyone get out?" Neal was deadpan. He didn't want Doyle to guess how much hung on his story — he might begin embellishing it.

Doyle shifted in his seat, put a hand to his ear as if searching for a cigarette, and stroked his glossy mop of black hair. "Might have," he said, still looking at Ava.

Sometimes Neal wondered how his sergeant put up with it. Though her looks could be useful sometimes . . . Now he was aware of Ava crossing her legs and leaning forward in her seat. He felt his own pulse quicken, and was embarrassed.

"What might you have seen, Mr Doyle?" Ava asked. Her voice was a touch huskier than normal.

Doyle leaned back in his seat. Neal felt a twinge of amusement as Ava sat back too, no doubt slightly peeved at her failure to charm him. A moment's silence ensued.

Neal cleared his throat. He looked across at Hammond Bell who was leaning against the wall behind Doyle. "PC Bell, in your opinion is there enough evidence to prosecute Mr Doyle for his activities?" Before Bell could answer, Neal added, "Or is there room for some leeway?"

"I suppose you might say that Mr Doyle's role was perhaps less active than others in the gang," said Bell.

"The ones who got away?"

"Yes, sir."

"Now, Mr Doyle, if you can just help us out on this other matter, I think PC Bell here might find that his memory of your part in this morning's events is somewhat hazy."

Doyle looked behind him and caught Hammond Bell's reluctant nod.

"Well now," he said slowly, "seems to me that I do know a bit about that car."

Neal's patience was running out. "Get on with it, Doyle."

"I saw a car parked up at the old abbey that night. It was a Ford, I think, not in the best condition. I would have walked past it except I noticed the key was in the ignition and I couldn't help trying the door handle. Anyone would have done the same. It wasn't locked. There was a wallet and a few other bits on the passenger seat. Talk about putting temptation in a man's way." Doyle looked around as if for approval. "I got in, thinking to drive a little way up the road in case the owner came back. I'm no car thief, you know? I just wanted to check it over, see what else I could find."

Neal nodded.

"I stopped in the woods up near the farm—"

"Ridgeway Farm?"

Doyle nodded. "I thought to leave it a bit hidden, you know?"

Neal caught Ava's eye. Finally, an explanation for the car being found so far from the crime scene. He said, "You helped yourself to what you wanted and threw away the rest?"

"There was a fair bit of cash in the wallet, but I had no need of the driver's licence or any of the other bits."

"Did you see anyone when you were near the abbey? Or hear anything?"

Doyle tilted his head as if listening. "There was a dog barking. I was in a bit of a hurry to get going, you know?"

"And you were in the car when you saw the farm thieves?"

"Sure, there was quite a commotion."

Not enough of a commotion to wake the farmer, though, Neal thought wryly. "Thank you, Mr Doyle, you've been most helpful." Doyle nodded, smiling hopefully. Neal added, "Pity you didn't come forward when Mr Cameron's murder was made public. An anonymous tip-off would have been enough." To Ham, he said, "Get him out of here before I change my mind and throw the book at him."

Chapter 16

Laura finished reading Rowan and Holly their bedtime story and kissed them goodnight, hoping they would settle quickly. She was a little surprised at how readily Rhona and David had accepted her offer to babysit while they went out for the evening. Now, sitting downstairs with Shaun asleep in her lap, she wished she could put Gabe North off. He would already be parked somewhere in the village, and had probably even spotted David and Rhona drive past on their way to Stromford. Too late to bottle out.

Less than five minutes after her call, she moved the curtain aside and caught sight of him emerging furtively from some bushes at the side of the drive and making his way across the lawn towards the house. Afraid that his knock might wake the children, she crept to the door and opened it slightly to let him see the light. Within seconds he was standing in the Pines' tiled hallway, shadowy in the orange glow of a night light on the landing, halfway up the stairs. With a finger to her lips, Laura pointed towards the sitting room and Shaun, now asleep in his Moses basket. "This was a stupid idea," she said.

"I had no idea the Pines were so well off. This is a beautiful house," Gabe said, peering into the room.

"We need to get started. There isn't much time," Laura said. "I don't feel good about this."

"Are you sure there's no chance of finding something among Ewan's things at home?"

"I told you, he shredded everything."

"We'll split up — it'll be quicker. You do the bedrooms. I'll look around down here." Gabe said, taking charge.

Laura began her search in David and Rhona's bedroom. As far as she could tell, Rhona had been telling the truth when she said that she and David did not always sleep in separate rooms. There were traces of David's presence here, crumpled pyjamas on the pillow, his razor in the en suite bathroom.

She tried to think of places where she would hide a picture or a drawing, and went through all those places first. This is futile, she thought. Why would David or Rhona keep anything that could implicate them in a young woman's sudden disappearance? Still, she continued, and for the next hour Laura pried into the minutiae of Rhona and David's personal lives. She turned out drawers and cupboards, pockets and handbags, and boxes crammed with everything from old bills to snapshots. She looked under beds, lifted rugs, moved pictures and ran searching fingers under furniture she couldn't shift. There was no sound from downstairs.

Abandoning her own search at last, Laura checked on the girls and carried Shaun upstairs to David and Rhona's bedroom where she gently put him, still fast asleep, in his cot.

She joined Gabe in the kitchen. His look told her his search had revealed nothing. He said, "We should look in the loft." The suggestion made Laura nervous. She glanced at her watch. Rhona and David would not be back for at least another couple of hours, but what if one of the girls woke up?

Reluctantly she agreed.

Back upstairs, she stood guard at the bottom of the ladder while Gabe disappeared into the loft. Laura grew increasingly uneasy as she waited. The silence in the house was oppressive. She wondered again why she had come to stay with David and Rhona. She gazed up the ladder at the dark, yawning opening. What did she know about Gabe North, this stranger in David and Rhona's loft?

Unable to bear the silence, she climbed the ladder and poked her head into the roof space. In the torchlight, she could make out Gabe North's silhouette. He was stooped over an open suitcase, which she recognised as the one Rhona had used years ago when she went to visit David in Stromford.

"That was Rhona's weekend case. What's in it? Have you found something?" Her voice startled him and he dropped the torch. It landed in the suitcase, which for a moment seemed to glow from within. Laura pulled herself into the roof space and knelt beside Gabe and the open case. She focused the torch beam on the contents and gasped. She picked up the sketchbook which was lying on top of the other stuff. It had Ewan's name on the cover. She opened it and looked at the first page. There Steph was, so like Tess, looking back at her with an amused expression. Ewan had drawn Steph seated on the floor, her legs folded at her side and her arms around her breasts in a classic pose.

Laura turned to look at Gabe and saw him swallow. Page after page revealed drawings of the same young woman. Ewan had scribbled his signature on every one.

"Tear out a page and put the notebook back," Gabe said. Laura obeyed him mechanically. Together they repacked the case and climbed out of the loft. As she descended the ladder, Laura's foot slipped. She missed a rung and Gabe grasped her arm to steady her. A memory, sudden and unexpected jolted her. Their first date. Ewan, grasping her arm when she tripped over a tree root in Princes Street gardens in Edinburgh. Their first kiss.

"Thanks," she mumbled to Gabe, suddenly awash with nostalgia for lost innocence.

Downstairs in the Pines' kitchen, they stared at the drawing on the table.

"It's getting late. You'd better go," Laura whispered.

"The drawing?" Gabe asked.

"I'll keep it safe." For a moment she thought he might grab it and run for the door. Instead, he nodded. At the door their hands reached for the handle at the same time. Gabe's hand closed around hers, and she gasped. He pressed, gently.

"I know this must be hard for you," he said. Laura didn't move. Her heart was beating fast. "I want you to know how grateful I am, and how grateful Tess will be when the truth comes out."

"This only proves he knew her, not that he killed her," Laura managed. She understood but did not share his enthusiasm for the drawings. Artists sketched the human form all the time and for that they needed models. But did they draw the same woman over and over to the point of obsession as Ewan had done? Would the police see what she and Gabriel could see in Ewan's drawings of Stephanie? How much they spoke of his love?

Gabe nodded and removed his hand. "I'll be in touch." Suddenly he bent and kissed her on the cheek. Then he was gone.

"Who was that man?"

Laura froze. She turned to see Holly standing in the doorway, rubbing sleep from her eyes.

"What's the matter, sweetheart? Did something wake you up? Would you like a glass of milk?" She went into the kitchen, crossed to the fridge and opened the door. Holly padded, barefoot, across the kitchen floor.

"Who was that man?" she asked again, in a small, insistent voice.

"Just a friend," Laura said, smiling.

"Is he your boyfriend?"

"No. Just a friend."

"He kissed you."

Laura wondered how much Holly had seen. How much had she heard? "Friends kiss sometimes," she assured Holly. "Do you want to sit on my knee to drink your milk?"

Holly nodded. "What's that?" she asked, pointing to the kitchen table where the drawing of Stephanie lay on the polished surface.

"Just a drawing. I did some drawing after you went to sleep."

"She's pretty. Why isn't she wearing any clothes?"

"It was just easier to draw her that way."

This seemed to satisfy Holly's curiosity. She nestled against Laura, drinking her milk, her eyelids beginning to droop. She yawned.

"Are you sleepy? Do you want to go back to bed now?"

Holly nodded. Laura took her in her arms and carried her upstairs. Rowan stirred as they entered the bedroom. Please don't let her have another nightmare, thought Laura.

She stroked Holly's hair until the child drifted off to sleep, and then went back downstairs. The drawing was still on the table. She snatched it up and took it to her room where she hid it in her suitcase. Her nerves were ragged. She poured herself a scotch and sipped it slowly, feeling her anxiety ebb away. She poured another and began to feel relaxed and even sleepy. She kicked off her slippers and ruffled the shaggy cream fireside rug with her toes. Soon she was asleep.

She woke to the sound of laughter from the kitchen. There she found Rhona and David embracing by the back door. She coughed, and Rhona and David disentangled themselves. Rhona blew her a drunken kiss. Laura hoped they were too drunk to notice that she too had been drinking. Then she remembered that David had been driving, and that he didn't seem to drink these days. He was looking at her. "Right. I'll just pour myself a glass of water and get off to bed. The kids are fine. No problems."

Rhona giggled. "We're going to bed now too, aren't we, David?" She gave him a lascivious smile and tickled him under the chin, swaying in his arms. They look like the perfect couple, Laura thought. Their affection for each other seemed genuine, but how could she be sure that it was love that bound them together and not some terrible secret from their past?

Laura helped David guide Rhona upstairs. She was feeling giddy herself after the scotch, but Rhona was clearly drunk. Laura had just begun to undress when there was an urgent knocking on her door. She opened it to see David standing outside, Rhona hovering anxiously at his back, suddenly sober.

"Where's Shaun?" David asked. "Is he in there with you?"

Laura stared at him, puzzled. "He's in his cot. He's been asleep for hours."

David strode across the landing to the girls' room. He opened the door and went inside.

Laura frowned. "I didn't hear a sound from the baby monitor."

"Wake up!" David's voice hissed from their bedroom. Laura went to the door in time to see him shake Rowan awake. Holly stirred in her bed and sat up, rubbing her eyes. Shaun was not with them.

By now Rhona's anxiety was approaching hysteria. "Where is he?" she cried, as first Holly, then Rowan began to cry.

David barged out of their room and stood in front of Laura. "What's going on? What have you done with our son?" he demanded.

Laura's heart lurched. She stared from David to Rhona, her head still fuzzy with alcohol. "I . . . I don't know what to say. He was asleep in your room . . . I . . ."

Holly tugged at her father's trouser leg. "It must have been the man who kissed Laura," she said.

"What man? What is she talking about, Laura?" said Rhona.

Laura's head spun. "I . . . don't know." She looked down at her tiny betrayer.

Rhona took a step towards her.

"Gabe North was here earlier," Laura blurted out finally.

"North? What the hell was he doing here?" David said.

Rhona tugged at his sleeve. "David! We're wasting time. We have to call the police."

David kept his eyes on Laura. She took a step back but he reached forward, grabbed her wrists and dragged her roughly into the hallway. Holly began to sob again. Rowan wrapped her arms around her little sister and drew her close. Their pale, frightened faces made Laura feel ashamed. She was responsible for this.

"Get dressed," David commanded. "You're coming to North's house with me. You know where he lives, right?"

Laura nodded, tearful. "Rhona's right," she said. "You should call the police."

David ignored her. He turned to Rhona. "No police, all right? I'll get our son back. Trust me, Rhona."

Rhona nodded, and her eyes met David's. Then she said in a thin voice, "Our son's life is more important than any secret. You have until morning. Then I'm calling the police."

* * *

David half-dragged, half-pushed Laura across the drive and into his Land Rover. "Where to?" he asked as the vehicle bumped down the lane.

Laura croaked out Gabe's address. Her thoughts were racing furiously and she wondered what she should say to David. There were few other cars on the road at this hour and the Land Rover sped along the Stromford Road at a reckless speed. All at once Laura became aware that she was crying. She touched her cheeks in wonder. She had shed no tears at the news of Ewan's death. Poor Shaun, she thought. How sad that an innocent child had to be caught up in all of this.

The Land Rover screeched to a halt outside Gabe's house. David leapt out and began battering on the door. Laura shrank back in her seat, wishing she could slide across to the wheel and drive all the way to Edinburgh without stopping. Instead she ran to David, begging him to calm down. David shook her off and resumed pounding on the door with his fists.

Gabe's silhouette appeared in the opaque glass panel and then he was standing in the doorway. "Laura?" he asked, sounding sleepy and puzzled. He peered at her over David's shoulder, but David grabbed hold of him. Laura stood by, watching helplessly.

"Where's my son?" David yelled at Gabe.

It was immediately evident to Laura that Gabe had no idea what David was talking about, but David repeated his question with his hand balled into a fist, close to Gabe's face.

"Stop it! Please stop it! Can't you see he doesn't have a clue what you're on about?" she pleaded.

David took a step back.

"Laura? What's going on?" said Gabe.

"Someone's taken Shaun."

For a moment Gabe stared at her, then at David. "Your baby?"

"Yes, yes." Laura answered. "David knows you were at the house. He thinks you took Shaun."

"No. I swear. I wouldn't do that." Gabe looked at David. "I would never harm a child." He said to Laura, "You believe me, don't you?"

Laura nodded.

"Then who did, dammit?" David rounded on Laura.

"I think it might have been Stephanie Woodson's daughter," she said quietly. "Tess."

"What the hell are you talking about?" asked David.

Before Laura could answer, a voice called out, "Everything alright here?" She spun round to see that a small group of people had gathered nearby. The speaker, a man in his thirties, was making his way up the path towards them.

Gabe waved at him. "Everything's cool, Greg. Just a misunderstanding."

Greg looked dubious. Then he said, "Alright, mate," and retreated to the gate. "Give us a shout if you need help."

"Please, come inside," Gabe said.

Laura and David followed him into the small sitting room where Laura had met Tess. Gabe disappeared for a moment, and then returned with a bottle of scotch and three shot glasses. Laura shook her head, but he insisted on pouring her a drink, saying, "I think we all need something to calm our nerves.

"Would someone care to explain what's going on?" David asked.

"Tess Woodson contacted Gabe recently and asked for his help in finding out about her mother's disappearance," Laura told him.

"So that's what you were talking about at Ham's party?"

"Actually, no. That was a couple of days afterwards when we met again," Laura informed him coolly. "Tess got in touch with Gabe a few weeks ago. She remembered him because he was looking after her the night her mother disappeared. Gabe wasn't sure how to help her. Then Ewan was murdered, Tess saw it on the news and she had the idea that Gabe could approach me and ask me to—"

"Spy on us?"

"Find out what you knew about Stephanie's disappearance."

"You spoke to Rhona about this?" David sounded wary.

"Yes."

"And I assume she told you what we told the police at the time. We were together, the three of us, all evening. We were up until three in the morning playing poker and drinking, then we went to bed." He glared at Laura. "Were you aware that North here was questioned by the police about Stephanie's disappearance? That he was arrested and released because of lack of evidence?"

Laura stared at Gabe. "You never said you'd been arrested."

"It wasn't an issue. I was released almost immediately because I was babysitting Tess that night."

Laura felt a surge of anger. "But you weren't, were you? At least not all night." She turned to David. "And you weren't all at your flat, were you? When are you all going to stop lying?" Suddenly she realised she was shouting.

David shouted above her. "What do you mean he wasn't babysitting? That was his bloody alibi! And how the hell would you know whether we were at home that night or not?"

"Because Gabe went round to your flat and there was no one there."

"He told you that? And you believe him, do you? A stranger, someone you've hardly known for five minutes?

You believe him instead of the people you've known for years? I thought you knew us better than that, Laura. Rhona was your best friend."

"Was she? A best friend doesn't shut you out for ten years because her husband falls out with your husband. I'm beginning to wonder if I ever really knew any of you at all. Especially the man I was married to for ten years! Why didn't I hear about any of this at the time? And please don't say it's because you didn't want to distract me from my studies."

David shrugged. "But that was the reason. And, besides, we didn't consider it that big a deal. None of us knew Stephanie Woodson."

"Oh come off it, David. Rhona's already admitted to me that Ewan was — in her words — 'besotted with Steph.' And we," she looked at Gabe, "have proof that he knew her." David went pale. "Your wall of silence is crumbling, David."

"What proof?" David asked.

"Drawings by Ewan. Of Stephanie."

David stared at the floor. "It's possible she did some modelling for the art college. That would explain any drawings Ewan might have made of her. A bit of a jump to assume he knew her personally."

Laura put her hand to her forehead and groaned.

"Look," Gabe intervened, "This isn't helping us find out what happened to Shaun." He looked at Laura and sighed. "I think you could be right that it was Tess who took Shaun. She told me she'd kidnap the Pines' baby if she didn't get to the truth soon."

Laura gazed at him in disbelief. David looked ready to explode.

"I'm sorry. I really didn't think she meant it. I certainly didn't think she'd actually do something so stupid."

"You're all pathetic. Why can't you just be truthful about things?" Laura said, shaking her head in disgust. She turned to David. "If you want your son back safely, you need to speak to the police. And you need to start telling the truth as well."

Chapter 17

Tess stared down at the child. He was finally asleep in the carrycot she'd picked up at a charity shop earlier in the day. If the dreadful crying had gone on much longer she might have become completely unhinged. Prior to snatching him she had thought she'd made all the necessary preparations. She'd taken care of all his likely physical needs by stocking up on nappies and formula milk and an assortment of other items that the baby book she'd looked at told her were essential. But she hadn't prepared for the child's distress. He'd cried non-stop from the moment he woke up in her car until about half an hour ago, when he'd fallen into an exhausted sleep. And now she was exhausted too. She needed to put her head down and get some rest before he woke up again, but first she had to send a couple of texts.

The first message was to her Aunt Eloise to let her know she was sleeping over at a friend's house. Eloise had been pleased. She was always encouraging Tess to go out more.

The second message was to Rhona Pine. An ultimatum. Tell the police what she knew about her mother's disappearance or she would never see her son again. Even as she sent the message off, Tess wasn't certain she could carry out her threat.

She'd arrived at the Pines' place a little after Gabe and parked in the lane before the turn-off for the track leading to their property. That way her car could not be seen from the house. From there, she had sneaked into the house using the back door, which had been left on the latch. If they found her, she was going to say that she had been unable to wait to hear the result of their search and had followed Gabe. She had watched Laura disappear into the loft after Gabe. All she had had to do was creep into the bedrooms and look for the baby. By another stroke of luck, she had chosen the right bedroom straightaway, and Shaun had stayed asleep until she placed him in the carrycot in the back of her car.

Tess zipped herself into the sleeping bag on the floor of the unfurnished room. It was cold and she wondered if it was too cold for the child. She reached over and touched his flushed cheek with a finger. He was warm. No need to risk waking him by lifting him from the basket and bringing him into the sleeping bag with her. She curled into a ball, bringing her knees up against her chest and, despite the cold, was asleep in seconds.

* * *

Ava woke to the sound of her phone playing yet another unfamiliar ringtone. Her brother Ollie liked to surprise her by changing them without warning, usually to something he was into at the time. At least this morning it was something she recognised — the theme tune to a nineteen sixties TV series, *The Champions*. Thanks to their dad's nostalgia for the TV of his childhood, she and Ollie had been introduced to many of the classics of that era. Her own particular favourite was *Randall and Hopkirk Deceased*.

"Ava?" Neal said.

She muttered a sleepy hello.

"The Pines' baby has been abducted."

"Come again, sir?"

Neal's tone was impatient. "You heard. Get yourself down here immediately."

"Yes, sir."

She padded into Ollie's room and shook him awake. "Get up, bro'. I gotta go."

"Duh?"

Ava had got up to go to the bathroom at two in the morning and seen a light still shining under Ollie's bedroom door.

"You heard," she said, echoing Jim Neal. "Downstairs in fifteen if you want a lift to school."

"I'll take the bus," Ollie muttered, pulling the covers over his head.

"Suit yourself."

Ava took a two-minute shower and was soon downstairs and pulling her down-filled parka off its peg in the hallway. Another minute and she was starting up her car. She glanced at the clock on the dashboard. Only fifteen minutes since Neal's call. She pulled out of the lane leading from her cottage and turned onto the main road into Stromford. It was still dark this early in the morning, but Ava could see frost glistening on the grass verges. Instinctively, she slowed her speed, conscious of the lurking danger of black ice.

Neal was waiting for her when she got to the station. Ava hoped there would be time for coffee but Neal was in a hurry.

"Come on, I'll fill you in on the way," he said. They used Neal's car. "Rhona Pine called 999 at five this morning. She said that Shaun had gone missing."

"Missing? As in kidnapped, d'you mean?"

"Something's not right," Neal answered grimly. "They discovered Shaun was missing last night. The Pines had been out and Laura Cameron was babysitting. The Pines returned and went upstairs to bed only to find Shaun's cot empty. Laura Cameron apparently thought he was safely asleep."

"Huh? They discovered he was missing last night and didn't contact us until this morning?" Ava was incredulous.

"I know. Like I said, something's not right. We've no other details but I'm guessing David Pine thought he knew where to find Shaun."

"At Gabriel North's house?"

"That would be my guess. But why dash off there instead of involving the police?"

Ava shook her head. "You're right. Something's wrong there." She thought for a moment. "Remember when we paid Tess Woodson and her aunt a call and how we both got the impression Tess had been in touch with Gabe, even though she claimed she hadn't?" Neal nodded. "You don't think that Tess and Gabe kidnapped Shaun because they believe the Pines know more about Stephanie's disappearance than they're letting on? They could have engineered the kidnapping to force their hand, make them admit what they know. Tess and her aunt were very bitter when we wouldn't promise to reopen Stephanie's case. What if they — or Gabe North — kidnapped Shaun to focus police attention on Stephanie's disappearance? Remember what I said about Tess or Gabe North luring Ewan to Stromford? Doesn't seem all that fanciful now, do you think? Tess is desperate for closure." She looked at Neal.

He nodded, his eyes fixed on the light spilling from the headlights onto the dark road ahead.

When they reached the house, David Pine's Land Rover was parked in the drive. They parked beside it and walked briskly to the front door.

The Pines' house was a hive of activity. Forensics were already searching the property. Equipment to monitor calls to the house was being set up. By the end of the day, police officers would have conducted a house-to-house search of the village and all the other properties in the area, including farm buildings and lock-ups. In this case the press would be welcome, because the publicity could speed up the process of gathering information.

At the centre of it all, Rhona Pine sat, ashen-faced on the sofa in the sitting room, clutching a toy rabbit. Laura Cameron was sitting beside her, looking strained. Ava was startled to see Gabe North there too. Only David Pine was missing.

Neal spoke to Rhona in his soft Scots accent. "Mrs Pine, I realise this is distressing for you. I'm a father myself and I'd be distraught if my son were missing. However, it is vitally important that you give us as much information as you can, so we can get your child back safely. I'd like to begin by asking why you delayed contacting the police when you discovered Shaun was missing."

Rhona held the rabbit, stroking its long, fluffy ears. "We thought he'd taken Shaun." She nodded towards Gabe North, who was shaking his head. "So David and Laura went to his house."

"I take it Shaun wasn't there?"

"Of course he wasn't." Gabe said.

"Why would you think Mr North had anything to do with Shaun's abduction?"

Rhona stared down at the rabbit in her lap. "I . . . that is . . . we . . ." She gave a sob.

Suddenly David Pine was in the room, and crossing to his wife's side. He placed a hand on her shoulder. Ava had the impression that he was warning rather than consoling her.

David Pine answered for his wife. "It was my fault, Inspector. I persuaded Rhona not to call the police because I was convinced that Gabe North had taken our son." He looked at Laura. "Laura had already admitted that North was here earlier in the evening while we were out. When my wife and I came home we could see that

Laura had been drinking. She'd fallen asleep. Someone could have walked off with all our children and she wouldn't have known."

"That's not fair," said Laura.

"Are you seeing Mr North?" Ava asked.

"No . . . at least, not like that. I . . . we've met a couple of times since I got here."

"May I ask why?" Ava was aware of a tightening of the atmosphere. It was as though everyone in the room was afraid and suspicious of everyone else. David took a step towards Gabe, who stood up, adopting a defensive pose. Ava and Neal looked at each other.

"Why don't you ask him?" Gabe muttered. "Ask him what he knows about Stephanie Woodson's disappearance."

"How many times do I have to say it? Ewan Cameron had nothing to do with your girlfriend's disappearance. He didn't even know her, for pity's sake. None of us did." David was almost shouting.

"Yes he did," Laura said quietly. She turned to Ava and Neal. "They all knew Steph Woodson. Rhona told me Ewan was besotted with her. I found countless drawings of her in his studio and he shredded them before he left for Stromford. Gabe and I found some more in a suitcase in the loft here while Rhona and David were out last night. That's why Gabe was here. To help me search."

"Thank you," said Gabe.

David turned to Ava and Neal. "And I've already told you that North will say anything to try and implicate Rhona, me and Ewan in Stephanie Woodson's death."

"Steph disappeared. No one can say for sure that she's dead," Gabe said.

Neal cleared his throat. "Enough! In case you have all forgotten, we have a missing child and you lot bickering is wasting time."

"It's all connected," Gabe North insisted, "I know it is. I think Tess might have taken Shaun."

"Tess Woodson? Stephanie's daughter?"

"Yes. Tess approached me when she heard about Ewan Cameron's death. She asked if I would help her find out about Ewan's involvement in her mother's disappearance."

In a flat voice, Laura added, "Gabe's right. Shaun's kidnap is all tangled up with what happened in the past. You need to get to the bottom of it, officers." With an apologetic glance at Gabe, she told them what he had said earlier about Tess's threat to kidnap Shaun.

Neal had taken his mobile out. He gave PJ a stream of terse instructions, finishing with, "Get over to Eloise Woodson's house immediately. Take a couple of uniforms with you and conduct a thorough search of the property. Use extreme caution. It's unlikely that Tess and Shaun are there, but we do not want that baby coming to any harm."

Rhona began to sob.

Ava wondered if Tess was getting her revenge. Her aunt had assured them that Stephanie had loved Tess and that she would never have abandoned her, yet she had left her daughter in the care of someone — Gabe — who was practically a stranger. What had Reg Saunders said? That Tess would be better off 'without a mother like her.' Was that why his inquiry had been so slapdash? Who else might have thought the same way? An image flashed through Ava's mind of Eloise and Tess on the sofa.

"Sir?" she said to Neal, "A word?"

They withdrew into the hall and Ava told Neal what she had been thinking.

"Eloise Woodson? You think she was involved in Steph's disappearance? And Shaun's abduction?"

"It's a possibility. She's clearly devoted to Tess. Maybe she thought the same way as Saunders — that Tess was better off without her mother."

"Maybe," said Neal. "Call PJ and ask her to be cautious with the aunt."

"Is my brother dead?" Ava looked up to see the Pines' elder daughter sitting halfway up the stairs, her arms wrapped around her knees and her cheeks wet with tears. Neal and Ava exchanged a look. Had the child been listening?

"Oh no," Ava said. "We're going to find Shaun and bring him safely home to you all. Don't worry."

Rowan burst into tears. "It's all my fault!"

Ava went and sat beside her. "How could it possibly be your fault, sweetie?"

Rowan lifted big, sorrowful eyes. "I promised. I promised Zak I wouldn't tell. I promised on Shaun's life and now he's gone missing."

Ava frowned. She looked down at Neal. "So you *were* out late on the night Mr Cameron died. Is that right, Rowan?" she asked.

Rowan sniffed. "Yes, Zak and me. We were looking for the ghost at the old abbey."

"Tell us what you saw, Rowan. Tell us everything you saw that night."

* * *

PJ was beginning to appreciate how frustrating a murder investigation could be. One step forward, two steps back. Ava had warned her, but she had not expected to be looking so much into the past. She didn't dare suggest to Ava that maybe Reg Saunders was right when he declared that there was no point in pursuing a link between Stephanie Woodson's disappearance and Ewan Cameron's murder. Sometimes a coincidence was simply that.

She had striven to unearth some details about Stephanie, who seemed to have led a pretty low-key life in Stromford ten years ago, judging by the number of people who claimed not to remember her. The ones who did had little information to impart. One of Tess's old teachers recalled that Stephanie had seemed to be a good enough mother. She'd always picked her child up from school on time and attended parents' evenings and sports days. Tess had seemed happy, certainly not neglected or mistreated.

It seemed that Stephanie was a young woman who looked after her child, kept herself to herself and had few or no friends. She had rented a two-bedroomed flat in a converted house in a cheap part of town and her landlady mostly remembered her because she had often been behind with the rent. PJ had shown Ewan Cameron's photo to everyone she spoke with, but no one could recall seeing the two of them together. How had they even met? She was a single parent and had worked part-time in a café in the centre of town — it had closed down years ago and was now a Costa. Ava had said Stephanie might have done some nude modelling at the art college, but again no one seemed to remember her.

PJ sighed. She drove to the address DI Neal had given her. Two uniformed officers were going to meet her at the property. She parked her car in the street and walked up to the front door, feeling slightly self-conscious about her uniformed bodyguards. A slender, fair-haired woman opened the door. She seemed surprised to see them.

"Eloise Woodson?" PJ asked. The woman's hand went to her throat.

"Oh God! Has something happened to Tess?"

"No. At least not that I'm aware of," PJ stammered. This was her first solo interview as a detective and she felt she wasn't making much of an impression on her colleagues.

"Well, what then?" Eloise asked, still looking worried.

How was she supposed to answer this? PJ wondered. *We think your niece might have kidnapped a baby and that you might be a murderer.* She explained as best she could, still standing on the doorstep. She was conscious that the uniformed officers might be attracting attention. As if reading her mind, Eloise invited them in. Her hand trembled as she pointed to the living room.

"We'd like to search the house, please, Ms Woodson, if you don't mind." PJ tried to remember her assertiveness training.

"Be my guest. The whole idea's laughable anyway." But Eloise wasn't laughing.

"Is your niece at home, Ms Woodson?"

"No. She's on a sleepover with a friend."

"Ah," said PJ. "Do you mind if I start in Tess's room? My colleagues will look in the rest."

Eloise led them upstairs. Tess's room was a typical teenage girl's, except for one thing. On the wall above her desk was a huge corkboard that resembled a police incident board. It was covered in photographs of her mother, of Ewan and Laura Cameron, Rhona and David Pine, along with other people she didn't recognise. To PJ's surprise, there were even pictures of Jim Neal and Ava Merry taken from a distance. The board was dotted with post-it notes and connecting red arrows and a couple of old newspaper clippings with reports of Stephanie Woodson's disappearance.

PJ stared at it.

"You can't blame Tess for wanting to know what happened to her mother. This past year it's been practically all she's thought about." Eloise gave a small laugh. "Believe me, I've tried as hard as I can to discourage her."

"She's certainly been busy," PJ remarked. "Is this your niece's laptop?" She lifted the lid of a pink Apple Mac. The screensaver was a picture of a smiling mother and daughter — Stephanie and Tess.

"May I?" PJ asked. Eloise shrugged. PJ scrolled through some of Tess's emails, aware that what she was doing was probably not legal without a warrant. Conscious of Eloise looking over her shoulder, she clicked open a file entitled, 'Stephanie,' and scrolled through it until she came to a document labelled, 'Shaun Cameron.'

PJ turned to Eloise and said, "I don't think your niece is on a sleepover at all, do you, Ms Woodson?"

The sound of laughter came from the bedroom next to Tess's. PJ went to investigate.

"What's the joke, lads?" The young officers looked embarrassed. One of them pointed to a number of framed photographs arranged on top of a large chest of drawers. PJ leaned in closer to take a look. She easily recognised the man standing with his arm around Eloise Woodson's slender waist, although he was thinner and less hirsute. She looked across at Eloise who was standing in the doorway and asked, "How well do you know the man in this picture, Ms Woodson?"

Chapter 18

After calling Olivia Darby, Ava drove round to their house. As she parked her car, she glimpsed Zak looking out from an upstairs window.

Olivia was standing at the door, looking edgy. "I'm so shocked about little Shaun. What's going on, Sergeant? And what does it have to do with Zak?"

"Please can you call Zak down, Mrs Darby? I'd like to ask him some questions."

"Is Zak in trouble?"

"I don't think so. Rowan Pine has just confirmed that she and Zak were out on the night of Ewan Cameron's murder. They saw a man dragging a body towards the woods at Stainholme Abbey. He might be our killer."

Olivia called up the stairs to her son. He came down slowly, and Olivia placed a hand on his shoulder. "Right, young man. You told the sergeant here that you and Rowan Pine weren't out in the middle of the night when that poor man was murdered. She knows you were lying, so you'd better make sure you tell the truth this time. Do you understand?"

Zak nodded. He looked at Ava, his eyes wide and fearful.

"Hello, Zak," Ava said. "Rowan told me you both ran away after seeing the man dragging the body from the car. Then you had an asthma attack and had to hide in the woods. Is that right, Zak?" A nod. "Did the man see you? Did he speak to you?"

Zak looked at his mother.

"The truth, Zak." Olivia put her arm around her son.

"No one's going to hurt your mother, son." Ava said, gently. "Just tell us what happened."

Between gulps and sobs the story came out. "We were watching for the ghost — the White Monk. Then we heard a car. Then we saw a man get out and pull something out of the boot. He started dragging it towards the woods, then Belle barked and he started running towards us. I couldn't breathe so I hid in some bushes and Rowan ran on with Belle. Then the man stopped chasing them. He was going back to the body but then he saw my inhaler and he picked it up and started looking around. He looked right over to where I was hiding but he didn't see me." Zak was beginning to wheeze and Olivia told him to take some deep breaths.

Forcing herself to stay calm, Ava spoke gently. "Did you recognise the man, Zak?" The boy looked at his mother, who gave him an encouraging smile.

"I . . . I . . . think it was Mr Gallagher."

Olivia gasped.

"Are you sure, Zak? Did you get a good look at his face?" Ava said.

"Nnn . . . not really. It was really dark, but he was really big, just like Mr Gallagher."

Ava and Olivia exchanged looks. Ava continued. "Uh huh. So, to be clear, you didn't actually see his face. He was a big guy so you thought of Bran."

Zak looked downcast. "I guess so. He came round the next day and said something about not wanting any harm to come to my mum, and I thought he must have seen me in the woods after all and was giving me a warning."

Ava nodded, thinking that maybe Zak had seen too many creepy movies.

"Why didn't you just tell me, Zak?" Olivia asked.

Ava answered for him. "You were worried for your mum, weren't you? You were worried someone might hurt her if you told anyone."

Olivia began to sob. She hugged her son. "Oh, Zak . . ."

"We don't have any proof it was Mr Gallagher you saw in the woods that night, Zak." Ava said. Then, seeing how dejected the boy looked, she added, "No one can blame you for looking out for your mum. And you've done the right thing in telling us now." She gave Zak a smile.

"I just can't believe this is happening," Olivia said. She hugged her son closer. "What if something bad had happened to you that night?"

"I'm afraid I'm going to have to ask you both to keep another secret and not discuss any of this with anyone for the time being," Ava said.

Mother and son walked her to her car. "Poor Rhona," Olivia commented, as Ava pulled her seat belt around her. "I hope you find that baby soon, Sergeant Merry."

Let's hope so. Ava thought grimly as she drove away. She pulled over, intending to call Neal, but just as she reached for her mobile, her radio crackled. It was Hammond Bell asking for her location.

* * *

Neal held the phone away from his ear as an enthusiastic, over-loud PJ explained what she had discovered.

"Thanks, Constable. Good work," he said. What she told him seemed to confirm Stephanie Woodson's disappearance, Ewan Cameron's murder and Shaun Pine's kidnapping were all linked, though Neal was still unsure how. David Pine came into the hallway and looked surprised to see Neal standing there alone. "Sergeant Merry is following up a lead," Neal said without thinking.

"Is it to do with Shaun's kidnapping?" David asked.

"Er . . . I can't really say."

"Well, what's happening? Do you think this Tess Woodson took him? What are you doing to find her?"

"We're doing everything we can, Mr Pine. The best thing you can do is stay calm and look after your wife and your other children," Neal answered.

David glared at him and returned to the lounge, banging the door behind him.

Neal stood, rubbing his chin. He spoke to one of the forensics team and learned that they had found nothing so far. A team of dog handlers was on its way with sniffer dogs, and an army of volunteers and police officers would be mobilised to carry out a search of the surrounding countryside. Was it possible that Laura Cameron was involved in Shaun's disappearance? Had she suspected the Pines of killing her husband and sought revenge?

Neal's phone rang again. It was Hammond Bell.

"DI Neal?"

"Yes."

"I've just had a call from Bran Gallagher — you know, the ranger out at the lime woods?"

"Yes, yes, I know who you mean, man. Go on."

"Bran told me he saw a car he didn't recognise driving down the track out at Holby Wood. He thinks the driver was a young girl. He called me because he'd just heard from Olivia Darby about the Pines' baby being abducted and he thought it might be worth letting us know. That road's been closed for years. There's a dilapidated cottage down there, nothing else. Do you want me to drive down and take a look?"

Neal pondered for a moment. "Sergeant Merry's at Olivia Darby's house right now. Radio her and ask her to meet you near the cottage. Wait for her to arrive before you proceed."

"Yes, sir."

Neal faced the door David Pine had just slammed shut. He turned the handle and went inside.

* * *

Ava turned off the main road and followed a lane that dwindled into a dirt track about a quarter of a mile further on. She saw Ham's car parked in a muddy lay-by near a leaky trough and some rusting farm equipment.

She pulled in alongside him and wound down her window. "Is it far from here?" she asked, straining to see what lay ahead, but her view was obscured by high hedgerows. Ham shook his head. Ava noted that he had a pair of binoculars dangling around his neck.

"About another half a mile up the road. There's a spot I know where we can park up without being seen from the cottage."

"I'll follow you." Just short of half a mile further on, Ham indicated right and took a sharp turn off the track into what looked like unused grazing land surrounded by hedgerows. Ava could make out orange pantiles and a ridged rooftop through the tangle of woodland encroaching on the cottage's garden. They parked in the field and walked close to the treeline to avoid being spotted.

"It looks derelict," Ava commented.

Ham held his binoculars to his eyes. "It's been empty for a while, but it's not so bad inside. Rosie and I rented it for a month or two before we moved into our caravan."

"Can you see anything?"

"Not so far." Ham trained his binoculars on a downstairs window, then tilted them upwards. "Nope. Not a thing."

"Where's her car? It must be round the other side — if she's here at all, that is."

They edged along the side of the field until they could see the other side of the house. A Mini Cooper was parked at the rear.

"Bingo," said Ham. "What now?"

"We need to confirm that it is Tess Woodson in there."

A few seconds later, the cottage door opened and a girl stepped out. She looked around her and then walked to the car, opened the boot and took out a large holdall.

Ham handed Ava the binoculars. "That's her. The baby must be inside, if she has him. Do you reckon she could be armed?" The thought had not occurred to Ava. She stared at Ham and he shrugged. "A lot of folks around here have guns. Farmers and the like."

"Tess isn't a country girl. I don't think she's likely to be armed, at least not with a gun. Still, she could easily harm the baby if we alarm her."

"So how do you want to play this?" Ham asked.

Ava fingered the phone in her pocket. Should she call Neal? Chances were, he would advise her to wait for backup. There was no way of assessing how Tess would react, and Ava wasn't trained in negotiation techniques. She pictured the slender young woman she had met at Eloise Woodson's house. Supposing she were to threaten Shaun with a knife? An image came into Ava's mind of Maggie Neal with a knife slicing across her throat. She couldn't provoke an incident like that again.

Ham stood quietly by, waiting for orders.

Ava looked at him. "I'm going to take a closer look. I need to know if she's got Shaun in there. Probably best if you keep your distance, we don't want to overwhelm her — we don't know what state of mind she's in."

Ham nodded, but he looked uncertain.

"Don't worry. I'm not going to do anything rash," Ava reassured him. Ava took a deep breath and began to edge along the hedgerow until she reached the ground floor windows. With her back against the wall, she sidled up to a window. She sneaked a look inside and then gave Ham the thumbs up. He stood watching from where the field met the garden.

Tess was sitting in an old armchair, feeding Shaun from a bottle. There was such a look of tenderness on her face that Ava longed to believe that Shaun was not in any danger. But she couldn't take that chance. She edged back to the door and tried the handle. Tess had forgotten to lock it. Quietly, Ava turned the handle and opened the door. In front of her was a flight of stairs, and to her right, the room where Tess was feeding the baby. Ava moved towards it silently, afraid of startling Tess and causing her to panic.

"Tess?" she said, softly, pushing open the door.

Tess leapt to her feet, still holding the baby. The bottle dropped to the carpet and lay there, oozing droplets of milk. They stared at each other. Tess said, "I haven't harmed him."

"I know." Ava could see that Tess was tense. She was suddenly afraid of misjudging the girl and everything going terribly wrong.

"You can't keep him here, Tess. We have to take him back where he belongs, with his parents."

"I can do what I want with him. I could take him somewhere far from here. I could end his life if I chose to. A life for a life." She gave a shrill, hysterical laugh.

"Tess, Shaun's just an innocent baby. He isn't responsible for what his parents did or didn't do."

"I don't care. What about the damage they did to me? They took away my feelings. I didn't just lose a mother, you see, I lost whatever it is that makes us human. So I don't care about this brat."

"But you *have been* caring for him." Ava pointed at the tin of formula milk visible through the kitchen door, the opened pack of disposable nappies on the sofa.

"I needed to keep him alive, that's all."

Ava shook her head. "You didn't have to keep him dry, well-fed, comfortable."

"It stops him crying. How did you find me, anyway?"

"Hammond Bell saw your car. He's outside. It won't be long before the rest follow. What was your plan, Tess? Surely you realised half the county would be out searching for a missing baby? You must have known you'd be found."

A blaze of anger lit up Tess's face. "It's not fair!" she cried. "I tracked down Ewan Cameron so I could prove that he harmed my mum and then someone killed him. He probably didn't even suffer."

"He suffered. Someone suffocated him. They had given him a drug that paralysed him but left him aware of what was happening to him. He would have felt real terror. He would have known his life was about to end."

Tess didn't flinch.

"Shaun's innocent," Ava said again.

"His parents aren't. They lied to give Ewan Cameron an alibi. Gabe said he went to their flat that night and they weren't there. I just want them to tell the truth!" Tess began to sob.

Ava's heart ached for her. She looked so young and fragile. The eight-year-old child, who had woken up one morning to find her mother gone and her whole world shattered, was still hurting. Ava knew that Tess would not hurt this child.

Tess stepped forward and placed Shaun in Ava's arms. "Will I go to prison?" she asked, her wide, frightened eyes still focused on the baby's face. "I wouldn't have hurt him. I just wanted to make them feel what it's like to lose someone you love."

"I know," Ava said, and added, "I honestly can't say whether you'll go to prison." Shaun squirmed in her arms. "Let's begin by taking him home."

A sudden noise behind the door made them both start. "It's only Ham," Ava said, and looked round. But it wasn't.

"DI Saunders?"

"That's right, Blondie. Nice work finding the baby. I'll take him now. You drive young Tess here back to the station. I'll let DI Neal know the kid's safe."

Ava stared at him, sensing that something wasn't right. But Saunders did outrank her. "Come on then, hand the nipper over. I'm looking forward to seeing his mum's face when I bring him back safe and sound."

So Saunders wanted all the glory for rescuing Shaun. How predictable. The three of them walked to the car and reluctantly, Ava passed him over to Saunders and he made some unconvincing cooing noises. Ava watched him strap the car seat in.

"How did you know we were here?" she asked him.

He didn't reply immediately. Then he said, "I heard Ham on the radio asking you to meet him. I was on my way out to the Pines' place and thought I might be more use here if a situation was developing. You're only a DS, remember, Merry. I've had experience of this sort of thing before."

Ava thought the only thing Saunders was experienced at was being an arsehole, but she kept it to herself.

Close behind her, Tess whispered, "I think I know him. He used to go out with my Aunt Eloise, when I first moved in with her."

"DI Saunders? Are you sure?"

Tess nodded.

"After your mum went missing?" It was quite possible they had met in the course of the investigation. Saunders would almost certainly have come into contact with Eloise, and probably even questioned her.

But Tess said, "And before. She knew him before too. I didn't know he was a detective."

"He was one of the detectives who investigated your mother's disappearance." Ava stared thoughtfully at Saunders, slowly reversing his car. Her mind was working overtime.

Ava pulled out her phone and called Hammond Bell's number as Saunders pulled out into the side road. There was no answer.

"Shit. Where's Ham?" With Tess following, Ava ran back to the place where Ham should have been waiting.

"Ham?" The young officer lay face down on the ground a few feet away from the hedge. Ava ran across to him and saw blood trickling from the side of his head. "Oh no. Ham! Ham! Wake up!"

Ham stirred and groaned. He felt his head and squinted up at Ava.

"Ham, are you okay? What happened?"

"*Uncle* Reg whacked me on the side of the head."

Ava turned to Tess. "Call an ambulance and stay with him. He's been unconscious, he shouldn't be left alone." Before Ham could protest she added, "That's an order, PC Bell." Ava began running towards her car. Over her shoulder she yelled back, "Call Neal! Let him know that Reg Saunders has Shaun and that he could be our killer."

She had no idea where Saunders was headed and to her dismay, Ava failed to catch up with him before the junction with the main road. She guessed he would go back into Stromford. The alternative would have been to make his way deeper into the Wolds and eventually to the coast, effectively a dead end. From Stromford, he could get on to the town bypass and head in any direction he chose.

As she pulled onto the main road, Ava slapped on her police siren, forcing startled motorists to move aside.

A car in front of her drifted into the middle of the lane. Ava slammed on her brakes and yelled a string of expletives as she overtook it. At the approach to a roundabout, she slowed down and looked along the line of cars ahead of her. She caught a glimpse of a flash of red and shouted, "Yes!" It was Saunders's red car.

Ava pulled out and put her foot hard on the accelerator. She wove between the cars in front, dodging oncoming vehicles and drawing nearer to the red car. Saunders must have seen her for he pulled out and sped across the roundabout, narrowly missing a van coming from the right.

"Shit!" Ava yelled. The same van had swerved, and was blocking her way. She struck the wheel with both hands in frustration.

She put in a call for backup. There was a burst of static, a couple of seconds' silence. Minutes later, control informed her that Saunders's vehicle had turned off the main road and had been intercepted by two patrol cars.

The turn-off lay just ahead. Less than half a mile along she saw the two patrol cars, one on either side of the road, doors flung open, lights flashing. Saunders's car had crashed into the hedge of a lone house set back from the road. She pulled up alongside the first police car and waved her ID. "Sergeant Ava Merry, Stromfordshire Police. Where is the driver of that car?"

The police officer pointed at the house. "He went in there."

"Was he carrying a baby seat?"

"Yes. Is it his kid? He threatened to hurt it if we intervened."

"No. Look, I don't have time to explain now. The man in there has probably killed already and he's using the baby as a hostage. Do you know if there's anyone in that house?"

The police officer shook his head.

Ava drummed her fingers on the roof of his car. She pictured Shaun as she last seen him, snuggled under a blanket in his baby seat. With a sigh, she said to the officer, "I know the man. If I go in, I might be able to persuade him to hand over the baby."

The officer looked uncertain.

Saunders's car had flattened the section of hedge that faced the road, but the rest was still dense and thick enough to conceal her. Ava crept along behind it, crouching low until she reached the end. Then she did a forward roll to the side of the house, straightened up and sprinted round to the rear. A long back garden ended in an open field. If Saunders decided to run, he wouldn't get far.

A window at the back of the house revealed an empty kitchen. Expecting the back door to be closed, Ava tried the handle and it turned. A laundry basket full of wet washing lay just inside. Someone had been disturbed on their way out to the dryer.

The kitchen door was ajar. Ava crept over to it and paused, listening. She could hear quiet sobbing coming from the front room. It sounded like a woman. Ava inched along an endless hallway and peered in through the half-open door. Sitting on a chair in the corner of the room was an elderly woman. Shaun's car seat was on the floor near her feet. The child seemed to be fast asleep. Saunders was standing by the window, peering out through the partially closed curtains. He seemed to flicker and jump as the patrol car flashing outside sent striations of light pulsing through the room. Ava tried to swallow but her mouth was dry. Her heart hammered in her ears. She took a deep breath and stepped through the door.

Saunders spun round and levelled a gun at her.

"Reg? What the fuck?" Ava instinctively raised her hands. It had never entered her head that he might be armed. The whole situation was so surreal that Ava could feel no fear. "Oh come on, Reg. You're not really going to fire that thing, are you?"

Saunders swivelled and pointed the gun at the terrified woman. "I could shoot her instead, I suppose," he said.

The woman screamed, waking Shaun, who began to yell.

"Reg, you're not thinking straight. There are two patrol cars out there and more on the way. This can only go badly for you unless you put that gun down and give yourself up." Ava had no idea if she was saying the right thing. What if her words provoked him further?

She saw the gun shake in his hand. Shaun cried louder, and Saunders was clearly rattled by the noise. He glanced at the child almost fearfully. Sweat made its way down his forehead into his eyes.

He blinked. "Move out of the way, Merry. I don't have time for this."

"What's going on, Reg?"

"You and Scotty make a crap team, Blondie. I thought the two of you might have figured it out by now."

"Figured what out? That you killed Ewan Cameron? Why? What happened to Steph, Reg? Did you kill her too?" It seemed important to keep Saunders talking, but Ava had no real plan. She sensed that he too was floundering.

"My car's outside, Reg. Leave Shaun here with this lady and take me along as your hostage. Drive anywhere you like. I'll tell Neal not to have us followed. You can get away."

Saunders seemed to consider this. Then, still pointing the gun at Ava, he cocked his head towards Shaun. "The kid comes too. Pick him up."

Ava moved gingerly across the room towards the crying baby. She bent to pick up the car seat and as she straightened, she glimpsed a shape flit across the lawn outside the window. She felt a surge of relief mixed with fear. Saunders had his back to the window and the person outside could not know that he was armed.

Ava tensed. She kept her eyes on Saunders, trying to think how she could distract him, giving the figure outside a chance to take him by surprise. Without much hope, she acted. Ava gave an exaggerated start and looked straight over his shoulder at the window. Saunders took his eye off the gun. It was all she needed.

She dropped Shaun's car seat to the floor and lunged at Saunders, delivering a swift kick to his groin. She grabbed his wrist and tried to wrest the weapon from his grasp, but Saunders held it fast.

A figure burst through the door. "He's armed!" Ava yelled.

They collided in the middle of the room, and three pairs of hands fought for control of the gun. The old woman and Shaun screamed, and the gun went off.

Suddenly there was silence. Ava clutched her ringing ears, and shook plaster from her hair and face. Hammond Bell, still bloody from the cut on his head, grappled the gun from his startled uncle, and threw him to the floor in a single deft move. Ava gave a slightly hysterical laugh at the look of sheer surprise on Reg's face.

Chapter 19

Ham snapped the cuffs on his uncle's wrists. "Is anybody hurt?" he asked.

"I think we're all good." Ava looked at the elderly woman, who was now holding the crying Shaun. She appeared shocked but unharmed. Ham got to his feet, brushing plaster from his clothes and shaking it from his hair. Ava coughed, tasting dust. "You're bleeding, Ham. Are you okay?"

"Never better," Ham said, sounding shaken.

"You followed me? You were supposed to wait for an ambulance."

Ham grinned at her. "Lucky for you, I didn't."

Ava pulled out her phone and called Neal. "Shaun's safe. Please let his family know they'll see him in about half an hour." She turned to Ham. "Where's Tess?"

"Outside. In my car."

They took their charges outside, leaving the elderly woman with the two patrol officers. Ava thought briefly that this woman remained a shadow. She'd never recognise her if she met her again, yet they had both been through this shocking incident together.

Ava strapped Shaun into her car and gave Tess a little wave. Her heart went out to the luckless girl. Maybe now she would find out what happened to her mother. First though, Ava was obliged to arrest Tess for child abduction. She did so reluctantly, after reassuring her that no harm had come to Shaun.

Ham drove off with Saunders and Tess. Ava drove slowly out to the Pines' place with Shaun. As soon as she drew up in their driveway, the Pines ran towards her car, with Neal close behind. Laura Cameron stood at the door.

Neal and Ava waited while the Pines took their baby inside. Ava told Neal what had happened.

"We need to question Saunders immediately," he said. "Are you sure you're okay?"

Ava nodded, though she was feeling shaky. "I'd like to speak with Laura," she said. "She deserves to know who killed her husband."

"Whom we suspect of killing her husband," Neal reminded her. "We have to follow procedure, Sergeant." Then he smiled.

Ava went upstairs and found Laura in her bedroom, packing. On the bed lay a piece of paper. Ava picked it up and saw that it was a sketch bearing Ewan Cameron's signature. "This is the picture you and Gabe North found in the Pines' loft?"

"Yes. There's a notebook full of them up there," Laura answered, dully.

"We are fairly certain we know who killed your husband, Mrs Cameron."

The jeans Laura had been folding dropped to the floor. She sat down heavily on the bed. "David? Or Rhona? Gabe North?"

Ava sat beside her on the bed and took her hand in hers. "No. It was most likely a police officer, a Detective Inspector Reg Saunders. It's still not clear what his motive was, but I'm going back to the station now with Inspector

Neal to question him." Still holding Laura's hand, she told her most of the story.

"I knew it couldn't be my friends. There's more though, isn't there? What are you not telling me?" Laura sighed. "I'm so tired of people keeping things from me."

"I'm sorry, Laura. I don't know any more than what I've told you. I promise I will get in touch with you as soon as I know the full story."

At last, Laura was crying. "He . . . he changed when he moved to Stromford. I knew he didn't really love me when he begged me to marry him. I'd begun to fall out of love with him too. Then suddenly he was more like the old Ewan again and I thought we could just go back to how we were before. It was around the time of his falling out with David and I sensed something terrible must have happened. I should have insisted on knowing the truth."

Ava listened. Ewan — and the Pines too — had made use of Laura and her passive nature. Even now she was blaming herself.

"You're not to blame for any of this, Laura," Ava said.

Laura wiped her eyes. "Did . . . did Ewan kill Stephanie?"

"We still don't know." Ava felt inadequate. She left Laura to finish packing and went downstairs. She joined Neal in the kitchen, where he was standing with one of the uniformed officers.

"You sure you're okay?" he asked again.

Ava nodded. "Thanks to Hammond Bell. We should make sure he gets some sort of recognition for his action."

Neal nodded. "Let's go. We'll take my car. I'll get one of the uniforms to drive yours back the station."

* * *

Less than an hour later, they confronted Reg Saunders. He had declined legal representation and seemed willing to cooperate. He appeared to have aged several years since Ava had seen him earlier in the afternoon. He looked like a broken man. Next to her in the interview room, Neal seemed edgy.

"Sorry I almost shot your girlfriend, Scotty." Saunders gave Ava a half-hearted leer.

Neal's voice was cold. "Start talking, Reg. We know you and Stephanie's sister Eloise were in a relationship before Stephanie disappeared. Your actions this afternoon show that you are guilty as hell . . ."

Saunders straightened in his chair. He seemed to regain his cocksureness. "But what am I guilty of? Still bloody clueless, aren't you?" he sneered.

"Give it up, Reg. It's only a matter of time before we establish that you killed Ewan Cameron. This afternoon you kidnapped a baby, took a woman hostage and almost shot two police officers. That's plenty to be charging you with while we puzzle out the rest. It will be very interesting to hear what Eloise has to say when we talk to her."

Suddenly it dawned on Ava, in a flash of intuition. "It was Eloise who killed Stephanie, wasn't it? You botched the investigation to protect her, didn't you?"

Saunders's tone was still mocking but sweat was running down his forehead. "Well done, Merry. Not such a dumb blonde after all."

Then he broke. Ava and Neal waited. Saunders sat, head in hands. Neal pressed him to explain what happened the night Stephanie 'disappeared.'

Saunders's voice was flat and expressionless. "It was an accident. Steph called Eloise and asked her to come to Cameron and Pine's flat, saying there was an emergency. When Eloise got there she found Ewan Cameron out of his head on drugs. Steph was scared that he'd overdosed and she wanted Eloise to get something to bring him round. She was — *is* a pharmacist. Eloise took a look at Cameron and didn't think he was in imminent danger. She advised Steph to call an ambulance. Then Steph asked her for money. They quarrelled and Eloise pushed her sister.

She hit her head on the hearth. It was a freak accident, that's all, but Eloise was scared no one would believe that. She called me. I had to act quickly. I staged things to make it look like Ewan had pushed her. They were both high. I thought it would be easy enough to steer the investigation a certain way to make Cameron seem guilty. He wouldn't be able to remember a thing."

There was a long pause. "And?" Neal asked.

"And then Steph's body disappeared and the Pines gave Ewan Cameron an alibi. They covered things up to protect him."

"Christ. What a bloody mess," Neal said under his breath.

"Those two idiots must have got rid of Steph's body. Don't ask me what they did with it. In a way it made things easier. No body, no evidence. I just had to make sure the investigation was closed as quickly as possible."

"And no one really cared what happened to a 'woman like Steph,' anyway," Ava added.

"It was better for everyone. Steph had been a drain on Eloise financially and emotionally for years."

"Convenient for her, wasn't it? Steph falling over and hitting her head like that," Ava said.

"It was an accident."

"Yeah, right."

"And Ewan Cameron?" Neal asked. "Why did you kill him?"

Saunders shrugged. "He came to me because he knew I'd investigated Steph's disappearance. Said he was tired of living with Steph's death on his conscience. He wanted to confess and serve his time." Saunders paused. "Obviously I didn't want the case to be reopened. Cameron's confession would have opened a whole can of worms. Forensics has moved on a lot since the original investigation, not to mention the fact that the flat Cameron shared with Pine had never been examined. And

Cameron had no idea what became of the body of the woman he was supposed to have killed."

Ava glanced at Neal.

Saunders had nothing to lose now, and so he went on. "I made up some story about having to drive him out to the Pines' place to consolidate the evidence. Before we left my house, I slipped him a roofie in a glass of brandy. The rest was easy enough. Or it would have been if it hadn't been for those damn kids. I'd planned to bury his body in the woods by Stainholme Abbey, but I had to abandon that plan when I thought they'd seen me. Then Cameron's bloody car disappeared, so I was forced to dump his body and leg it home. Fucking farce."

"You must have loved her a lot," Ava said.

Saunders gave a bitter laugh. "Fat lot of good it did me. As soon as she got what she wanted, she got shot of me faster than a dog can lick its arse."

Ava didn't understand. "What did Eloise want?"

Saunders shook his head. "Tess. Eloise wanted Steph's kid. Couldn't have any of her own and she didn't give a shit about being with me. Once she had the kid she didn't need me anymore."

* * *

While Ava waited for Neal in the staff kitchen she congratulated PJ on her good work in finding the link between Saunders and Eloise. PJ invited Ava to join her and Steve at the Crown for a meal, but the case wasn't finished yet. There was another car journey to be made.

David and Rhona Pine sat next to each other at the kitchen table. At last they told the truth about what had happened on the night Stephanie Woodson left her home and never returned. As they spoke, Laura crept into the room and sat perched on a stool, listening.

David spoke first. "Steph was modelling for an art class at the college. The moment Ewan set eyes on her, he was bewitched."

Laura flinched.

"Steph wasn't the least bit interested in him, but she slept with him a couple of times. Ewan gave her money and bought drugs for her, even though he had hardly any money himself. Steph made Ewan swear he wouldn't tell anyone about their 'relationship.'" David paused, glanced over at Laura and went on. "Rhona and I guessed what was going on. We urged him to stop seeing Steph, stop taking drugs, but he was hooked — on both."

Rhona sat clutching David's hand, her face white.

"That night, Rhona and I were out. We were going out for drinks then on to a party, but it was called off at the last minute, so we got home early."

Quietly, Rhona began to sob. David squeezed her hand.

"When we got back to our flat, we found Steph lying on the floor in Ewan's room. There was blood on the carpet around her head and . . . and . . . she wasn't moving. I knelt by her side and felt for a pulse in her wrist, then her neck, though I knew she was dead. Her eyes were open, they looked glassy . . ." David faltered.

"Was Mr Cameron in the bedroom too, Mr Pine?" Neal asked.

"He was lying on the bed, unconscious — or so it seemed. Drugged up. He had blood on his hand and . . . well it seemed obvious what must have happened."

"You made the assumption that Mr Cameron had killed Stephanie Woodson?" Neal's stare took in both of them.

Rhona, still speechless, managed to nod.

"May I ask why you took it upon yourselves to make that judgement? Why didn't you contact the police?"

David mumbled something inaudible. "Louder, Mr Pine, please," Neal said.

"Ewan was my best friend. I wanted to help him."

"And you, Mrs Pine?"

Rhona looked at Laura. "I . . . Yes."

"Yes what?"

"I wanted to help Ewan too," Rhona sobbed.

"It didn't occur to you that Stephanie Woodson had people who cared about her? She had a daughter, for pity's sake. That same daughter was so desperate to learn the truth about her mother's disappearance that she abducted your son, making a criminal of herself."

"Rhona had nothing to do with it. It was all my idea. I'm willing to take all the blame," David Pine said quietly.

"How very gallant of you."

"I . . . don't understand," Rhona said. "If Ewan didn't kill Steph, who did?"

"We believe it was Steph's sister: Eloise Woodson. Steph called her because she thought Ewan had overdosed. She hoped her sister, who is a pharmacist, could help."

Rhona looked puzzled.

Ava added, "Another person arranged the crime scene to make it look as though Ewan killed Steph." With an apologetic glance at Neal, she added, "It was a policeman who was seeing Eloise at the time."

Suddenly Laura Cameron jumped down from her stool and crossed to the table. "You believed Ewan had killed someone? And whose decision was it not to tell me any of this? To let me marry a man you believed was a murderer?"

Rhona stared at the smooth surface of the table, unable, it seemed, to meet Laura's eye. Finally David spoke. "You have to understand, Laura. We were just kids. We didn't know what to do. We were thinking of you and Ewan, Laura. The life you could still have together. Ewan had loved you once. We were sure he could again and that resuming his relationship with you would help him—"

"Atone?" Laura spat out.

"Be a good person again," David finished.

"You're despicable, both of you. Your perfect life, here in your lovely home, with your lovely children." She laughed. "Some penance you're doing!"

Ava decided to intervene. "Mrs Cameron, let the police deal with this matter. Why don't you bring your case downstairs and I'll arrange for one of our officers to drive you to a hotel?"

Laura turned to go. At the door, she paused. "I never want to see you again, either one of you. Ever!"

Neal asked the Pines what they had done with Stephanie Woodson's body.

"We put her in the boot of our car and drove up towards Edinburgh. We stopped somewhere in the Borders and buried her in the woods," David said.

Neal sighed. "Somewhere in the Borders? We're going to need you to be a bit more specific than that, Mr Pine. Tess Woodson deserves to see her mother's remains respectfully laid to rest."

"I . . . I think I could find the spot again," David said.

"We wrapped her in a sheet," Rhona added. "It was a silk one. Pale blue. My grandmother gave it to me for Christmas because she knew I had delicate skin."

Perhaps, thought Ava, Rhona's 'atonement' had begun the moment she pulled the sheet from its drawer.

"What happens next, Inspector? Are my wife and I under arrest?"

Rhona stared at her husband. Tears rolled down her cheeks.

Ava looked at Neal, thinking of the three children upstairs.

Neal sighed again. "You'll be advised in due course," was all he said.

* * *

Ava followed Neal out to the car.

"Feeling exhausted?" he asked. "It's not every day you have to relieve a colleague of his gun."

"I'm fine. When did you realise Saunders was involved?"

"PJ messaged me to say there was a photograph of him in Eloise's house. She didn't know what it might signify but she thought it was noteworthy. Saunders must have picked up where you were when Ham radioed in his location."

"What a mess. Makes you feel sorry for him, doesn't it? *Almost.*"

Neal shook his head. "We still have to prove that Saunders killed Cameron. Despite his blabbing earlier, he'll probably plead not guilty once he's lawyered up."

"There's the inhaler Zak dropped when he ran away. Saunders picked it up and put it in his pocket. I found the top when I was searching the woods the day we found Cameron's body. Dan in forensics has it bagged and tagged. If we can find the other part at Saunders's place . . ." Ava frowned. "Then there's the fact that he had a motive. And he *did* try to shoot me . . ." Ava was feeling very tired now and feared she was babbling.

Neal laughed. "That should be enough to be getting on with, Sergeant."

Ava stopped talking. What was happening to her boss? That was at least three times she'd heard him laugh. His trip to Scotland must have done him some good after all. She smiled, and shook her hair loose. A few strands clung to the sleeve of Neal's jacket. Out of the corner of her eye, Ava caught her boss looking down at the silky blonde threads. Ava smiled again and closed her eyes.

THE END

Thank you for reading this book. If you enjoyed it please leave feedback on Amazon, and if there is anything we missed or you have a question about then please get in touch. The author and publishing team appreciate your feedback and time reading this book.

Our email is office@joffebooks.com

www.joffebooks.com

ALSO BY JANICE FROST

DEAD SECRET
DARK SECRET
HER HUSBAND'S SECRET

Manufactured by Amazon.ca
Bolton, ON

38585912R00136